PRAISE FOR THE SILVER MYSTERY SERIES

Susan Reiss captures the magic, mystery and charm of that quintessential Eastern Shore town – St. Michaels. Secrets lay hidden for generations among the stunningly beautiful estates along the Miles River. Can't wait for her next "silver" adventure.

—Kathy Harig, Proprietor of *Mystery Loves Company* Bookstore

"This is a series that captures the local flavor of our area – St. Michaels, the food and the quirky characters who live here and visit. The descriptions of all the real places make me feel like I'm there. The mystery kept me turning the page. This is a series I recommend to my library patrons... and to you.

—Shauna Beulah, Branch Manager, St. Michaels Library

"This series will transport you to the Eastern Shore of Maryland, but will remind you of whatever town has a special place in your heart—hopefully without murder. It leaves me wondering what other secrets this quaint little Eastern Shore town is hiding and I'm waiting for Susan Reiss to tell us."

—Barbara Viniar, Retired President
Chesapeake College, Wye Mills, Maryland

Silver Mystery Series

Tarnished Silver
Sacred Silver
Painted Silver
Hammered Silver

HAMMERED SILVER

SUSAN REISS

Best,
Susan Reiss

Author Photo by Bob Bader

Website: www.SusanReiss.com
Facebook: Susan Reiss
Twitter: @Susan Reiss
Goodreads.com: Susan Reiss, Goodreads Author

For
Jimmy and Jeanie Wilson
who introduced me to the joys and finer points of sailing
and
All those hearty souls
who would rather be on the water

Rays of sunshine warmed my skin. Fingers of a gentle breeze ran through my hair. The boat engine hummed softly. A serene moment.

The boat lurched with no warning. Knocked out of my reverie, I grabbed for the rail. The engine revved then quieted. Screams pierced the silence.

"Help me, Abby. HELP ME!"

Who was calling out to me? I wanted to run from the ghostly terror in that voice. The rail held me prisoner on the bow. There was no escape.

"Abby! Help me, Abby!"

Other voices joined in screaming for help. Only he cried out my name.

"Abby, help me!"

Invisible threads drew me to the stern of the boat. Step by step. Closer to the voice calling.

I looked over the side and saw a white cloud floating just below the surface, as if pulled down from the turquoise blue sky, held there against its will. Ruby-red tendrils twisted and turned in an eerie dance against the ghostly white backdrop.

"ABBY!" His voice tugged at me. "Abby! Help me!"

The body of the voice drifted into view. A pulsating torrent of crimson hid his face. His hand rose from the water. Reaching for me. Red droplets flew from his fingers as they clawed the air. Closer, closer, they came. At the touch of my shirt, they clamped shut and pulled me into the sea of blood.

CHAPTER 1

arnish can cause serious damage to a silver piece. If it is not removed, the damage may become permanent.

"The Butler's Guide to Fine Silver"
Mr. Hollister, 1898

I JERKED STRAIGHT up in bed, lungs heaving for air. There was no water. The only thing clutched in a fist was my sheet. My skin was damp with sweat, not river water. And no one screaming my name.

The only sound was the contented snuffle of Simon, my black Lab, snoozing on the corner of my bed.

It was a dream. But not a dream. A memory.

I fell back on the pillows and closed my eyes. They popped open again. I didn't want to fall sleep if that nightmare still lurked in the dark behind my eyelids. At least the sun was coming up. Waking up like this was bad. Waking up in the pitch black of night was the worst. I thought I might as well make the most of the early hour. Maybe if I wore myself out during the day, I'd sleep through the night.

I relaxed my clenched fingers, swung my feet over and heaved my body off the bed.

And collapsed to the floor with a yelp. "SIMON!"

He awoke with a jolt, jumped to the floor and scanned the room, not knowing if he should attack or sit for a cookie.

I pulled myself back up on the bed and rubbed the bottom of my right foot that had come down squarely on his rubber hedgehog toy with hard nubs all over its body.

"I told you not to leave your toys where I can step on them." I flung the cursed thing at him.

Simon whimpered as he hunched down to avoid the incoming missile. Safe, he turned his golden brown eyes to me.

My hands went to my mouth in horror. *What did I do? I threw something AT my Simon?*

I reached out to him. He flinched. And I felt sick. Tentatively, he inched forward until I could wrap my arms around him. I cooed and stroked him with love and apologies. It took some moments before he licked my face, but we were friends again. He followed me to the bathroom and sat patiently on the fluffy white bath mat while I showered off the wretched start to the day.

Dressed and downstairs in the kitchen of my cottage, I realized that this wasn't a morning for sipping a cup of coffee alone in quiet contemplation. No, this was a morning that needed friends and a good breakfast. I opened the door and Simon was off like a shot, dancing around, darting after a dragonfly, smelling everything to find out what happened during the night. I'd only taken a few steps before my sandals and feet were soaked with morning dew. It was a small price to pay to see the beautiful vista of the rolling lawn and slow-moving Miles River.

There was something about the movement of water, from the tiny curls on the surface swished up by the breeze to its languid flow to its unseen destination. I could look at the water for hours, but I didn't want to be in it. Something about getting my face wet. And I wasn't born to spend time on the water either. The constant movement was a challenge, but I was getting better. The little pink pill helped keep my stomach settled so I could enjoy the places a boat could take me. Yes, I'd already piled up some wonderful memories spent on this river. Would there be more?

I kicked my melancholy self. It must be the aftereffects of the nightmare. Right now, I needed the comfort of friends and some excellent coffee. It was only a short walk to the kitchen door of the main house and the domain of Mrs. Clark, the longtime cook and kitchen magician of Fair Winds. For years, she had *whipped up*, as she liked to say, everything from Chateaubriand to creamy potato salad. She believed in tasting as she worked and it showed at her rounded waistline. Funny, I don't think I'd ever met a good chef or cook who was skinny. The waistline was probably a good barometer of culinary skills.

"Oh, Abby," she said, with a grin, dressed in kitchen whites. "You've got great timing, as usual. The biscuits are just now this minute, done." She peered around at the empty room with squinty eyes. "Are you sure you don't have a spy in my kitchen?"

It was wonderful to be in a place where joking around was comforting. My mouth watered as she took a plate out of the cabinet, popped two of her heavenly biscuits on top and put it on the counter in front of me.

I reached for the butter she always kept out so it was soft. To her, rock-hard butter was no good to her in the kitchen. She knew refrigeration was important, but if it was good enough for her grandmother, or mom-mom, it was good enough for her. I slathered on the butter and took a bite. I didn't care if I burned my tongue. I deserved it. It was the perfect way to reset the morning. I closed my eyes to concentrate on the taste. Mm-m-m. She'd taught me that this was the only way to eat a biscuit and she was right. Sheer delight. When I opened my eyes, Mrs. Clark stood with her hand on your hip, staring at me as if I was a bug under a microscope.

"What?" I grabbed a napkin to catch the butter dripping down my chin. "What did I do?"

She paused for a moment. "What are you doing up so early again?" She finished pouring a mug of coffee for me, topped off her own and came to sit down at the kitchen island.

The memory of the nightmare drew a dark cloud over the bright morning. I slowly returned the biscuit to the plate.

"Ah, you've had another nightmare, haven't you?" It was more of a declaration than a question.

"I'm trying—" I started to defend myself as if the fault lay with me and I should be able to control my dreams. She held up a plump hand and I stopped.

"It's perfectly normal for such a ghastly incident to haunt you. Oh, what do they call it on those TV shows?" She pursed her lips. "Yes, post-traumatic stress. No surprise you've got it. It's not every day that you see somebody dying right in front of your eyes."

"Who is dying?" The tall, thin man floated into the kitchen carrying a white towel with dark gray smudges. Great. He wasn't the person I wanted to see on any morning. After the nightmare, dealing with him would be even more difficult. "Oh, you're talking about the accident. You can probably expect it haunt you for a few months and then it should fade away."

As usual, Dawkins had a clear understanding of every situation. It was maddening that he was almost always right. Silently, I prayed he was wrong this time. "If I have this nightmare for the next couple of months, I'll collapse and die from lack of sleep. That would upset the schedule, wouldn't it?"

"Nonsense. You're just projecting." He tossed the towel he was carrying into the trash. "But if you insist on dying, don't do it before you tell where to put this." He gently placed a small silver Revere bowl on the counter. "I polished it again and the engraving is easy to read now. Where do you want it?"

My stomach clenched and threatened to send up the biscuit. I pushed my chair back from the counter. "I don't want it anywhere." Secretly, I wished I'd never found it in the corner of the closet and touched its natural chill of sterling silver... and death.

CHAPTER 2

*I*mportant pieces of silver that represent the accomplishments
of the Family must be carefully maintained. No matter how
old or out-of-date they are, they must be kept free of tarnish and
accorded a proper position in the silver collection.

"The Butler's Guide to Fine Silver"
Mr. Hollister, 1898

IT HAD all started on what seemed like a normal day. I was doing
my job, cataloging and appraising the Fair Winds silver collection
owned by Lorraine Andrews. We first met on the eBay website
when she purchased a silver angel food cake server in her pattern.
It was part of the inventory of silver I'd inherited from Aunt
Agnes. Lorraine offered me a job and I moved to Fair Winds, her
waterfront estate and working farm. Simon, my oh-so-cute Lab
puppy, and I settled into our fresh start on life.

The work was challenging, much more than writing down
how many knives and forks were in a certain pattern. Discovering

unusual serving pieces as well as the history was always a delight. On that particular day, getting my job done was more challenging than usual. Dawkins was in my way. He was Lorraine's highly-efficient… What was he? A butler, house manager, majordomo? I wasn't sure about his title, but he seemed to be in charge of or had an opinion about everything at Fair Winds. To me, Dawkins was always a pain—friendly sometimes, surprising often and a little creepy the way he floated around the house, anticipating our needs before we knew we needed anything.

It was a beautiful mid-summer day and we had ended up in the windowless silver closet together. True, there should have been enough room for both of us since what we called the silver closet was more of a room. Its floor-to-ceiling shelves were designed for the express purpose of storing Lorraine's vast collection of sterling silver. But Dawkins was preparing for a whirlwind weekend of political guests with sensitive egos that included a welcoming buffet, a fishing trip, a seafood feast and a reception for the governor of the state of Maryland. Dawkins had memorized the menus, of course, and now needed to select the appropriate table settings and serving pieces. Like a general planning an assault, he lined up the pieces on the huge dining room table so he could assess their condition and set aside those that needed polishing. Normally, he was cooler than an icicle when Lorraine entertained, but the uniqueness of the situation and unexpected stress was cracking his calm exterior.

Frankly, he was driving me crazy. I needed to get on with my inventory work which was behind schedule. I had to be sure I had identified everything in the silver closet for the first round of appraisals. I shuddered to think about the boxes stored in the attic, but that was a project for another day. At least Simon was content to play outside with the other dogs instead of being underfoot.

Down on my knees, I reached into a dark corner and touched something hard and cool. *Great, another piece jammed out of the way.*

With a little groan, I pulled piece into the light. It was a small Revere bowl, engraved on the side: *Governor's Cup 1945.* Not sure if it should be part of the Fair Winds silver collection, I walked down the hall to ask the boss.

I found Lorraine sitting at the desk in the library. The sage green walls held floor-to-ceiling bookcases filled leather-bound books, many of the titles printed in gold gilt. An exquisite marble fireplace brought warmth and comfort on many a cool evening when we sat in the two overstuffed chairs solving the problems of the world and talking through personal conundrums. On an antique walnut table stood photographs mounted in silver frames. There was the bridal portrait of her as a young woman wearing an exquisite gown and a breathtaking diamond necklace. A candid shot of Lorraine wearing a dazzling diamond pin on the lapel of her dark suit showed her chatting casually with President Reagan. When I'd noticed that many photos had disappeared, she'd explained they held too many memories.

Morning sunshine shone through the wall of windows over-looking the lawn running down to the Miles River. This was the heart of Fair Winds, the library along with the kitchen. Here, Lorraine managed her many social and business activities. Lorraine, tall and trim, just teasing the age of sixty, sat at her large, carved mahogany desk. Instead of enjoying the grand view of the land, water and sky, she leaned over a mass of papers. Her light brown hair softly framed her sun-kissed face that was now scrunched up in a frown.

I paused in the doorway. "Oh, is this a bad time?"

She leaned back in her chair and groaned as she tossed her reading glasses on the papers. "It seems always to be a bad time lately, but come in. Please, save me from all this."

I stepped across the plush oriental rugs on the highly polished wood floor as she continued her rant.

"I don't know why I ever allowed myself to be talked into

hosting this party to celebrate Governor's Cup race. The only good thing is that it will all be over by Sunday night."

"I think we'll all be glad when it's over. I've never seen Dawkins so wound up. It's out of character for him and almost makes him normal."

"I think we're all wound up about it." She rubbed her forehead as if a headache was building behind her eyes. "This is more than a social event. It's turned into a political weekend like the ones my daddy hosted years ago." Lorraine's father, a well-respected advocate for the Eastern Shore, often hosted fishing excursions and small dinners so political leaders from Annapolis and champions of different causes and competing opinions could talk quietly in hopes of building consensus. "I've invited local leaders and state politicians from the capital. It's good for them to network and build consensus." She sighed. "It's been a long time since I've done this sort of thing. I'd forgotten how much work it is juggling all the personalities, egos and agendas to keep things calm and productive. I've tried to insulate you from the chaos."

"And you've done a good job." I smiled, hoping to reassure her. "It was inevitable that Dawkins would invade the silver closet." She sat up quickly, ready to remedy the situation, but I hurried on. "I'm not here to complain. I found something in a dark corner of the closet that I thought you should see. I'm not sure it should be included in the inventory of the Fair Winds Silver Collection."

Lorraine smile made her eyes sparkle. "Good, I'm ready to face a problem that is easy to solve. Let's see what you found."

I held out the engraved silver Revere bowl for her inspection. Her hand shot forward and grabbed it.

"There you are, you little stinker." She giggled. "You're the whole reason for this hysteria." She rubbed her thumb over the tarnished silver and read the inscription. "Daddy won the Governor's Cup that year with *Flying Wing*. Oh, she was a work of art when he sailed her."

"Did someone say she was ready for a break?" Dawkins said in his precisely enunciated style. As usual, Dawkins had glided silently halfway across the room before we noticed him. His posture was painfully erect as he carried a large tray laden with drinks and snacks. He always appeared with what was needed a moment before Lorraine realized she needed it. She thought it was a talent. I thought it was a little creepy, but at times like this, the refreshments were appreciated.

"Perfect timing, as usual," Lorraine said as she pushed the papers and ledger aside to make room for the goodies. "Abby found a treasure in the silver closet."

"Another one? Maybe we should call it the silver treasure chest instead of just a closet," he suggested as he pour iced tea into tall chilled tumblers.

Yes, Dawkins was a pain in my neck, but he did have his uses, I thought as I helped myself to a couple of small shrimp salad sandwiches with the crusts cut off. I eyed Mrs. Clark's tiny fruit tarts with great anticipation. I knew they would be a sweet experience. It had been more than a year since Lorraine's longtime housekeeper and childhood friend Evelyn was murdered right down the hall from the study. It was only recently that Lorraine had given Mrs. Clark permission to use some of the old recipes. They were too delicious to ignore, but they still reminded us of some difficult times. They say time heals, and thankfully, Lorraine's pleasant memories were starting to balance out the sad ones.

Lorraine grinned. "Thank you, Dawkins. This is perfect."

He drifted out of the room silently, as usual, while we spent a few silent moments together. After touching her lips with a napkin, Lorraine picked up the little bowl again.

I put my empty plate back on the tray. "I don't think it's valuable, but I thought I should check with you."

She took the corner of her napkin and gently began to polish the tarnished metal. "Valuable? Maybe not in the silver world, but it's a racing trophy coveted by every log canoe captain on the Chesapeake Bay."

I looked at the little trophy in Lorraine's hand in astonishment. "They covet that little trophy? Maybe it's appropriate to have a small trophy for a canoe."

Lorraine hooted with laughter. "Oh Abby, I'm sorry. I always forget that you're just learning about the Eastern Shore." She waved the bowl in the air. "This isn't the Governor's Cup. It's just a little memento that a log canoe captain or owner can put on his mantle to remind him of his victory in a very famous race. The actual trophy is a large bowl made of hammered silver. It's too valuable to be loaned out to a winning captain for a year, so it lives year-round at the Miles River Yacht Club, the sponsor of the race each year in St. Michaels."

"Hammered silver?" I considered the term. "I don't think I've seen anything like that."

"I'm not surprised," she sighed. "It's almost a lost art. I seem to remember reading an article several years ago that there were only three or four silversmiths left in the world who have mastered this technique. If anything ever happened to our Governor's Cup, I don't think they'd be able to replace it."

I hesitated to ask, but I needed to know. "Why do they have such an impressive trophy for a canoe race?"

She countered my question with a question. "You've never seen a log canoe, have you?"

"Of course. I learned how to canoe at camp when I was a kid, but those canoes were made of fiberglass. Isn't paddling a log canoe uncomfortable?"

She dropped her hands in her lap in a rather dramatic way. "Oh, dear. We have a failure to communicate." She bounced up from her desk, glad to be distracted from the details of entertaining. "Let me show you a picture of a log canoe." She went to one of the bookshelves and found a large framed picture.

"My father commissioned this portrait and meant to hang it here in the family library. The display was one of many projects we never completed after Daddy died so suddenly." She beamed with pride as she held up the framed painting. "This is *Flying Wind*, the log canoe Daddy sailed to win the Governor's Cup."

I gasped. "That's not a log canoe. It's a magnificent sailing ship."

"Magnificent, yes. But her hull is a canoe made of logs. Building and sailing a log canoe are art forms that deserve a Governor's Cup Trophy made of hammered silver."

I glanced through the windows overlooking the Miles River. "I don't remember seeing anything that like that in the boathouse."

There was a tinge of sadness in her voice. "No, *Flying Wing* was sold after my father died. My mother had no interest in racing, but knew that if the boat wasn't properly maintained, she would disintegrate and be lost forever. It was a sad day when the new owner came in his power boat and towed her away." She sighed a little. "It was sad, but it was the right thing to do. At least Daddy crossed the finish line first with her and accepted the trophy from the governor himself."

I picked up the little trophy and the napkin already smudged with black tarnish. "Then we should keep this little bowl in a special place."

Lorraine didn't say anything and when I looked up, I saw tears filling her eyes, then a determination that usually meant I was about to receive a new assignment.

"Okay, what are you thinking?"

She hesitated.

"Come on, tell me," I urged playfully.

"Well, I was thinking the little trophy shouldn't be buried in the silver closet. It should be on display. Maybe we could make a place for it, the portrait, and may be a little book about *Flying Wing*. What do you think?"

"That's a great idea. One evening, you could tell me about log canoes. I could print something up on the computer."

Lorraine shook her head. "I'm sorry. I told you just about all I know about log canoes, but," she added quickly, "I know just the person for you to interview."

I started to balk. "I have a lot of work to do on the silver inventory."

"No,," she said with a smile. "This is important. My friend knows everything about everything. He's a librarian. I remember he has an impressive collection of books about log canoes. I'm sure he knows about the silver trophy and the technique of hammering silver. When you talk to him, you'll get a lot accomplished." She opened a large desk drawer and took out an old-fashioned Rolodex. "I have his number here somewhere."

"You really should convert your contacts to an electronic format." What was I saying? I'd suggested yet another assignment for myself. Fortunately, she rejected the idea immediately.

"Why would I do that when I have everything I need right here at my fingertips? And I don't have to worry about it crashing. Yes, here it is." She pulled out a card and handed it to me. "Give Dr. Phillips a call and arrange an appointment. I guarantee you'll learn a lot from him. He retired from the United States Library of Congress."

I expected to learn about silver and sailboats, not murder.

CHAPTER 3

*U*nderstanding the fine art of caring for sterling silver is vital. Only those members of the staff with the proper training and awareness should handle the silver. To do otherwise invites damage to a piece.

"The Butler's Guide to Fine Silver"
Mr. Hollister, 1898

THE REVERE BOWL trophy was nestled in a soft towel in my tote as I parked my Saab convertible and walked to the entrance of Dr. Phillips' home. It seemed like a comfortable home though a little modest in comparison to many waterfront houses. Modest, except for the large two-story addition on the left. *Maybe it was built for the grandchildren,* I thought as I went up the front walk edged with well-tended flowerbeds on either side. The front door popped open before I touch the doorbell.

"Ms. Strickland?" asked an older woman dressed in a plain navy blue dress

"Yes, I have an appointment with Dr. Phillips."

"He's expecting you." She gestured for me to enter. "Please follow me to the library."

She led me through the living room and family room, both comfortably furnished but unremarkable. So I wasn't prepared when I stepped through a pair of French doors made of beveled glass into his library. The addition wasn't for the grandchildren. It was for his books.

The cavernous room was two stories high with bookshelves running floor to ceiling on almost every vertical surface. And they weren't just any bookshelves. They glowed with the natural warmth of rosewood. Carvings in certain corners begged closer inspection. A wooden ladder attached to a brass railing near the top allowed easy access to the leather-bound books sitting patiently on many of the shelves. Suspended from the vaulted ceiling was an elaborate crystal chandelier, its gentle light glinting off the gold-embossed titles.

A deep resonant voice softened by age called out to me. "Come in, come in, Ms. Strickland."

I stepped forward, a little embarrassed that I'd been caught staring. "Dr. Phillips?"

"Yes, I'm here in the reading area. Come forward."

I followed his voice toward the windows with a panoramic view of the Tred Avon River. He was getting to his feet the way older people do when they're feeling the ache in their joints. Standing, he was a short man, a little roly-poly, with wisps of silver hair combed back from his forehead. I suspected that there was nothing phony about this man. He was a man of truth.

I walked over to him and shook hands. "I must apologize. I feel like my chin is dragging on the carpeting. I don't think I've ever seen a room like this."

He chuckled. "Don't worry, my dear. My guests often have that reaction when they visit for the first time, or the second or… Actually, I feel a certain thrill every time I walk in here. You are in very good company." He motioned to an upholstered club chair that looked perfect for curling up with a book. "Come and sit down."

WHEN I DID, I moaned softly with pleasure. It was truly the most comfortable chair I'd ever experienced. It seemed to enfold my body while supporting it in all the right places.

"Ah, I see you appreciate my furniture as well." His eyes twinkled with delight.

"I've never sat in a chair like this," I gushed.

"And you probably never will unless you spend rather a lot of money."

I ran my hand over the smooth light blue upholstery. "Maybe someday, I'll be able to—"

"For now, you must come and sit anytime you wish." He dismissed the discussion of money as if it was a crass topic of conversation. "A friend of Lorraine's is a friend of mine. And it's even better that you appreciate my little experiment in design."

I jumped a little in surprise. "You mean you designed this chair? But I thought you worked for the Library of Congress."

"Yes, I did for many years. It became of hobby of mine to try and design a wonderful chair where one could sit and enjoy books. It was such a waste if one was uncomfortable looking at the books I'd acquired for the Library and for myself. A furniture manufacturer was kind enough to make my dream a reality. I'm afraid that chair is one of several generations of trial and error." He grunted almost to himself. "Fortunately, some of his customers were delighted to purchase our rejects."

I noticed his suit was beautifully tailored. It was a light steel gray suit worn with a pearl gray shirt and a tie of mauves and blues that reminded me of a Monet painting. He was ready for a meeting in Washington, D.C. instead of his home on the Eastern Shore.

I felt uncomfortable as I looked down at the cotton capris and sleeveless, shapeless top I was wearing. "I'm afraid I'm a little underdressed for our meeting."

He waved away my comment. "Nonsense, you look cool and comfortable. There's nothing like seeing a young woman in a summery outfit."

"If I had known you were going to wear a suit…"

"Oh, but I always wear a suit when I'm in my library. Partly out of habit after working so many years at the Library of Congress, but partly out of respect for the books." He looked around at the many shelves in the room. "Think of all the hours these writers spent to create these volumes. I dress out of admiration for their efforts. It's the same reason I wear a suit to a theatrical performance, out of respect for the playwright and the actors." He scrunched up his face as if a bad smell had just floated into the room. "I can't imagine wearing jeans and a T-shirt to the theater as so many people do. If I were an actor, I'd refuse to perform. Why should I do my best when certain members of the audience thought so little of the experience we were presenting."

"Oh, now I really feel—"

"Abby, the books and I are glad you're here. Please relax so we may enjoy your company. Now…" He laid an ivory bookmark with a slim tassel on the end across the page and closed the book on the ottoman. "I know you didn't come here to discuss chairs or my suit so I won't waste anymore of your time with my ramblings. Lorraine said that you found a captain's trophy from a Governor's Cup race."

I reached into my tote and drew out the silver Revere bowl. He looked at it and nodded. "That's nice, but it truly pales in comparison to the real Governor's Cup."

"Lorraine hoped that you could tell me a little about the trophy," I said as I tucked away the engraved bowl. "She also said that you could make me smart about log canoes, especially *Flying Wing*, her family's log canoe."

At that moment, the lady who had answered the door walked in with a large tray and promptly served each of us a cup of tea and a small plate of pastries. I was beginning to think that talking about log canoes always involved something to eat and drink. At this rate, I was going to have to hit the gym more often.

After he finished every one of the pastries on his plate, he settled back in his comfortable chair. "I do enjoy my afternoon tea and now I have the energy I need to answer all your questions about the log canoes."

"Actually, I don't have any questions, because I don't really know what to ask. I'm embarrassed to admit that until the day I found the little silver bowl, the only canoe I knew about was the one I learned to paddle at summer camp."

He smiled. "That's not unusual. Many people have the same reaction. The only place in the world where log canoes are sailed and raced is here on the rivers of the Chesapeake Bay. I have to check my references, but I believe the first person to build a canoe out of more than one log and to add sails was Sydney Covington from Tilghman Island, right down the road from Fair Winds."

I took a small notebook out of my tote and began to make notes. "Do you have any idea what happened to *Flying Wing*?" I almost winced as I asked, hoping he would not say she was now a pile of splinters someplace.

"Fear not, dear lady, *Flying Wing* is still sailing. In fact, she is sailing in this year's Governor's Cup race."

"Oh, and when is that?"

I was shocked when he took a Smartphone out of the inside pocket of his jacket and tapped the screen a few times. "Yes, the race is this Saturday. Would you like to go?"

I sat up on the edge of the chair. "I'd love to go with you."

He grimaced as he put his phone away. "Oh, Ms. Strickland, my days of going to a log canoe race are long over. However, I can make a call or two and see if I can arrange for you to watch the race from one of the chase boats." He brought his white eyebrows together in a frown. "You don't get seasick, do you?"

I shook my head and made a mental note to take the magic pill that would keep my tummy in place. "Is there anything I should bring?"

"Not really. Just an awareness of what's happening around you and to stay out of the way. You must understand this isn't really a social event. The sailors take this race very seriously. The captain's first priority is the log canoe and her crew, not you. You might also take a camera because it is a unique opportunity to see these magnificent boats up close during a race."

Slowly, he pulled himself out of the chair. "As a general introduction, you should know that a boat or log canoe runs about thirty to thirty-five feet in length with two masts and three large sails: mainsail, foresail and jib. That's a lot of canvas for a hull that sits only eighteen inches above the water line. If a captain takes too long to respond to needs of his boat or the challenge for position by another boat, or if he misjudges the wind, the log canoe and all aboard face potential disaster. If she heels over too far and cannot regain her balance, she will settle into the water."

"She capsizes?" I asked horrified.

"That's right. If she goes over, the sailboat race is lost and a new race begins, the one to account for every member of her crew. Once they know all the people are safe, it's time to take care of the boat. When a modern sailboat capsizes, the crew probably can right it with the right maneuvers and weight positioned just right. That's not true with this type of sailboat.

"A log canoe must be dismantled like a giant jigsaw puzzle and towed to a dock to be put back together." He took a sip of coffee. "But a log canoe can lose more than the race. She can lose a mast heralded by a mighty crack that splits the air as the wood splits apart. A rough sea can swamp her. She might settle gently on her side or go over violently, becoming a weapon that injures her crew or worse."

"Log canoe racing almost sounds like gladiators doing battle with the wind and each other."

He gave me a sweet smile. "That's very good, Abby. I think your analogy works well. Now, let's see if I can find one or two treatises to give you a general introduction to log canoes."

He led me to the library shelves focused on sailing, boat construction, racing and even North Atlantic crossings by sailboat. They surrounded a glass display case with intricately-tied knots of thin eggshell-white rope. Across the top, the knots were labeled Chain Plait, Sheepshank and Surgeon's. The bottom row began with the Carrick and Double Carrick knots. I looked closer to try to see the difference between the two, but resolved that it required a more experienced eye than mine. The Figure of Eight knot filled out the row. I liked the way it symbolized the optimism required by every captain and crew entering a race.

He noticed my interest and said, "I've always been fascinated by the more complicated knots. I guess I'm a frustrated engineer at heart."

"Did you tie these?"

He chuckled. "You must think I am a master of all trades. No, I had a dear friend who captained a beautiful yacht in the Newport-to-Bermuda race for many years. He was a braver man than I. Bluewater racing is not for the faint of heart. He's gone now, but I keep his knots as a reminder of a good man and the exciting life he led. I have the book he wrote of his memoirs, but I think we should save that for another time."

He ran his finger along leather bindings and fine paper dust jackets. "Now, let me see. We're talking log canoes." His voice brightened. "Yes, here is one title." He gently drew a volume from the shelf and then another. With the books came a flutter of a few sheets of paper.

"Oh dear. No, no, no," he grumbled.

I bent down quickly to retrieve them so he wouldn't have to exert himself. "Here they are."

He exchanged the books for the papers. "This will never do. About a year ago, I allowed myself to be talked into hiring a library assistant to help with the cataloguing and shelving. She didn't last long. She wasn't willing to work to my high standards. After all, when one works for the Library of Congress, one can't let the arrangement of a personal library fall below par." He shook the papers gently. "This is an example of her idea of proper filing. Well, I shall take care of them properly."

He tapped the books in my hand. "If you scan these two volumes before this weekend's races, I think you'll gain a basic understanding of log canoe racing. It's about precision, mechanics, construction and understanding the elements of wind and water. Remember, there's no factory representative to call to come and fix or fine-tune something on the boat. Each log canoe was built by hand, some more than a hundred years ago."

And I'd thought sailboat racing was a recreational pastime.

"It's not a sport for the faint of heart. It takes a lot of determination and an iron will just to finish a race, let alone win it. And there's the money, of course. A new set of sails these days can cost upwards of $50,000. If a mast breaks, a canoe can be out of commission for months, even the rest of season, while a suitable tree is found, trucked down to Maryland and fashioned into a new mast at a substantial expense. These captains finance their own boats. They don't have sponsors." He raised his left hand and stroked his chin. "Here's a thought that might put things into perspective for you, Abby. The state of Kentucky has its gentleman's sport of thoroughbred horse racing. Think of log canoe racing as the gentleman's sport of the Eastern Shore of the Chesapeake, considering its long tradition, pedigrees and high costs. Yes, I think it's an appropriate comparison. Racing has strained more than one marriage. In many cases, the boat came first in the heart of her captain."

"It sounds like this is about more than just winning a race. Would you say it's a way of life?"

He nodded. "That it is."

"Thank you, Dr. Phillips. Lorraine said you'd give me a firm foundation and, as usual, she was right." Carefully, I put his books away in my tote and then he walked me out to the front door.

"Your library is truly remarkable," I said.

"Now that you know where it is, I hope you will visit me often. " He handed me a card on heavy ivory paper. "I really can't call it a business card now that I'm retired," he said with a chuckle. "It has my contact information."

I looked at the information presented without a big corporate or government logo or other extraneous wording. It listed his name, telephone number and... "Oh! You have an email address." The words popped out with warning. I was so embarrassed. "I'm so—"

He held up his hand and gave me a big smile. "Don't apologize. People don't expect an old fossil like me to use the latest forms of communication." He leaned closer and lowered his voice to a whisper. "I'll let you in on a secret. I've been known to text from time to time. That's a cell phone number on the card. I hope you'll use it and come back to visit."

Once again the Eastern Shore had revealed an unexpected surprise. "Yes, I'd like to do that."

"Good, I think you will find many treasures here in my library." He raised his index finger and shook it a little. "You may even uncover a secret or two."

As I walked to my car, I glanced back and saw him standing in the doorway looking at the papers that had fallen off the shelf. Little did I know that he was holding the key to the future.

CHAPTER 4

*he beauty of repoussé may be lost if the delicacy of the
workmanship are ignored. Care attention must be paid to the
intricacies of the pattern. If tarnish is allowed to build up in even the
smallest corner, the beauty of the design may be lost, perhaps forever.*

"The Butler's Guide to Fine Silver"
Mr. Hollister, 1898

THE NEXT DAY, I walked into the living room at Fair Winds and
settled into a wingback chair upholstered in soft rose velvet by a
window that overlooked the driveway. There was still time before
my ride was due to arrive. Dr. Phillips had arranged for Charlie
Malone to show me the Governor's Cup at the yacht club, as part
of my introduction to log canoes racing, since he was a member
of the *Island Memory's* crew. While I waited, I read about the technique used to create the trophy. Hammering silver to raise a
design from the surface of the metal dated back to antiquity.
Three thousand years before Christ, the Greeks used the tech-

nique to create bronze plates of armor. Also, it was used to create detailed works in gold and silver as well as copper and tin.

This way of working with metal had more refined names to describe it than *hammered*. One of the most well-known was *repoussé*. Craftsmen used a variety of hammers and other tools to stretch the metal to force the design to appear above the surface. A silversmith used *chasing* to refine an element of the design by sinking or chasing a line, groove or other feature into the metal. These two techniques created a finely-detailed finished piece, whether it was a water serving pitcher for the table, a communion chalice for the altar or a large metal sculpture.

In 1927, the Governor's Cup Trophy was donated to the Miles River Yacht Club for the annual log canoe race. It was named for the then-governor of Maryland Albert C. Richie who agreed to sponsor the race and so it continues in perpetuity.

I was looking forward to seeing this coveted sailing trophy as an outstanding example of a silversmithing technique that is almost lost in today's world. Of course, many jewelry makers, both amateur and professional, used the hammered silver technique to create a unique surface for earrings, bracelets and other pieces. But to capture the image of a log canoe under full sail on a large trophy was a challenge to the silversmith.

I closed my reference book when I heard the sound of a car pulling up to the front door and peeked out the window. The man getting of the black Jeep Wrangler was about my age and a little taller than me. The broad shoulders under his white polo shirt showed that he took care of his body. His ink black hair was short and wavy. His vehicle with the top down suggested that this was a man who liked to have fun. He took his time walking to the door to take in the details of the Fair Winds house. I remembered the first time I saw the two-story pillars that held up a portico over the steps of the large house painted brilliant white and the lush bushes heavy with roses and hydrangeas that almost it. It was worth taking a look.

When the doorbell rang, I called out "I'll get it." But, as usual, I wasn't fast enough. As I moved away from the window, I caught sight of Dawkins slim figure in his usual dark jacket, gray slacks and a plain tie floating across the foyer to the door. He'd probably been at the back of the house, but somehow always knew what was going on and where to be. His efficiency sometimes made me feel unnecessary, like now.

The heavy black-paneled door stood open with Dawkins blocking entry as I got to the foyer. Poor Charlie, challenged by our valiant gatekeeper. I'd forgotten to put his arrival on Dawkins radar. I grabbed my little purse and hurried across the blue marble floor tiles and around the table with a cut-crystal vase brimming with pink hydrangeas to rescue my new friend.

"It's alright, Dawkins. Charlie is here to see me." I smiled in welcome as I took control of the situation from Dawkins, a rare event.

"Hi, I'm Abby," I said to the man who stood about an inch shy of six feet. "I really appreciate you picking me up. I could have met you at the yacht club."

He looked surprised. "Why would I give up the chance to see Fair Winds from this side?"

"Excuse me?"

"Sorry, what I meant was, I usually see Fair Winds from the water, when I'm racing in log canoes and sailboats on the Miles River. This is my first chance to see the house from this side." He looked around at the brass door knocker in the shape of a sail. "It's just as beautiful from this angle. Well, if you're ready, your chariot awaits."

I pulled the front door closed and skipped down the steps. "I've always wanted to ride in one of these Jeeps. It looks like fun on wheels." While he opened my door, I noticed in the mirror finish of the car that a couple curls had escaped my barrette, as usual. I smoothed them back into place as I slid into the soft leather seat. The interior felt like a luxury sedan.

"Not what you expected, is it?" Charlie said, his face glowing with health from spending a lot of time outside. "I think that's why I like it. People say your vehicle says a lot about you and I think this one describes me perfectly. Fun-loving and full of surprises. Here we go."

We went down the long drive overhung with a leafy green canopy above created by the old majestic oak trees on either side, then past the flat stone panel chiseled with the name *Fair Winds* and out to the main road to St. Michaels and the Miles River Yacht Club. The Governor's Cup was housed permanently in a secure display case there. But first, on this Friday afternoon we had to get through the oceans of tourists. The people visiting St. Michaels seemed to forget the purpose of sidewalks and tended to wander in the roadway looking at the old stone church or the many shops and restaurants that lined the main street. I guess they trusted that drivers would stop or swerve to avoid them. Personally, I wouldn't want to take the chance.

The village of St. Michaels was about ninety minutes of Washington, D.C. and light years away from that lifestyle. People came by car and by boat. Its reputation as a sailing destination was well known. The town, stores and restaurants not only welcomed adults and children, but catered to four-legged canine visitors as well. Water bowls were strategically placed around town and some restaurants even featured a canine menu on their patios or enclosed outside serving areas. Visitors thought it was a great place to visit. I was lucky to live here.

"Oh, look!" I pointed to a large purple sign by the side of the roadway. It read *4 out of 5 people who use heroin started with recreational use of prescription painkillers.* "Do you know why signs like that one are popping up all of a sudden?"

"As a matter of fact I do. It's all part of Project Purple, is meant to raise awareness about opioid epidemic led by the county sheriff. There are always people who think drug addiction problems happen someplace else, but it's happening everywhere. Good people take a doctor-prescribed painkiller after surgery or injury and get hooked. And it can become a downward spiral that leads to heroin." He reached into his glove compartment. "I just happen to have a pamphlet here that tells you all about it."

My eyebrows shot up in surprise. "You're well prepared," I said as I opened the purple and white piece brimming with information and contact telephone numbers.

"I should be. It's one of our Rotary projects," he said with pride.

"Is that why you're so involved?"

As we rode together in the sudden silence for a several minutes, I wondered if I'd said something wrong. Then Charlie took a quick look at me, not once, but twice. "My dad walked out on our family when I was in high school so it was just Mom, my sister and me. Dad was the disciplinarian in the family. Since he wasn't there to bust my chops when I acted out my anger, I started experimenting with drugs."

Now it was my turn to take a quick look at Charlie. He didn't seem the type to use drugs, but what did I know?

"Mom went back to work to make sure we had enough money, because he said he wasn't going to pay for us anymore. So, I had plenty of freedom to dive into drugs to deal with the craziness and to find some peace. I started slow, with marijuana. Then people told me I deserved to have some fun and I hit the prescription drugs in my mom's medicine cabinet. Fortunately, an old coach saw me, brought me up short and helped me get clean. Who knows where I'd be today if he hadn't recognized the signs or written me off as a *bad kid*. Now, I can have a beer occasionally, but when I want or need a high, I jump on a boat. The people in the racing community are like my second family. That's what I need, to be around people who love and care about me. So, if Project Purple can help somebody the way my coach helped me, I'm all for it."

I didn't know what to say so I thought it was best to keep

things light. "It sounds like you're involved in a lot of things. What do you do when you're not sailing, ferrying newbies around or fighting a drug epidemic?"

"I wanted to make my living sailing, but that's almost impossible to do. Now, I have a landscaping… more of a lawn maintenance business. At least I'm outside. A desk in an office would kill me. And it didn't take long for me to realize that to make some real money I had to work on big properties. That's how I met Dr. Phillips. He's incredible!"

"Yes, he is. He knows something about everything, I think." I turned to him. "I really appreciate you taking the time to do this. I didn't mean to take you from your work."

"No problem. Sailing always comes first with me. And I have a couple guys working for me now. They can handle things this afternoon." He hit the blinker. "Almost there."

We followed a meandering road that lead to the yacht club. He slid the little Jeep into an open space and I got out almost in a daze. What a perfect spot for a yacht club. The sprawling one-story building presided over an area of bucolic beauty and serenity. Leaves of the tall, decades-old trees swayed gently in the breeze and offered shady areas on a manicured lawn that ran down the hill to the docks. In almost every slip, a large boat swayed on her lines. This was not a world of little runabouts or small rubber rafts with a motor on the back. Those boats were used as dinghies for the sailboats, cabin cruisers and trawlers waiting patiently for their captains and mates to take their next trip on the Miles River and beyond. While the view of the river from Fair Winds was breathtaking, the view of this cove offered a different perspective. Across the water stood large houses designed as second or retirement homes. Behind us, giggles and wild splashes came from the club's swimming pool where children, parents and grandparents were enjoying themselves.

"Abby?"

Charlie drew me from my reverie. "Oh, I'm sorry. I got lost for a second."

"It's a perfect place, so peaceful right now." He grinned with a mischievous glint in his eye. "But this weekend, it will be chaos, sometimes controlled, sometimes not. People will meet up with friends. There will be some posturing, sometimes friendly, sometimes not. I think you'll find it interesting."

"What are the people like, the ones who race the log canoes?" I asked.

"You could say most of us are a different breed of sailor," he said with a laugh. "First, if we had a choice of being on land or on the water, most of us would turn and head to a boat. I think our first choice would be a sailboat, but it probably wouldn't matter if a power boat was the only kind available." He turned and looked out at the Miles River, almost a mile and a half wide here, beyond the cove. "Most people don't understand, but it really is a different world out there. Things are constantly changing. You're going head-to-head with Mother Nature."

He turned and looked at me. "Don't laugh, okay? If I can take a cue from Charles Dickens … Sailing is the best of times and the worst of times. And it definitely brings out the best and the worst in people. You'll see…you are coming to the seafood feast, aren't you?"

"You said something about it on the phone, but I don't know where to sign up."

"Consider yourself a Friend of the *Island Memory*, the canoe I sail on. You'll love meeting the crew." He leaned closer and lowered his voice. "I'd love to hear your impressions of the different people who come out for the races. Friday night will be a blast if you love to people-watch." He paused for a moment and cocked his head to the side. "Actually, I think each crew has a little different personality."

"Are there rivalries?

He snorted. "Rivalries? Some of the captains are out for blood. You'd think their whole lives depended on the result of a race."

He'd piqued my curiosity. "What about your captain?"

"Dominick? He's the best. Calm, easy-going. But don't get the idea that he doesn't care. He sails to win with a quiet, almost brooding, intensity. Yes, that's a good way to describe him. He loves being out there and that feeling transfers to everyone on the crew. That's why I love being on his crew."

"What about your main opponent?"

Charlie's face darkened. "You mean *Flying Wing?* She was built on Tilghman Island just like our *Island Memory.* But her captain is a piece of work. I'd rather be on a chase boat then crew for him. He's wild. They call him Black Jack and he loves the name. Says it makes him sound ominous. He completely misses the point that he only sees black if he doesn't win." He held up his hands in mock defense. "Don't get me wrong. He wins sometimes, but not all the time as he'd like." He shook his head. "But his way isn't the way I like to win. What do they say? It's not about the winning. It's about the journey. My skipper, Dominick, makes it a total package."

Charlie's observations fascinated me. "So, why do you sail log canoes?"

Charlie's eyes drifted away, almost in a trance, taking in the beauty of the water, pondering my question. Then he said, "I think there are two reasons. There's the thrill of sailing on the edge of catastrophe. The other reason is the feeling of belonging. I guess every winning sailboat crew is close. They have to be if they're going to work as a unit. But there's something different on a log canoe. You're facing the threat of capsizing, together. You're harnessing the wind, together. You celebrate the hard-fought win, together. And face the disappointment of defeat, together." He had a bewildered look on his face. "Does that make sense?"

I smiled, feeling a little envious. "Yes, it does. I think you call it *family.*"

A smile spread over face. "Yes, I think you're right. We're a family." He shook his head. "A family, warts and all warts."

"And you all are vying for one trophy in the afternoon race, the Governor's Cup ?"

Charlie snapped back to reality. "Yes, of course. The Governor's Cup. That's the whole reason you're here. Come on, it's inside." He led the way to the front door. "I didn't mean to go off on a tangent.

"That's okay, it helps make this whole experience more interesting. I'm learning it's about more than silver."

He reached out to open the door and found it locked. "Oops, forgot my key card," he said. "Be right back."

That's when I heard him call out, "Hey, stranger."

"Hey, yourself," was the response. It was that voice that sent an electric shock through me.

Could it be? Ryan? I thought. *No, he's thousands of miles away doing something important. If he'd come home, he'd have let me know... wouldn't he?*

I turned around.

Ryan was home.

CHAPTER 5

he techniques used to work metal date back to the times of the Ancient Greeks. They have been modified for use with silver. It is tragic that with the passing of great silversmiths, some of these techniques are falling into disuse or lost entirely.

"The Butler's Guide to Fine Silver"
Mr. Hollister, 1898

THE DEEP RESONANT voice belonged to a strikingly-handsome man who greeted Charlie with a strong handshake and man-hug. Ryan. Last year, he stole my heart then disappeared on a months-long business trip. His face looked weary, his tan faded. I watched silently, stuck in place, as snatches of conversation reached me.

"...Buddy Skyler in Oahu." "Hong Kong..." "Beach at Corfu." "London... West End... compared to New York."

"Abby?" Charlie was walking toward me with his friend.

What should I think? How should I act? Ryan was back and he

hadn't let me know. I put my hands behind my back and held on to my fingers so the men wouldn't see them shaking.

"Abby, forgive me," Charlie said. "I'm being rude." Ryan started walking toward me, his face filled with delight. "This is my good friend, who I haven't seen in months. Let me introduce you. Abby, this is—"

"Introductions aren't necessary." I hoped my voice sounded steady. "Ryan and I have met." My words were like icicles.

We've met! MET? What was I saying?

We were more than casual acquaintances. I was drawn to him from the moment Lorraine introduced us at the festival on Tilghman Island where we watched the docking competition and ate crabs until I thought I'd burst. There was the excitement of my first Christmas in St. Michaels with Lorraine's lavish holiday party at Fair Winds and the ride on his sailboat decked out with twinkling lights in the magical Christmas Boat Parade. And the romantic cruise up the river to the cove by the Abbey ruins. He recounted the local legend of the star-crossed lovers who returned every year as regal white swans, always together. Then he kissed me. I thought, I thought— shortly after that afternoon when we caught a murderer, he disappeared without a word. Well, he didn't exactly disappear. He left on what his message said would be an extended business trip. A business trip? This man who seemed to fill his days with sailing and spending time with friends. He never talked about his business or profession until he left in a whirlwind.

"Yes, Abby and I are—" He hesitated for a moment. "Friends."

My heart squeezed.

Charlie could sense the tension between us as he sputtered, "Friends. Great." His head whipped back and forth between the two of us as he tried to get a handle on the situation. "Yes, we're all friends here." He took a deep breath. "Well, I am supposed to show Abby the Governor's Cup trophy inside."

Excited that he'd found a neutral topic, Charlie turned to

Ryan. "Hey, did you know this Sunday is the 90th anniversary of the race? It's good that you're back for it. Things are really…" His voice trailed off when he noticed we really weren't listening to him. Our eyes locked in the steaming heat rising from the asphalt parking lot.

"I called when I got back," Ryan said in a soft voice.

It didn't help. I was still mad, still hurt. He'd left town like a thief in the night. No warning. No explanation. And couldn't be bothered to keep in touch. I'd called his cell, but it always went to voicemail.

During one late-night conversation, Lorraine floated the idea that he'd forgotten his phone. As the days went by, she speculated that he might be using a satellite phone. Later, she suggested that he was using a business cell phone since he was away on business and wasn't allowed to make personal calls. Away on business. Lorraine couldn't shed any light on his business, because she'd never thought to ask. The Eastern Shore was another world, so different from the cities of Washington and Baltimore just miles away. Here, it was more of what kind of person you were, not what you did for a living.

Chase shifted his weight from one foot to the other, not sure what to say or do, then he cleared his throat. "Well, I guess I should show Abby the trophy."

I wasn't going to make it easier for Ryan. It was up to him to make things right. Not me. "Yes," I said with a gay lilt. "Let's see this special silver trophy." I turned toward to the front door.

But Ryan got to the door first and swiped his key card to unlock it. "I need to talk to the dockmaster about my boat anyway."

He let me enter the long hallway first. It was cool, such a relief after the August heat and strain outside. I stepped around the pennant or burgee of the club done in tile and set in the floor. I didn't know if it was bad luck if one stepped on the symbol of the organization. There was enough bad karma right now from the raw feelings that welled up inside me at seeing Ryan again. Yes, they were raw and that surprised me. I'd pushed them down for months, out of mind. Now, here they were again, bright red and angry.

"The trophy cases are in the main dining room. This way, Abby."

It was time to bury those feelings again and go to work. I followed Charlie down the hallway to the club's formal dining room decorated with a subtle nautical theme. What really captured my attention was an entire wall of trophies, many of them silver, winking in the special lighting that shone from above.

"Not all these trophies are for sail racing," he said as he moved to the far section. "Some of them are for power boating and some are for fishing tournaments."

I was amazed at the variety. Somehow I thought of a trophy as being a small loving cup or set of pillars with one of those figures on top like a baseball or football player. Of course, I knew about the Heisman Trophy, Stanley Cup and the America's Cup, but they were for big championships and had international recognition. These trophies varied from fine crystal to ornately-worked silver. Some were mounted on wooden pedestals surrounded with small engraved plaques that begged closer examination. But Charlie wasted no time looking at them. He went to stand in front of a large silver trophy placed in a prominent position.

"Here it is," he announced. "The Governor's Cup of Maryland."

I had seen pictures of it, but nothing prepared me for the real thing. The term *cup* was misleading. "I can't believe how large it is," I said in surprise. "It's more like a punch bowl than a cup."

Charlie chuckled in embarrassment. "Funny you should say that. It's a magnificent piece, but sometimes the captain and crew get a little carried away when they win."

I was almost afraid to ask, "What do you mean?"

"Well, sometimes the trophy is turned into sort of a punch

bowl. The winners might fill it with champagne or beer, depending on their tastes, and drink out of it."

I looked back at the trophy and shook my head. "The wooden base looks really heavy and awkward."

"Yeah." The skin crinkled around his eyes as he grinned. "I didn't say all the champagne went down the gullet. Usually a fair amount ends up on the floor and dousing the people all around. That's why we do it outside. The crews have been known to swamp their captains the way teams do in the NFL."

I looked at him in horror. How could they use such a treasured piece of silver like that? What if it slipped? What if it hit the ground? It was too awful to contemplate. But I didn't dare say a word. I didn't want to embarrass this man who had probably been sailing all his life on the Chesapeake Bay and was kind enough to introduce me to this special world. I looked at the trophy and had to trust that since it had survived ninety years, it would likely make it to its centennial.

I flashed him a big smile. "Well, I guess they earned it."

He relaxed and returned my smile as I leaned closer to the trophy. "The workmanship to create the boat under sail in repoussé is amazing, "I said. "The sails look like they are full of wind and the boat seems to be racing across the front of the trophy," I said.

"The canoe," he said gently. "We call it a log canoe or a canoe. The term sailboat seems to refer to a more modern boat like the ones at the slips outside."

"Ah, I understand. I'll try not to make that mistake again," I said, hoping I'd remember.

"You might be interested to know that the canoe on the trophy is not a figment of the silversmith's imagination. It is a representation of an actual racing log canoe called *Island Bird*. She was built by William Sidney Covington right down the road on Tilghman Island. The name of the all his log canoes began with the word Island to show his pride in the place where he was born, raised and worked."

I was intrigued. "Names like ?"

"*Island Bird* and *Island Blossom*, those canoes are still racing today along with the canoe I'm on *Island Memory*."

As we walked back to his Jeep, I realized how these boats had captured my imagination. "I'm really looking forward to seeing my first log canoe race this weekend," I said. "I've been on what you call modern sailboats but…"

Charlie his face lit up with excitement. "There's nothing like a log canoe race. The masts are made from tall thick trees soaring high over your head. The yards and yards of canvas are right next to you, straining against the wind, propelling your canoe through the water at a breakneck speed. And you always face the challenge of counterbalancing the pressure of the wind with your weight just to keep it upright." He shook his head in awe. "It's quite a rush to be part of the crew, flying along just inches out of the water, working together as a team dancing on the edge between winning and disaster."

I envied him the thrill and his commitment to something that he loved so much. "How long have you been doing this?" I asked.

He glanced up at the sky with a smile, lost in a memory. "I've been sailing since before I was born."

"I don't understand."

"My mother was the main trimmer on *Flying Wing*. It was really the only position for somebody small and light. She sat on the outrigger, the seat that is back beyond the stern of the canoe. She didn't let a little thing like expecting a baby keep her from doing something she loved. She must have passed that passion on to me in the womb. Like so many other kids, I took the tiller at a young age. Before I knew it, I was competing in regattas around the Shore in my very own little sailboat called an Opti, for Optimist and I've been doing it ever since, whenever I get the chance."

What a friendly and open man. "Sounds like you plan your life around sailing."

"You've got me pegged. As soon as the season starts in May, I'm on the water. And in the winter, I'm involved in training and helping to get the boats and crews ready for the next season. When you're facing the water, wind and weather, you need your wits. I do everything I can to sharpen my skills. What I learn could make the difference in where we finish or just keeping our log canoe upright." He walked away from the trophy case. "I need to get you back to Fair Winds then I've got to get back. There's a lot to do."

What a joy it was for Charlie to live in a place that fed his passion for sailing and racing. I too had found a feeling of belonging at Fair Winds and was grateful for it.

Feeling light and happy, I wasn't prepared for the look of desolation that met me when I returned to the cottage at Fair Winds. My roommate barely lifted his head from his paws when I stepped on to the porch though his brown eyes followed me as I put down my things and sank down next to him. Gently, I lay my hand on his head and I kept telling myself, *Stay calm.* If he was sick, I'd learned it was very important for me not to panic. He would react to my reaction and we'd both be hysterical in moments. *Stay calm.*

"What's the matter, buddy? Don't you feel good?"

I don't know why I always asked him questions, expecting a response, but it seemed like the most natural thing to do. Except this time, he didn't move. He just looked at me with those brown eyes that always made me melt. It was time for the ultimate test and if he didn't react, I'd spring into crisis mode.

I stood up slowly and asked The Question. "Simon, do you want a cookie?"

HE ALMOST KNOCKED me down as he scrambled to his feet. He licked my bare toes, my new sandals, my legs.

"Okay, okay. I get it. There's nothing wrong with you that a little attention and a cookie or two can't fix." I opened the front door and Simon dashed passed me, his nails skittering on the wood floors all the way to the kitchen. I took the lid off the his dog cookie jar. He wagged his tail in ecstasy.

"Nope, it's not that easy." I took out a cookie, showed it to him and put him through the hand signals for Sit, Down, Sit, Stay. Then I flipped the cookie into the air. He jumped and caught it on the downward arc. His jaws made fast work of it. He always did, since he was a pup. I felt a wave of sadness. He wasn't a pup any longer. He'd passed his first birthday several months earlier and tipped the scale at almost eighty pounds. The vet said early on that he was going to be a big one. I remembered cringing at that piece of news. It was funny that my first dog was the size of Mack truck!

Fortunately, Lorraine was my mentor in dog ownership as well as so many other things. She didn't replace Gran in my heart. There was no way anyone could replace the woman who'd raised me, but I guess my heart had grown to make room for this woman who'd become more than an employer. She was my closest friend. It was obvious that Simon was getting too smart for me. I'd have to consult with her about teaching him new tricks. But it would have to wait until after the weekend sailing events.

Feeling like my life was back in balance again, I thought I was ready to deal with the whole Ryan situation. I sat down and tried to make sense of the fact that somehow it was my fault that I missed his calls since he'd returned. Unlike most people under 30, I did not walk around with my cell phone plastered to my body. I'd done that in my past life when I worked as a software developer, first for a defense contractor who expected an instant response no matter the hour, then as part of start-up run by a friend who would give me creative room to put my ideas to work. I thought I'd get time for a more normal life. Only it was worse. Sharing a Friday night pizza at the pub became a staff meeting. My phone even stayed by my pillow in case someone had a *brilliant idea* in the early morning hours. When a bloody murder and a bullet from Lorraine's old gun put an end to all that and I started my new life on the Eastern Shore, Lorraine and Dawkins and later, Ryan teased me about ignoring my phone or missing text and voicemail alerts when I was busy researching and writing. It had been a struggle finishing the magazine article by the deadline earlier in the week. The only way I could get it done was to ignore everything else. If Lorraine had needed me, she knew where I was.

I looked at the list of missed calls and noticed that I'd missed a text alert from the day before.

I'm back! Can't wait to see you! I brought you a present! Call me!

Great, now what was I supposed to do? I could hear Dawkins prim-and-proper voice in my head. "Do nothing. Let him pursue you." Lorraine would counter, "Don't be ridiculous. These aren't the dark ages when I grew up. Call him!" But neither of them had witnessed our reunion at the yacht club. They didn't see freeze him out. They didn't see his chilly response. No, this had to be my decision. I powered down the phone and put it on the kitchen counter. Maybe time would sort out this awkward situation. At least, that's what I hoped.

Besides, he wasn't the only one with a business to run. I was still behind on doing the inventory of Lorraine's silver and I owed an article to an elite magazine for silver aficionados. Maybe I didn't have a business that took me around the world, but what I was doing was getting some attention in the world of sterling silver.

CHAPTER 6

It is prudent to insist that any member of the staff handling silver pieces wear white gloves. They are a reminder that special care is needed and carelessness can cause damage to a piece.

"The Butler's Guide to Fine Silver"
Mr. Hollister, 1898

THE NEXT MORNING, I had breakfast in my cottage rather than the kitchen in the main house which would be a busy place. Mrs. Clark prepared all the meals for the political chat weekend. The guests would start arriving tonight for drinks and a buffet. A few were staying at Fair Winds, but most would appear early Saturday morning to board the fishing boat for a day of talking *across the aisle*, as Lorraine called it. Actually, they would also be talking *across the Bay*, because she had invited some people who had the interests of the Eastern Shore dear to their hearts. No press was allowed so they a chance for them to get to know one another as people and explore ideas.

Armed with a mug of coffee, I went straight to the Lorraine's library and found her on the phone. I was about to slip away when she waved me into the room.

"Fine. Thank you, Frank." She put the phone down with a sigh of relief. "Quick, tell me how you are, before that blasted thing rings again," she begged.

"I'm fine."

She peered at me and sensed something was wrong. I didn't want to complicate her life this weekend with the news that Ryan was back. She had enough to juggle without straightening out my life.

I gave her a big smile. "I wanted to make sure you're surviving. Is there anything I can do?"

She sat back, grateful for a moment's rest. "Yes, I'm surviving. This kind of weekend creates a whirlwind . Someone, who wasn't invited, heard about it, called a mutual friend who called me to beg for another invitation. I had to listen to all the reasons why he would be a valuable addition. Now, I can say the fishing boats are full." She giggled. "Maybe we'd be better off if the boats sank with all aboard." She threw her arms up in the air. "OH MY! What am I thinking? Abby, if you ever tell anyone I said that, I shall deny it to my dying day."

I laughed, too. "Your secret is safe with me. Is there anything I can do to help?"

She put her hands together in prayer. "You could come to the buffet dinner tonight. I can't believe I agreed to hold an open house. We'll be lucky to lock the front door by eleven."

I shook my head. "I can't, and it's all your fault," I accused her in a playful way. "You want me to learn about log canoe racing and the silver sailing trophy. Dr. Phillips contacted someone who is on a crew. He took me down to the yacht club ..." My words trailed off. Lorraine was staring at the view outside. "Lorraine?"

She continued to gaze outside as she said with a gentle softness. "I wonder if I should call Rupert to come..." Her eyes jumped back to me as if she'd suddenly remembered I was right there. "I mean Dr. Phillips. He's such an old and dear friend and would be such good company to balance these stuffy politicians." With a quick shake of her head, she sat up. "I must be losing my grip. That is a *terrible* idea. Once they found out he knows everything about everything, they'd ring him dry for that one factoid that would make an argument… or even an election! No, no."

She picked up a pen and was about to make a note somewhere on the papers in front of her when she looked at me again. "I'm sorry. Did you say you're coming to the dinner buffet tonight?"

I had to suppress a giggle. Lorraine was normally calm and in control. This weekend of entertaining had really thrown her off her stride. "I'm afraid I can't. Charlie offered to take me to a special seafood buffet tonight sponsored by one of the log canoe captains for all the crews and friends to kick off the weekend."

"Hmm, that's a little unusual," she commented while shuffling papers. "The crew party is usually Saturday night, if I remember correctly."

"Charlie— that's Dr. Phillips's friend—said one of the captains is sponsoring it because it's Governor's Cup weekend."

"That explains it. Well, what about my big dinner tomorrow night? Think of it, an evening of exaggerated stories about the one that got away. Won't you please…?" The hopeful glint in her eye faded when she saw me slowly shaking my head again. "Abigail, what event could possibly be more enticing on a Saturday evening?"

"If I have any energy left at all after a day on the water, Charlie asked me to go to the party at the club that night."

Lorraine raised her eyebrows and sent a silent question my way which I quickly answered. "No, it's not a date. It's just part of the whole log canoe race weekend experience."

She pulled her attention away from yet another list of details. "I'm glad you're making friends. A word of advice: be sure to watch out for a Dark 'n Stormy."

"A what? It sounds like the beginning of a bad mystery novel." I got the desired effect of lifting her mood without trying.

"It's as far from literary as you can get. A Dark 'n Stormy is a sailor's drink. You pour dark rum over ice and then add ginger beer and a lime. It's delicious and deceptive. Don't drive after a couple. Call and we'll pick you up. Too bad it's so early in the day. One of those could help me through these last-minute details."

I headed to the door. "I'd better let you get back to it. I'm sure it will be great."

She sighed. "Thank you for your vote of confidence. I wish there were two or three of me to handle all these details."

"I'll look in on you tonight."

Lorraine smiled. "It would be good to see a friendly face."

"Good luck this weekend. I think you're doing a good thing."

Lorraine nodded. "Yes, I think Daddy would be proud. He always said that more good politics happens over good food and drink than on the floor of the chamber. We'll see." Her phone rang. She blew me a kiss and answered it with a sweet *Hello!*

Back at the cottage, I paced like a caged lion. The sound of toenails on the hardwood floor followed me until Simon got tired and jumped onto the sofa where he could watch me with expending any energy.

What was wrong with me? What was I feeling? Irritation? Anger? Desperation? I stopped. I was feeling none of those things. I was feeling guilty. Guilty about a friendship with Seth that developed during Plein Air Art Festival. Guilty? Ridiculous! Ryan and I didn't have an exclusive relationship. I wasn't sneaking around behind his back. He'd left as if I wasn't part of his life, supporting and encouraging him in whatever he wanted to do. Something came up and he didn't give me a chance to be part of it. He left. So, I went off on my own.

On my own. I learned what that meant when Gran and Aunt Agnes passed away. I was so deliberate about making decisions, trying to act grown up. But I was terrified of making a mistake. I sold the house and headed east to Washington, D. C. to start a new life and met Reggie. Together, we worked to build a new business. I didn't know Lorraine was his aunt. The story of what happened was so sad. I had no time for tears now.

I headed to the kitchen for more coffee and sat on the porch thinking about how I'd ended up here at Fair Winds. Deciding to accept Lorraine's job offer was different from deciding to selling the house in Seattle and driving across country. I knew Lorraine. We'd started our history together. She gave me a clear job description and delineated the financial arrangement that included a rent-free cottage overlooking the Miles River. It was my first real step to becoming self-reliant.

That's what I thought. I met Ryan and was almost swept off my feet. We shared a lot, but brought different experiences to the relationship. How did I let him distract me from who I wanted to be? I wanted to be an independent woman who could take care of herself. I didn't want a man to take control of my life. Why was I so distracted?

Simon curled up at my feet. I never expected this black fur ball to worm his way into my life. As I stroked his silky fur, I realized that he held the answer. I was missing *family*.

Everybody has a family by blood. Sadly, mine was gone. My mother died in a car accident when I was five. My dad was driving. He felt so guilty that he left me with Gran and returned to active duty as a naval officer.

And they say each person has a family by choice. That's the one I was building here on the Eastern Shore. Lorraine was more than an employer. She was a friend, confidant, sort of like a big sister. And Dawkins. Thinking about him as *family* made me wince. He was a strange bird, but I had to admit that when things got complicated, I could count on him. He probably filled the role of obnoxious big brother in my new little family. And then there was Ryan. Yes, I wanted a man in my life. Someone I could enjoy spending time with, going to parties, events or a sunset cruise. I wanted a man who could share my life and maybe someday grow to love. But I had to realize that we'd only known each other for a little over a year and we had only been dating for several months. If I was going to feel anything about my relationship with him, it might be guilt for trying to speed things along. An independent woman would have the confidence to let things happen naturally.

I stood up and declared aloud, "And that's what I'm going to do."

Simon scrambled to his feet, lost his balance and fell against my leg. He was growing up and out, getting bigger and stronger every day, but he was still a born comic when his puppy side came out.

"Come on, big guy. Get your ball." He scrambled to his toy box, got the red ball and raced outside.

CHAPTER 7

Be aware that a silver piece may be altered to increase its value. Know that the true value of an altered piece is its worth before the alteration. Any change to a finished piece, once discovered, reduces the value of the piece substantially.

"The Butler's Guide to Fine Silver"
Mr. Hollister, 1898

AFTER MY ROMP WITH SIMON, I showered and put on a comfortable pair of shorts and a top with a soft neckline. I was about to leave when my phone rang. It was Ryan. I couldn't let it go to voicemail, not again. I took a deep breath and answered the call.

"Hi, I'm so glad I reached you." His words rolled out in a rush. "I was wondering if you'd like to have a drink... or dinner?"

I asked when and his answer amazed me.

"Tonight, if possible?"

What nerve! Was I the one he called when he didn't have any other plans for a Friday night? I fought down the urge to verbally separate his head from his body. I plastered a smile on my face and tried to sound sincere. "Oh, I'm so sorry. I'm on my way out to the seafood feast at the club tonight and I'm tied up with the Governor's Cup all weekend."

He didn't say a word. Did I want to sever any chance of a relationship with him? Gran always said to leave my options open, so I did. "How about early next week?"

He stammered as if surprised by my response. "Oh, okay. I was hoping we could talk."

I felt my hard edge soften. "Yes, I think that would be a good idea. I just can't right now."

"Okay, next week then." I could almost taste his disappointment.

"Great," I said quickly. "I'm sorry, but I have to run."

I patted Simon, locked him in the cottage and headed to my car, mumbling the whole way. *Who does he think he is? Calling at the last minute like that?* I decided I wasn't going to let it ruin my evening and I headed to my Saab convertible. When I saw the cars coming down the driveway, I was glad I'd blocked the doggie door in the kitchen so Simon was safe from drivers not used to watching for a black dog running around in the dark.

I found a parking space way out in the field and hiked to the front porch where Charlie waited for me. Why hadn't someone snapped up this guy? He looked good in his navy blue plaid Bermuda shorts and white buttoned-down shirt with the sleeves rolled up to show off his tan. He was smart, nice and successful. If Dr. Phillips thought well of him, he must be a good catch. Not that I was interested. Not now anyway. No, I was just going to enjoy the weekend.

"Hi," I said in greeting as I walked up to him. "Sorry to keep you waiting. I had to park almost in the next county." I thought it was funny, but he took my comment seriously.

"Yeah, I should have warned you. It sounds like a small event— a seafood feast for log canoe sailors—but each canoe has a crew of eight to twelve or more people, depending on her size. Multiply that by the twelve canoes that are planning to start. Add friends and family and you've got a lot of people."

Quickly, I did the math and gasped. "They're feeding as many people as a medium-sized wedding. No wonder I had trouble finding a parking place."

"Wait until tomorrow. But you're here now and that's what is important. Let's check out the buffet before all the food is gone." He touched my elbow and we turned to walk down the spacious lawn where everyone was chatting, eating and drinking.

I put my hand on Charlie's arm and drew him a little closer. "I feel a little…"

He filled in the words for me. "A little like a fish out of water?" I looked at him and smiled. "No, I didn't mean to make a pun… or whatever that was. It's how a lot of people feel when they come to a sailing event, especially a log canoe event. Everyone knows everybody or at least speaks the same language. We don't say main sail. It's pronounced *mains'l*. Do you know you'd better watch out when we're jibing?"

"Exactly. I have no clue—"

He put his hands on my shoulders and put his forehead against mine. "Do you like eating?"

"Um, yes." I wasn't where he was going with this.

"Do you like oysters all different ways and corn on the cob slathered in melted butter?"

"Mmm, yes." I didn't realize that I was hungry, but now I was starving.

He squeezed my shoulders. "You'll fit right in. Come on." He grabbed my hand and led me down the hill to the buffet tables that were crowded with all the delicacies he'd described.

He stopped and surveyed the scene. "The line is too long. We'll come back. There's someone you should meet."

I waved away a cloud of gnats, a summertime nuisance, as I gazed at the table, my tummy grumbling, but followed Charlie to the spot where two men were talking. One was wearing a white chef's jacket and toque. The other was in black shorts and a black polo shirt with the name *Flying Wing* stitched on it in white. He was about six feet tall with light brown hair streaked by the sun, holding an open bottle of imported beer in his hand.

The chef was saying, "Yes, I can do that. I'll take care of it right away."

In response, he got a nod and a sarcastic comment. "You do that."

The chef scooted away and Charlie stepped up to the man in black. "Skipper, how are you doing?"

"Charlie! Good to see you, my man. Have you seen the error of your ways and decided to join my crew?" He took a swig of his beer. Up close, I could see a few pockmarks left from acne, but it was his eyes that had captivated me. They were deep Mediterranean blue and reminded me of that day on the beach at Mykonos that summer with Gran when the sea was the same color.

A smile of satisfaction flashed across Charlie's face. "No, I'm pretty well committed to *Island Memory*." He gave my hand a little tug and I ended up in front of the skipper. "But I do want you meet someone new to log canoe racing."

He looked me up and down. "Too big for a baler."

I wasn't sure how to take that comment so I pasted a smile on my face as Charlie jumped in with an explanation. "No, she's not a candidate for a crew position. This is Abby. You said she could catch a ride on your chase boat tomorrow. " He glanced at me. "Abby, this is Jack, the skipper of *Flying Wing*."

"People call me Black Jack, sometimes even to my face." He squinted and turned to Charlie. "And I said she could go out on my chase boat?"

Charlie responded by saying each word very carefully to give added meaning. "Yes, Jack. You did. This is the woman who works for Lorraine Andrews and lives at Fair Winds."

Jack's face lit up. "Yes! Of course." His hand shot out to shake mine. "And how is Lorraine?"

A little seasick by his sudden mood swings, I said she was doing fine.

"I'm happy to have you aboard. Maybe you'll bring us luck." He appeared to check me out again from top to bottom.

Somebody in the crowd called out to him. "Jack, over here,"

With the flair of a hack actor, he shrugged. "My public calls. See you tomorrow."

I leaned over and whispered in Charlie's ear. "If he doesn't win tomorrow, is he going to blame me?"

He raised his eyebrows. "Why would you say that?"

"Well, every sport has its superstitions. They say that baseball players are the worst."

He looked at me in surprise. "What do you know about baseball superstitions?

"My Aunt Agnes was a huge baseball fan. She loved to listen to the games on radio. She said television ruined the game. She preferred to *see it* through the words of the announcers who really knew the game."

He nodded. "There are still a lot people who prefer to listen then watch."

"That's how she learned about the superstitions. This player made sure he stepped on the foul line when coming up to bat. That player intentionally stepped over the line. When a team was on a winning streak, some players only ate chicken or a steak or macaroni and cheese. Or they won't wash their socks or their—"

Charlie held up his hand. "Okay, okay, I get it. It's going to take me a while to get that little piece of information out of my brain. No, I don't think sailors are quite that—"

I realized that I really wanted to go out and watch the race up close and blurted out, "Is he still going to let me go out on his chase boat?"

He took my hand. "Don't worry. He's already said yes." Then

he was quiet for a moment. "He doesn't go back on his word, usually," he mumbled.

I pressed. "So, if he loses the race tomorrow, he might think it was because I was nearby and breathing." I had to know what I was getting into.

Charlie began to chuckle, then the smile fell from his lips. "With Jack, you never know. There a reason they call him Black Jack. He's always ready to blame anyone or anything even if he was the one who made a boneheaded move as captain. He likes to intimidate the competition, too. He's really quite an act, but I don't think he's as superstitious as baseball players." He put his arm around me and gave me a little hug. "I think it's time to eat!"

As we neared the mile-long buffet table, Charlie slowed to stop. "Uh oh, that's not good." I looked around, but didn't see anything wrong. "Over there. Jack is talking to two of my crew mates."

The significance escaped me. "Why is that a problem?"

"Jack is the captain of *Flying Wing*, our big rival." I felt his hand against my back, applying a little pressure to move me forward. "Let's just wander by and see if we can catch what they're saying."

I let him steer me and the captain's voice was loud and clear. "You should come over to my boat. You're good sailors and I'll give you the freedom to do what you do best."

One of the guys noticed Charlie closing in on their conversation and made a quick exit. "Maybe next season, Jack. Gotta go."

He steered me away. "Okay, now we can get something to eat."

People clustered around the long buffet like bears to honey. While we got in line, I caught a glimpse of a walking floral bouquet. I couldn't help but stare at the young woman, petite with freckles sprinkled across her cheeks. Her hairstyle was something to behold. There were maybe five braids spouting from her head in different colors with matching flowers. I'd never seen anything like it and was about to point her out to Charlie when I stopped. No one else had reacted to the bright display. Could she be a regular part of this group? I closed my mouth and focused my attention on the buffet.

Tangy smells of the sea enveloped us as we stepped up to the stack of large dinner plates. Platters and bowls stretched down the length of the table. I started with a fried soft crab then moved on to the pile of fried oysters with spiced lumps of breading crumbling away. I took several. This was no time to think about cholesterol or calories.

Suddenly a muscular arm reached in front of me. His head of sun-bleached silver-blonde hair tickled my nose as he leaned past me. "Don't mind me, pretty lady. I just want one of these beauties." He waved a gnat off a broiled crab cake, grabbed it with his bare fingers and popped the whole thing in his mouth."

"Oh, come on, Dutch," Charlie growled. "That's gross."

"Hey, didn't mean to gross out your lady." Dutch opened his ice blue eyes wide and pouted, trying to look innocent, but it was obvious to everyone that he didn't mean it.

Somebody behind us challenged him. "Why don't you get in line like everyone else?"

The big man faked a shudder. "Oh no, that would interfere with my drinking." He held up his large plastic cup. "Don't have enough hands." And he walked away laughing.

Charlie had promised this was a great night for people-watching and he was right. I kept my eyes on what was next on the buffet, deviled clams, cold crab salad and crispy fried chicken, a staple at many Eastern Shore feasts. The side dishes were a meal in themselves: creamy coleslaw, two kinds of potato salad, fresh green beans, baby lima beans and stewed tomatoes. Mountains of golden rolls and biscuits and a wide variety of sauces came next. There were several tomato-based sauces that went from spicy to fire-engine hot. Small bowls of mayonnaise, capers, pickle relish and lemon wedges offered separate taste enhancers or the chance to concoct one's own. Fresh corn on the cob slathered in melted butter stayed warm in a special pan. I glanced at the dessert table and was excited to see several flavors of Smith Island cake, the nine narrow-layered wonder. Lorraine always said that the original was the best, so I promised myself a slice of yellow cake with velvety chocolate icing. Looking at my plate piled high, I wasn't sure if I'd have room. We followed the orderly crowd and moved into the next line, the long one, waiting for one thing. Fresh oysters on the half shell.

"Do you like oysters?" Charlie asked, almost drooling in anticipation.

"Yes, I do. Have you ever had a West Coast oyster?" I challenged.

He did a double-take. "Isn't an oyster, an oyster?"

"Well, yes." We moved forward a few steps in the line. "But people say that the oysters on the West Coast are sweeter than the ones here on the East Coast. I suppose it depends on one's taste buds."

"You're not trying to start an oyster war, are you?" he teased.

"Heavens no," I said with a devious smile. "It might be fun to have a taste-off sometime. After all, there's no cooking involved."

"I'm always in favor of that, but to me," he closed his eyes, a dreamy look on his face. "An oyster is a little taste of the sea itself."

I made a show of pushing myself in front of him. "I need to step up first or there might not be any oysters left after you fill your plate."

He put his hand to his chest. "Me? Eat a multitude of oysters?" He dropped his hand and winked. "You betcha, honey."

The two men at the front of the line shucking oysters were so fast that their hands were almost a blur. What they were doing was sheer artistry. Growing up in Seattle, I was familiar with the delicate process of shucking fresh oysters. The process required a firm hand and the right knife, sturdy with a pointy end.

One man, with a head of unruly brown hair, had the face of a man who'd spent countless days in the sun or standing in rain and punishing winds to bring us this delicacy. And now, he was working hard to free those gems from their shells. He cradled the rounded shell of an oyster in his hand. With a little wrist action, he inserted the tip of the knife in the back where the oyster hinged the shell with a wiggle and a little pushto make sure the tip was inside.Then he gently twisted the knife until the shell popped open.In one continuous move, he dragged the knife around the edge until the top shell was free.He flipped that shell went into a pile and zipped the knife around to free the oyster from the bottom shell without spilling any of the natural brine or liquor.With a swipe of a towel, he cleaned anyway any loose bits of sand and nestled the oyster on its half shell on a large bed of ice withlemon wedges, tabasco sauce and a spicy cocktail sauce close by. Without stopping, he picked up another oyster from a mound and repeated the process again and again.When it was almost our turn, I slipped up to the front to talk to him.

"I've been watching.You are a master at shucking.Do you ever cut yourself with the knife?"

"This knife?"I gasped as he ran the edge across his wrist."It only looks sharp. But you don't want to jab yourself with the point.It will draw some blood with it." His hand reached out for another oyster and went back to work.

I moved over to the ice holding the oysters and saw Charlie's hand shoot past me to grab a half-shell. I slapped it playfully. "Oh no, you don't. Me first. Wait your turn."

"Then hurry up," he whined. A man could starve here."

We both giggled as we juggled our plates and headed for the crew and friends of *Island Memory*, but paused when a guy with wire-rimmed glasses halfway down his nose clapped his hands and called for everybody's attention. When the group quieted, he called out a toast. "Here's to Black Jack for a great seafood feast."

The group chimed in. "Yeah, thanks, Black Jack!"

One woman, wearing a tank top to show off her tattoos, added her take. "Because when we see food, we eat it!" She held up a plate piled high and everybody hooted.

Jack stepped up in the center of the group. "Glad you're stuffing yourselves." He glanced at the oyster bar. "I don't think there's an oyster left in the Bay." Everyone laughed. "And tomorrow, I'm gonna drink out of that Governor's Cup. See if I don't."

The air sizzled with trouble as the crew of *Flying Wing* cheered and the others jeered.

CHAPTER 8

echniques used to work metal date back to the times of the Ancient Greeks. They have been modified for use with silver. It is tragic that with the passing of great silversmiths, some of these techniques are falling into disuse or lost entirely.

"The Butler's Guide to Fine Silver"
Mr. Hollister, 1898

SOMEBODY KNEW how to handle this crowd. The music level went way up. The thumping rhythm demanded a body move and the party was back on track.

As Charlie steered me over to the crew of *Island Memory*, a slim fellow with a shaved head that gleamed in the fading afternoon light bellowed, "Did I see you talking to the enemy? You're not thinking of jumping ship, are you Charlie?" The man drew himself up to his full height and became an almost threatening character, .

"It's cool, O.T. Not to worry."

"Come on, guys. We know which flag Charlie sails under," said an older man with midnight black hair. "We have a guest. Now, behave."

"Yeah," somebody called out from behind us, but I wasn't about to turn my back on the bald guy. "Charlie knows when he's got it good."

"Yes, I do." Charlie held up his glass in one hand while juggling his two plates on his other arm. "Here's to the best crew ever. Here's to *Island Memory*."

Everyone around us cheered. "*Island Memory*."

Charlie said in a low voice, "Don't let that guy get to you. O.T. runs on the straight and narrow. He always does the right thing. He must. He's a state cop. Now, let me introduce you to my captain."

I glanced over my shoulder for a moment at the man, only he wasn't so scary now as he sat talking and drinking with his friends. A cop? That explained how he could look threatening one minute, and normal the next.

"Abby?" I turned my head quickly. "This is Dominick, captain of our log canoe, *Island Memory*."

Captain Dominick was probably the shortest member of his crew, but when he spoke, he grew in stature. This man had *presence*. He made me feel like he was talking only to me, even though his crew and their friends were listening. And when I spoke, there was nothing in the world that could distract him. This man had a rare talent. Dominick and his lady friend Nina made room for us at their table.

As we enjoyed the mound of food on our plates, I turned to Dominick, "May I ask you a question?" He nodded as he slid a raw oyster between his lips. "Why a log canoe? Why not a regular sailboat?"

Charlie gave me a strange look, but Dominick didn't miss a beat. "It's the challenge." He put down the empty oyster shell and held his arm in front of his chest. "Here's the canoe." He motioned above his arm. "Up here, you have a huge amount of canvas or sail area the wind pushes against." He gestured below his arm. "Down here, you only have a centerboard to counterbalance the wind. That's not enough." He laid his fingertips perpendicular to his arm. "So we don't capsize, we put one, two or three big men on boards that stretch beyond the side of the boat to create a human counterweight or ballast."

"Do they stay out there for the whole race? Do they ever fall in the water?"

Dominick snickered. "They'd better not. When we *come about* or change the direction of the boat and the sails, the boardmen slide into the canoe, shift the boards to the other side and scramble out again before the wind sends us over. If the boardmen are working as one, it's a beautiful thing to see. If they're not, if they're slow or sloppy…" He looked down and shook his head back and forth slowly. "It's downright ugly and bad things can happen."

"Like what?"

He huffed in disgust. "The wind can spill out of the sails slowing the boat down or the boat capsizes."

"And everyone goes in the water?" I shuddered. That would be a nightmare for me.

"Yeah, but the important thing is the canoe is out of the race. It's difficult if not impossible to right a canoe after it's gone over. The chase boat can't help. You don't have the dock to stabilize the canoe. Your race is over."

Now, I could understand his intensity. Sure, in the scheme of things, losing a sailboat race isn't like getting cancer. But these people were dedicated to a way of life filled with keen competition. A person had to focus on the prize and execute each step with precision. I realized that it wasn't so different from writing elegant computer code or staging a play. Commitment and attention to detail was required in so many of the things before our efforts paid off.

I wanted to get back to the particulars. "What if someone falls off a board?"

There was a collective groan from the crew of *Island Memory*. Dominick shrugged. "We have to go back and get him."

"And kiss the race good-by," someone said.

"We have to finish with the same number of people we started with." Dominick smirked. "Or I suppose we could pick up somebody else along the way."

That idea led to a lot of arm punching and joking around with the men assigned to the boards. Things settled down and people returned to their food. Soon, Charlie and Dominick monopolized the conversation with talk about possible tactics in the upcoming races.

"Anybody check the latest weather forecast?" Charlie asked the group.

"We should be good," answered a man who was different from all the rest. He was shorter and definitely rounder. His place had to be on the boards. His bleached blonde hair and aqua blue eyes suggested his nickname, Titan. "No problems like they had for this race in what, 2008?"

"What happened," I asked.

Titan put his thick arms on the table, ready to tell the story. "It was ugly. The weather wasn't great and it deteriorating fast. It was blowing at 35 knots or over forty miles an hour. The rain was coming down like bullets."

"Didn't they call the race for weather?" I asked.

Titan grunted and his belly jiggled. "This isn't baseball where the players run for cover at the first sign of a drizzle. We sail through it all."

"But maybe they should have called that one," argued Dominick. "Twelve boats started the race. Nine of them capsized."

"So, only three boats finished?" I was shocked.

"Well, three boats crossed the line. Two were upright. One

capsized as she approached the finish line and the current and her momentum carried her across."

"That's unbelievable!" I looked around at all the faces of the crews of *Island Memory*.

"You asked why log canoes?" repeated Dominick. "It's the challenge and the people. They're hard as nails, and stupid as hell sometimes."

Everybody roared, clinked beer bottles and toasted themselves. The thought of being out on the water in 40-50 MPH wind made my stomach flop over.

Charlie looked at me and smiled. "Don't worry, the weather tomorrow is supposed to be perfect!" I tried to give him a brave smile, hoping he was right. "Besides, you'll be on the chase boat, not a canoe."

While the men downed a couple more oysters, I said, "You sound very confidant."

"You have to be when you sail log canoes," Dominick said. "You're riding on the edge. One minute, you're moving along like a hot knife through butter, but if you push her too far, over she goes."

"But you can keep her from capsizing, right?"

Dominick smiled at my naïve comment as Charlie clarified things for me. "Not always. It doesn't take much. A bad gust of wind, moving the tiller too hard, boardmen out of sync. You have to treat the canoe with respect. She's probably seen every condition in her 128 years. Our canoe was built by William Sidney Covington, the man who originated the racing log canoe."

Dominick held up his index finger. "Charlie, you have to give the old girl her due. *Island Memory* was built 128 years ago as a workboat. Her original owner used her to tong oysters and sail the catch to market. A log canoe had to earn her keep, but she was born to race."

Confused, I asked, "Did they race their boats on weekends?"

A couple of people from Tilghman Island sputtered. Titan said,

"A waterman doesn't know what a weekend is during the season. The local preacher is lucky to see him in church on Sunday. The season is the time for him to make the money he needs to feed and care of his family."

I tried to look contrite as Dominick continued my lesson. "After the waterman had his catch for the day, it was time to head to the market on land or a buy boat sailing the rivers of the Bay. They say that the first one who got to the buyer, got the best price. If a captain saw another boat heading to market, he'd set his sails as a challenge to see which boat was the fastest, the best. So log canoe racing was born."

"And it's been a tradition of more than 150 years," added Charlie.

"What was true back then is still true today." Dominick set aside his empty plate. "A successful skipper understands his canoe, her idiosyncrasies and he has to be able to read the temperament of the wind which can change in an instant."

Charlie added, "He won't tell you, but Dom studies the cut of the sails, does the math like trigonometry and understand the physics of the wind. He knows not only how the air is affecting the sails right at this moment, but he reads the water to see what's coming."

"That's enough," he warned. "You're making me out to be some kind of Stephen Hawking of sailing and I'm certainly not that smart. I'm just a guy who applies a little science to what we do and treats his boat like a lady. If you don't treat her right, she won't forgive you."

"You all are very brave," I said with true admiration and added with a grin. "And probably more than a little crazy!"

The group erupted again in cheers and toasts. I was accepted as a friend of *Island Memory.*

As we finished our dinners, people started to wander away for second helpings, dessert or to make a run. "Anyone want another

'Dark 'n Stormy'?" Several people yelled out. *Yeah! Make mine super dark. Me too!*

Dominick's voice undermined their call for more liquor. "You've got an early call tomorrow."

"How about some coffee and dessert," suggested Charlie.

Nodding, Dominick called out for all to hear. "Good choice! I want to see you all in the morning at eight o'clock, SHARP! You need your sleep. We've got *two* races tomorrow!"

The crew started the process of heading out.

I noticed Captain Black saunter by as if he was king of all he surveyed. His steps slowed as he noticed our little group and his eyes locked on to Nina, Dominick's lady friend. Trouble, I thought. And I was right.

"Well, you never know what flotsam and jetsam are going to wash up on the Eastern Shore." His eyes bore into the woman sitting next to Dominick.

"Jack, black as usual," Dominick commented casually. "You know that's no way to treat a lady." He snapped his fingers and threw his head back. "No, I forgot. You don't. That's why she's sitting next to me now." The gasp that came from the people around him seemed to bring him to his senses. "I'm sorry, Jack. I'm letting the competitive spirit get the best of me. Why don't we keep our little rivalry on the water?"

Jack ignored him as his stare drilled into Nina. She didn't seem to care. She stared right back with her emerald eyes blazing. She reached up and ran her hand through her absolutely straight raven black hair, a move that was both sensuous and defiant. Jack shook his head and opened his mouth to say something, but Dominick preempted him.

"Jack, I said we should keep it out there on the water?"

Finally, Jack tore his eyes away from Nina and directed his stare at the *Island Memory* captain. Each word dripped with contempt. "Anything you say, Dom."

A tense moment followed that made everybody but Jack

uncomfortable. Then he turned and walked away as if nothing had happened. We all seemed to breathe a sigh of relief.

Dominick put his arm around Nina, drew her close and gave her a kiss on the forehead. She gave him a warm smile then patted the table with her palms and stood. "Shall I get us some more oysters?" Without waiting for an answer, she headed over to the shuckers.

Dominick got up and came over to me. "I'm sorry you had to see that, being new to log canoe racing and all." He sat down on the bench. "After a while, you'll get to know the characters."

"There are characters everywhere in life," I said. "Why should a fun activity like sailing be any different?"

"I like your attitude," he said with a smile.

I glanced over at Nina, petite among all the big, tall men in line. "Is she okay? He was kind of brutal."

His eyes followed mine. "There's a lot of power in that small package. Size isn't important with her. Her power comes from her mind and her heart. She's a doctor who really cares about her patients. On the personal level, life has delivered a couple of wallops so she's a little bruised, but getting stronger every day. Give her a little time and she'll shrug off the effects of Jack." He patted my shoulder as he got up. "But thanks for thinking of her. Have a good time."

As I watched him walk away, I marveled at how truly nice he was. Not the kind of man you find every day. Not one who is a fierce competitor, who sails to win.

Charlie plopped down next to me on the bench. "Want anything else to eat? There's some –"

"STOP!" Playfully, I punched him in the shoulder. "If I eat another thing, I'll burst. Right here in front of all your friends."

He covered his head with his arms. "Oh, no! Not that!" The big man who stole some crab cakes in line distracted him. "Hey,

Dutch!" The big man acknowledged the greeting with a quick nod, but used his thick legs to continue his trip up the hill. He was a man on a mission.

The atmosphere of the party was changing. People sat with their own canoe crews. The competitive spirit needed for the upcoming races was growing. After all, this wasn't a friends and family weekend. These crews were racing for points toward the season championship and, of course, there was the race for the Governor's Cup. It was time to get serious. But not everyone was in good shape.

A man with a receding hairline and brown fringe swayed and staggered up to Black Jack who stood surrounded by his crew. The man grabbed Jack's shoulder and said in a slurred Southern accent. "Hey, man. We need to talk." Jack started to shake him off, but the man held on and moved closer. "We gotta talk. It's about the race."

Jack jerked out of the man's grip and walked away. He muttered something that I couldn't quite hear, but I bet it wasn't complimentary.

Dominique wiped his lips, stood and held out his hand. "Nina, what do you say?" It looked like the log canoe wasn't the only one in his life he treated like a lady. Nina flashed him a big smile, put her hand in his and rose. Let's round up the crew and get them on their way." We all said good night and went our separate ways.

As we walked up the hill, a figure almost staggered out of the shadows and stood inches away from Charlie, reeling slightly. He looked like one of the oldest people at the feast. His receding hairline and wire-rimmed glasses gave him a more mature look than the younger people around, though he wasn't acting very mature at the moment.

"I've got to talk to you." His ice-blue eyes were blood-shot.

"Kevin, not now." He nodded his head toward me. "Do you not see Abby standing right here."

The man didn't even glance my way, but focused his pained expression on Charlie. "I need—"

"This is perfect," I chimed in. "I need to make a stop before I made that long walk back to my car. Charlie, would you point me to the ladies room, please?"

"Sure, top of the hill, go in the front door and turn right at the burgee."

"Thanks." I set off to follow his directions then doubled back. "Burgee?"

"We've got to get you trained up on sailor's speak," he said with a smile. "The burgee is the club's flag that set in the tile floor."

"Got it."

As I walked away, I overheard Kevin say in a voice filled with tears, "I'm in trouble and I don't know what to do."

"Kevin, we've talked about this before," Charlie said gently. "If you're worried, quit."

"I can't." His words sounded more like a wail than a statement. "Too much invested."

Charlie put his arm around his friend's shoulders. "Okay, but if anything happens, don't blame me."

"No, I'd never do that," Kevin promised. "He'll blame me."

I wanted to pause and listen to the rest, but decided it wasn't my business. I quickened my steps to the building, found the burgee on the floor and slipped into a room decorated with a soft nautical theme. Afterward, I went to rejoin Charlie when sharp words on the other side of the door stopped me.

"I've been hunting you up all evening. You better not be avoiding me."

I recognized the Southern accent of the big man who sailed on *Flying Wing*. It was Dutch, the crab cake thief. I peeked through the slightly opened door and saw two men standing right outside. I didn't think this was the time to interrupt them so I waited.

"Will you keep your voice down?" demanded Black Jack, speaking in a strained whisper. "This is no place—"

But Dutch didn't let him finish. "I've got only one question for you. Have you got some? "

"I don't know what you're talking about," hissed Jack.

Dutch shot back. "You know what I want. I need a little help for the races this weekend."

"Can't help you," Jack countered. "Now, I've got to go—"

"You're not going anywhere. You're going to supply me." The nastiness in his voice made me shrink back. "I know you're running."

"Running, maybe. Not dealing. You've got a guy. Go see him."

"What you think I am stupid?" Dutch argued. "Running. Dealing. Same difference."

"There's a big difference between running and dealing." Jack sounded very sure of himself. "And I don't cross that line."

Dutch hissed. "You better cross that line if you want to win this weekend." The threat hung heavy in the air. "And you better have it for me by tomorrow morning. It's all on you." Dutch grunted and walked away.

I peeked out the door and saw Jack straighten the collar of his polo shirt and reset his sunglasses on top of his head. He took in a deep breath and walked off.

I hugged the door, shocked by what I'd heard. Was Jack involved in drugs? I had no time to process the idea, because I was almost knocked over by a group of ladies pushing open the door. Somehow this near accident set them off in gales of hysteria. It was definitely time for me to leave. I didn't know what to do with what I'd overheard and decided to keep it to myself.

I met Charlie outside and asked, "Is your friend okay?"

"Kevin? Yeah, he works for Jack and he's gotten himself in tough position."

"Jack, the captain of the log canoe?" I asked, gathering more information about the man.

"Yes, he's an employee and a member of the crew."

"That can get a little too close for comfort," I said, thinking about the arrangement I had with Lorraine. Not only was she my employer and good friend, we practically lived together. But she wasn't anything like Jack, so I counted myself lucky.

"Ready to make the hike back to your car?" Charlie asked.

"Yes, I think so." I wanted him to think that everything was fine so I flashed him a big smile. "This was an incredible event. Thank you so much for inviting me."

He looked at me and lifted his head. "Are you okay?"

Lorraine was right again. I'm a lousy liar. "Yes, I'm fine," I said, probably too brightly. "I'm just tired."

"Do you want me to drive you home?"

"No, not necessary," I insisted.

"Maybe I'd better walk you to your car." I started to protest. "No, I don't want to hear it. It's what a gentleman does. What if you twisted your ankle on the gravel or fell out there in the field?" He touched my elbow as he had at the start of the evening. "No, I'm walking you to the car... and I'll entertain you with stories about the Great Rivalry."

"The Great Rivalry?" I asked.

"Actually it's more rabid on one side than the other. You noticed the tension between the skippers Jack and Dominick. I know you picked up on it. Don't be embarrassed. Everyone knows about it."

So much for polite conversation. "Yes, I did," I admitted. "It seemed to make the lady, oh, what was her name?"

"Nina," he said almost like a schoolboy with a crush.

"Yes, Nina seemed to be a little uncomfortable."

"I think you're projecting how you would feel in that situation. That's how any normal woman would feel when confronted by the man she threw over for the man she's dating now."

I gasped. "Oh! That's awkward."

"But that's not the real story. The girl thing just makes it juicy. The real battle is on the water. Dominick has been racing *Island Memory* a lot longer than Jack. I think Jack is jealous of all the attention Dom gets, because he's won so many races. Jack is taking it personally, now. He doesn't get it that Dom is a really good captain."

"And now they're going head to head?" I asked.

"Yes, they are. All weekend." He closed his eyes and shook his head. "I'll tell you, sailboat racing attracts some odd personalities."

"Tomorrow should be interesting," I said, not quite knowing what to think. "Thanks for letting me on the background." Charlie was focused on the races. I didn't dare tell him what I'd overheard. As far as I knew, he was using, too. No, I rejected that thought. He didn't seem like the type. I took out my keys, hit the fob button and unlocked the car. "This is me. Thanks for walking me out here. I'm sorry to have taken you out of your way."

"No problem. I'm parked right over there. No special parking for crews." He shrugged. "I'm glad you came and had a good time." When I opened the door and started to get in my car, Charlie touched my arm. "Abby, one more thing. It would be a good idea if you left that at home."

Confused, he gestured to my wristwatch, a gift from Gran, my Piaget gold watch certainly didn't belong on a boat.

"Right! I put it on every morning like clockwork." I groaned. "Sorry about the pun. I'll leave it at home tomorrow."

"Don't forget," he said while he walked away. "Be here by 8:30. It's a little early, but you don't want to miss your ride."

No, I didn't want to miss it for the world.

CHAPTER 9

The Butler must not react if someone picks up the wrong fork. The Hostess may wish to salvage the situation by also using the wrong fork. Other guests should always follow the Hostess.

"The Butler's Guide to Fine Silver"
Mr. Hollister, 1898

I HAD to park way out in the field because it seemed like *everybody* was at the yacht club for the log canoe race. I remembered the tranquil scene the day before and marveled at what I saw. Organized chaos. I met Charlie by the front door of the yacht club. It was quickly becoming my spot.

"I'm ready to head out. I put on sunscreen and I wore my boat shoes," I said proudly.

"Okay, let's head down to the dock."

The dock was truly the area of intense activity. I didn't understand everything the people were doing. Whatever it was, there was no kidding around as they raised the masts and rigged the sails. On one canoe, a man carried a cooler toward the bow, positioned it carefully then sat down with lines to a sail in his hand. The skippers took their places by the tillers. On *Fixed Wing*, the big men—the boardmen—made some adjustments to the slick planks of wood they'd use to balance the boat during the race. As the boats were ready, their chase boats moved in, one at a time, took on a sturdy line and were towed out to the river close to the starting line.

Out of curiosity, I looked around for Dutch. He was so big and looked so strong, I was sure I wouldn't miss him *if* he was here. Based on the condition he was in last night, he should have been a wreck this morning. But when I saw him working with some sails, I was amazed. He was moving with confidence, his platinum blonde hair pulled back neatly in a ponytail. The guy I saw last night was tipsy and glassy-eyed. This morning, he jumped off the boat, picked up a line and stepped back without hesitating. From what I could see, his eyes were clear and he was full of energy. He didn't hesitate or tumble as he leaned over or tugged on the canvas.

Charlie walked up with a pouch slung over his shoulder. "You're looking at Dutch. He's a marvel."

"I saw him last night and he was so…"

"Drunk. I know. He's one man who can really hold his liquor and sail a good race the next morning."

"I know." I held out my open hands in surprise, hoping for an answer. How does he do that?"

"Advantage of being a big man, I guess." He looked over at the group of people at the dock readying *Flying Wing* for the race. "Jack's whole crew is like that. They all seem to know what they want and can make it happen. Makes them a good fit with Jack. He likes to think of himself as a pirate. Somebody who takes what he wants.

O.T. tossed out a comment as he walked by. "Takes whatever he wants on both land and water."

Charlie shook his head. "No love lost there. Not sure why, but he's right. To Jack, a rule is more of a suggestion than a line you don't cross. That's how Black Jack got his nickname. He'll do anything to win. I think he'd fly the Jolly Roger if the committee let him. He seems content with the colors he chose for *Flying Wing*."

"Which are?"

Charlie raised his chin toward the crew bunched around someone handing out black T-shirts. "Black with the name of the boat stitched in white."

"And that's the crew I'm supporting today?" Quickly, I was rethinking this whole idea.

"Well," said Charlie, almost apologizing. "You'll be on his chase boat. Sorry, it was the only way I could get you a ride. Our chase boat is full."

"Do I have to wear a black shirt? I mean, in this heat—"

Charlie laughed and shook his head. The moment of tension was gone. "No, you're fine. Only the crew gets to sweat in those black shirts, but they don't. You see Jack wasn't content with having his crew wear regular cotton tees. They're made of some kind of special fabric that wicks away the sweat or something."

"Lucky guys."

"Okay, let's touch base with the skipper." Jack was coming out of the club's main door. "I know you met him last night, but it's a curtesy." He waved to the tall man dressed all in black. "Jack!"

The skipper raised his eyes obviously deep in thought about something else. He gave Charlie a puzzled look as we hustled toward him.

"Jack, you remember Abby. You met last night and by the way, that was a great seafood feast." Jack mumbled something in response. "She's going out on your chase boat this morning."

"No, she's not," he said, speaking as if I wasn't there.

"But you agreed to this. How can you change your mind like that and at the last minute?"

"Because I'm the captain and I can do anything I want with my boats.

"Does that mean she can't go out at all?" demanded Charlie.

He answered in an off-handed way, "No, she can go out on my chase boat this afternoon. We'll be sailing for the Governor's Cup and she'll look good there for the photographers. She certainly better looking than Elliot, the chase boat captain."

Charlie is mortified by such a sexist comment but I waved it off. "He's thinking about the race, not some stranger. Don't worry about it. I'm happy if I can go out this afternoon."

He held up a massive pair of binoculars in matte black. "I have something for you." I hefted them as he put the wide strap over my head. "This way you'll be able to see the action up close. Don't worry if they get knocked around on the boat. They can take it and they're waterproof, but I don't suggest you let them go overboard."

A young woman in black short shorts and a black halter rushed up and gave Charlie a red shirt. He pulled off his blue T-shirt, tossed it to her in return and put on the new one with the boat's name *Island Memory* stitched in yellow on it.

"I have to run or I'll miss my boat, literally. Go up to the patio and have a cup of coffee until the race starts. You'll get a great view." And Charlie was off at a dead run.

Everywhere I looked, people were busy. Some were straightening ropes …or were they called lines? A big pickup truck was backing a trailer down a ramp into the water with a canoe lashed to it. Some big men were stepping a mast into place. Others were rigging sails. Coolers and pails for baling were loaded aboard.

"Hey, everybody," Kevin called out to the crew of *Flying Wing*. "It's time to go."

The last members of the crew stepped aboard. Items were stowed out of the way. Bear, leader of the boardmen, took off his shirt and flexed his arms, proud of his well-developed muscles. He swung his black shirt over his head like a lasso, grunting at each turn. The crew caught the rhythm and grunted with him, faster and faster. Then he threw his fists up to the sky and they all screamed *Go Wing!* A straggler in a black crew shirt rushed from the parking lot, wiping his nose. Dutch looked healthy and ready to go which mystified me after seeing how drunk he was the night before. I remembered what I'd overheard… and wondered.

At the top of the hill, Dutch stopped, drained the bottle of water in his hand and spiked the bottle on the ground like a football along with a growl. He caught up to Jack who was making his way down the hill. Dutch snorted when Jack said, "My mouth feels like the Afghan army marched through in their socks."

"I hear you," said the big man slapping his captain on the back.

This crew had its own routines to get itself psyched up for the race, but the show wasn't over yet. Jack held a bottle of champagne high over his head and waited until he had everyone's attention, then he challenged them.

"What is the best log canoe in the fleet?"

They cried out in unison. "*Flying Wing!*"

Jack strutted back and forth on the dock. "And who is the crew of the *Flying Wing?*"

"WE are!"

He held up a bottle of champagne. "Who wants some of this?"

"We do!"

Jack put his hands on his hips, gripping the bottle by the gold-foiled neck. "So, what to do you have to do to get this?" He thrust the bottle in the air.

"Win the race!

"So, what are you going to do?"

"WIN THE RACE. Go Wing, Go Wing, Go Wing!"

Jack stepped aboard, shaking the bottle like a rattle and gave his first order of the day. "Let's shove off!"

There was nothing else for me to see or do so I headed to the patio. All the tables were empty, except one. The woman from the three-way confrontation the night before was sitting by herself in a little red and white print sundress that looked comfortable and cool. Nina stood out, because she wore something so different from the shorts and T-shirts often seen around the club. And because her confidence added to her beauty.

"Ah, at last some company. Come and sit down with me." Her voice was easy, almost velvety. "I'm tired of thinking my own thoughts." I noticed she had a red T-shirt sitting in a wrinkled clump on the table next to her.

"Oh, are you part of a crew?" I turned and pointed toward the water. "Because they're – "

"A member of a crew?" She gave a little shudder. ""Heaven's no."

"Oh, maybe you're like me, a friend of the log canoe races, but I didn't get a T-shirt." I tried to match her light attempt at humor, but mine sounded strained.

"It's just Dominick staking his claim in a somewhat subtle way." She put her hand on the clump of fabric and seemed to consider some silent question. With a little nod, she put the shirt with her purse. "He doesn't expect me to wear it. After all, the only person who looks good in a tee-shirt is a big man with bulging deltoids and well-developed pectoralis majors."

"Wow, you sound like you know your anatomy. You must be a trainer or a doctor."

She dipped her head a little. "Guilty. Actually, I'm a cardiologist.

The girl from last night's seafood feast with the great floral arrangement in her hair started to race across the patio, carrying something that looked like a small artillery shell. Today, she her hair was tied in a flurry of black bows that flapped in the air as she skittered to a stop by our table. She held up what I thought was ammunition for us to see. "I almost forgot Jack's water bottle."

She looked around as if afraid to be seen, her cheeks turning bright red. "Hi, Nina."

Nina gave her a sweet smile. "Hi, Tiffani. Abby, I want you to meet this young woman who sails in a very important position on *Flying Wing*. She sits far away from everybody else, out beyond the back of the boat. She trims the main sail and, when she's not doing that, she is Jack's water girl." She reached out and slipped a sleek black container from her hands. "And this is the famous water bottle," she said with a sneer. "Jack can't bring himself to drink out of a regular bottle of water like the rest of the crew." She held it out for my inspection. "Have you ever seen anything like it? It holds more than 32 ounces of water and will keep ice frozen for ninety hours! That's almost four days! I mean, who needs a water bottle like that for a log canoe race that *may* last three hours? And there's a loop on the top so he can tie down his precious water bottle so he won't lose it if the canoe capsizes. "

Tiffani shrugged and, missing the point, said with awe and respect, "I guess he has to have a special one 'cause he's the captain." Nina shook her head in disbelief. "I've got to run or I'll miss the boat." She gave a nervous giggle, then shrugged. "Just wanted to say hi."

Nina smiled to be kind. "And hi to you. Have a good race."

Tiffani beamed with delight and gave us a small wave.

As we watched her skip down to the dock, I wondered if they'd wait for her.

"Oh, Jack wouldn't leave the dock without her. You know how they say that behind every successful man is a woman. Well, Tiffani is Jack's ace in the hole. She could handle that main with her eyes closed. She can read the boat as if it was part of her."

I was relieved to see Tiffani with her hair in a flurry of black bows crawl back to her position on the outrigger perched beyond the stern and only a couple of feet above the water.

"But she has a problem," Nina added casually, "She has a fatal crush on Jack, poor girl."

I didn't think it was my place to discuss matters of the heart connected to *Flying Wing*, especially after last night's scene. "At least she looks cute in her black T-shirt and those little ponytails all tied with black bows."

"It's her cry for attention." Nina leaned back and closed her eyes. "She tries to coordinate her hairstyle with the event and it often includes a complicated dye job, too. She has hairpieces and ribbons galore. Guess she got home too late last night to do her usual black and white checkerboard design." She sighed, opened her eyes and sipped her coffee. "It's amazing how people spend their time."

"Black and white checkerboard design? That sounds…" I struggled for a word. "Startling."

"Oh yes, it's something to see." She cast her eyes down to the table as if lost in a thought. "I too have a black crew shirt."

"You're on the crew of *Flying Wing?*" Now, I was truly confused since I thought she was dating the Dominick, the captain of *Island Memory.*

"No, I was once a friend of the canoe. Well, that's not true. Once I was a friend of her captain. We met when Jack was visiting a friend who was one of my patients. He drove all the way to Georgetown in D.C. to see him which proves that Jack has a heart… or an ulterior motive. We got to talking. Next thing I knew, a cup of coffee turned into dinner. He was charming and livened up things. I was bored and hurt, coming out of a divorce from my doctor husband. He fell for another pretty face and a tight ass in the halls of a hospital again, but this time he went for a nurse instead of a doctor. Less competition."

"At first, it was fun going to restaurants and clubs again. He suffered through evenings at the Kennedy Center when I got tickets, but tried not to let it show. His true interest came out when he asked me out here to spend a race weekend. That's when I found out who he truly loved and she is a jealous mistress during the summer." She inclined her head to the side as if reconsidering what she'd said. "Or what he truly loved was being the captain. Yes, I think that was it."

"Everybody likes being in charge, at least from time to time," I suggested.

"Jack likes to be in charge all the time. Dominick is nothing like him." A warm smile spread over her face. "Dom is takes things easy. What you see is what you get and that's pretty terrific."

It sounded like we'd strayed into some dangerous waters so I noticed that the fluffy white sails on the water. The twelve canoes in the race were massing together between an orange mark in the water and an old style cabin cruiser that looked like it was from the 1920's.

I stood up to look closer. "I think the race is about to start. Do you want to go with me to the other side where we'll have a better view?" I put the strap of Charlie's binoculars around my neck. "I'd be happy to share these high-tech binoculars."

Nina said with a sigh. "No, you run along. I've seen enough log canoe races to last me a lifetime."

We said good-bye with the idea that we'd see each other again later in the day.

CHAPTER 10

The silver for a particular menu must be place correctly on table. A simple mistake can lead to confusion and embarrass-ment for the Hostess and Family, a situation that cannot be tolerated.

"The Butler's Guide to Fine Silver"
Mr. Hollister, 1898

LOG CANOES WERE TETHERED to their chase boats. While they were towed out toward the starting line, crews made last-minute adjustments while underway. I caught sight of one captain sitting back comfortably at tiller, enjoying the ride out to the middle of the river. He called out to the other captains as he passed, "Have a good race, gentlemen." He reminded me of the civilized quality of racing at the highest level, regardless of the sport. Civilized, until the starting gun.

Using the binoculars, I watched the white sails of the racing fleet converge in the area near a sleek powerboat. It looked like mass confusion among canoes. I held my breath, hoping one boat didn't ram another one either by accident or on purpose.

A man's raspy voice interrupted my thoughts. "What are you seeing out there?"

I lowered the glasses to find a man wearing a lime green T-shirt and plaid shorts standing next to me. He sipped a beverage that was probably stronger than iced tea. To disguise my urge to burst out laughing at his outrageous outfit, I raised the glasses to my eyes again.

He missed my reaction entirely. "That's the second best way to watch a log canoe race if you're not on a boat." He cradled his drink as he folded his arms. "Log canoe racing is like no other sailboat race." I asked why. "Maybe because each canoe was built by hand. There still is no factory in the world that produces them. Maybe because many of the twelve boats in the race were built more than a century ago. One canoe, *Magic,* had been in the same family for more than ninety years. Maybe this kind of racing is special because this was the only the place in the world where log canoes have ever sailed." He took another sip. "The wind is fickle. It can change direction or gust without warning. The big question is which crew will keep the canoe balanced so the captain can sail right down the throat of his competition?"

Then he began a commentary of the action on the water that helped me make sense of what I was seeing. "That's the race committee boat out there. They hover around her because she acts as one end of the starting line. That large orange triangle float to the left is the other end. They'll cross the starting line when the gun goes off, not before. The race committee chair will make sure no one gets a head start."

I could make out several people in the stern with clipboards, watching the log canoes jockey for position. There was so much to see and hear. One boat moved up along the starting line and voices of people yelling drifted over the water.

My commentator moved closer to me and mumbled, "Oh boy,

he's too soon." He frowned as he took a sip from a plastic cup. "He's got to bear off. If he crosses the line early, they'll slap him with a penalty. A longtime race chairman in a male-dominated sport, who happened to be a woman, always said, 'Lose your start, you won't be first around the first mark. If you're not first around the mark, you might as well go home.'"

"So, the race is won in the first few minutes?" That sounded hard to believe.

"Oh, that's only part of it." The man might not know how to dress, but he knew something about sailboat racing.

I held out the binoculars. "Would you like to use these to identify the boat on the line?"

He gave his head a shake. "No need. I can see it's *Flying Wing*. I can't figure out what Jack is doing." He ran his hand through his thick white hair. "He has to fall off."

"One of the sails isn't tight. It's rippling in the wind."

"Luffing," he corrected. "He's luffing the foresail to lose momentum. That's not good."

A big bang sounded, black smoke rose from a double-barreled shotgun on the committee boat and the race was on. Only Jack's crew didn't react immediately. *Flying Wing* seemed to flounder while the other boats shot across the line into open water. Jack was screaming.

"Oh boy," my companion moaned. "That's gonna be trouble."

"Can you tell me what's happening?" I asked. "This is my first sailboat race."

He smacked his lips together as if he didn't know where to start. "Let's just say that's a tough way to start a race. He's lost time that will be hard to make up. I don't care what a boat's handicap is, it's all about covering the course in the shortest amount of time."

As one canoe approached the mark, she leaned over so far that I held my breath. Was I witnessing a disaster in the making? "She's going to capsize!"

"Not to worry," he clucked. "That's *Island Memory*. Watch."

I RAISED the binoculars and focused on Charlie's canoe as the men sat poised on the boards, ready for action. They whipped their heads back and forth from the captain to their lead boardman as they made subtle adjustments in their positions. Then, in what seemed like the last possible second, they slid down their boards, moved them to the other side and glided up to their positions just as the bow of the boat came around to a new direction and the sails gracefully swung over to the other side. The log canoe went tight around the mark and took off like a shot. The maneuver was like the choreography of a ballet. I wanted to applaud, but I didn't. It probably wasn't appropriate to applaud *Flying Wing*'s major rival when I was going out on her chase boat in the afternoon.

I watched other canoes make the turn, including *Flying Wing*. They were close enough that I could hear the order *Get In*, followed by the thudding sounds of the boards being moved from one side of the canoes to the other as they rounded the first mark. Sails snapped as the boats changed direction, followed by the order *Get Out* and the men climbed the boards again.

"Well, Jack has made up some time," said man in the plaid shorts. "I don't know if it's enough, but I think she's got a chance. How he handles the next mark will tell. I'll be back." He meandered off with his empty cup.

There wasn't much for me to do, but wait. Everyone else who had watched the start had wandered back inside or gone home. My commentator returned in time to see the approach to the next mark, his cup replenished. I was learning that crews and racing enthusiasts enjoyed their adult beverages.

Again, my companion uttered the words, *Oh boy.* I jammed the binoculars against my face to figure out what was wrong. Jack's voice thundered over the water. He was hot. I saw one of his sails start flapping in the wind. The boardmen scrambled down the boards into the canoe, but their movements didn't look coordinated. *Flying Wing* seemed to flounder. Another boat, I didn't know which, cruised up and by him, her sails full of wind.

"Jack just lost position. He has to give way. This isn't good," my reporter said with dismay.

"The wind probably shifted direction," I said, as if I knew what I was talking about.

"No," he declared. "Jack made a mistake and it's a costly one." He contemplated the ice cubes in his cup and sighed. "You'll see more of the action from the chase boat. It can get boring when you watch a log canoe race from shore. You'll have more fun this afternoon."

I was about to ask how he knew I'd be on the chase boat when the sound of a gun shot reverberated across the water as the first canoe crossed the finish line.

"There's the winner." It was exciting even though I had no idea which canoe it was.

My companion held up his index finger. "Don't be so sure. The first one across the line isn't necessarily the winner," he said. "Remember the handicaps? The committee has to do the computations before they declare a winner." He held his cup out toward the finishing line. "Here's to the winner, which ever she may be."

He was celebrating, but I felt a little deflated. How can a person cheer at a race if you don't know who is leading? Sailboat racing, or at least log canoe racing, was very confusing with its terminology, traditions and handicapping. Eight boats crossed the finish line in the next five minutes, but the group didn't include *Flying Wing*. She crossed the line all by herself in splendid majesty, far back from the first boats. Of course, the race was all about competition, but she looked regal as she sailed alone. A little spark of excitement went through me. I was eager to see the Governor's Cup Race up close from the deck of the chase boat.

My companion mumbled, "There's going to be hell to pay. A

poor start and that mess at the mark." He shook his head. "I'm glad I'm not on board *Flying Wing* right now."

"What about the handicap?" I suggested. "Maybe she finished better than we think?"

"In your dreams. A handicap can't make up that big a difference. No, we'd better find someplace else to be when she comes in."

Flying Wing's crew quickly dropped the sails and the canoe lost her dignity. She sat so low in the water, it was hard to see the canoe at all. Only the two masts stood out and they looked like two giant matchsticks on the water, swept back at a slight angle from the bow. There was action on the canoe. Somebody was standing up and waving his arms.

My buddy in the funny shorts stared at the canoe. "What's going on?" He grabbed the binoculars while the strap was still around my neck. His move yanked me within an inch of his shoulder.

I cleared my throat. "Do you mind?"

He dragged his eyes away from the binoculars and looked at me. "Oh, sorry." Realizing the problem, he pulled the strap up and over my head then glued his face to the lenses again.

"Tell me what's going on?" I was ready to yank the binoculars away from him if he didn't report.

"Jack is standing up in the canoe, yelling at the crew. No surprise there. Wait! Now, what?"

I couldn't wait. "What? Tell me."

"He's holding something over his head. Holy – it's the bottle of champagne. Whoa, I can't believe it." Then he stopped talking.

I couldn't stand it. I took the glasses from him and focused on the canoe.

"You won't see anything now. You missed it," he said, replacing his sunglasses on his nose.

I spoke between my clenched teeth. "And what is it that I missed?"

"Jack threw the bottle of champagne overboard," he said in awe. "It flew in a nice arc. The man has got an arm, I'll say that for him."

"He threw the bottle of champagne in the water?" Jack must be out of his mind.

The chase boat swooped in to take the canoe in tow. Someone on the crew pulled the canoe up close and the two boats floated together as one.

"Yeah," he continued. "Sometimes, he'll put a bottle on the canoe to motivate the crew. After the race, they can open it and pass it around on the way into the dock. If they win, that is. I've never seen him throw a bottle overboard." His head shot forward and his eyes squinted to see what was happening. "Now, what's he doing?"

I passed the glasses to him before he could grab them. He paused for a minute, realizing what a jerk he'd been, and thanked me. He raised them to his eyes and described what he saw.

"Jack is getting on the chase boat. That's weird. He could have capsized the canoe."

Even without the binoculars, I could see *Flying Wing* rocking violently from side to side. Then the chase boat gently moved in front until the line was tight. Under tow, they headed to the dock. It was easy to see Jack pacing around on the bow of the power boat. Captain Jack was in a black mood, but the drama wasn't over.

In the meantime, the winning canoe arrived at the dock. The crew of *Island Memory* was jubilant. Charlie came rushing toward me, scooped me up and danced around.

"Did you see it, Abby?" He didn't wait for an answer. "Wasn't it the best?"

People in red *Island Memory* T-shirts joined his victory dance with me at the center, hooting and hollering. "Best finish of the year." "We showed him." "Sweetest victory ever!"

I noticed *Flying Wing* pulling up to the dock. The captain of her chase boat was yelling. "Jack, come on back here!"

"Why? Why should I? I want to be as far away as I can be from that group of people in my boat who call themselves a crew. YOU'RE INEPT," he yelled to be sure his crew heard him. "You messed up the start so we had no chance. We could have sailed the race of my life and still lost."

"Jack, come back here," insisted the captain.

The yelling captured the attention of the people around me. Charlie lowered me to the ground and we all watched the drama in silence.

"Why should I?" Jack shot back. "Give me one good reason."

Elliot, the chase boat captain, barked. "Because you're in the way. Come on back here to the cockpit and let Sammy handle the lines so we can dock."

Jack stopped, noticed Sammy, a young teenage boy, holding the dock lines and trying to stay out of the way. Disgusted, Jack moved to the stern. "Happy now?" he snapped at Elliot who focused on making a safe approach. Ignored, Jack sat on the stern with his back to his crew and canoe.

A crowd drifted over so they had a good view of the dock where *Fixed Wing* would tie up. The crew of Charlie's canoe went to finish their chores so they'd be ready for the next race in just a couple of hours. As they worked, they kept an eye on Jack and his boat. I spotted O.T., the man with the shiny head and the curious nickname. He was such a cheerful guy now, having fun with his friends, doing menial work. I guess he was frightening until I found out he was a cop and a cop had to be frightening at times.

Then my attention was drawn back to the dock. The chase boat delivered the canoe gently to the dock and the crew secured her lines. Almost without a word, they started to stow things and make preparations for the afternoon race.

Jack jumped from his chase boat to the dock, stomped over to his canoe and blew his top. "You're all idiots! You lost the race for me. I don't know why I bother." He threw up his hands in the air. "You're a miserable crew..." He kicked the side of the log canoe. "On a miserable boat." He marched away leaving everyone in stunned silence.

I made my way over to Charlie by *Island Memory* just as Dominick walked up to Charlie and said softly, "That's the worst I've ever seen him."

Charlie shook his head. "I wonder if he'll have a crew at all for the next race."

"I bet everyone will show up for the Governor's Cup this afternoon. They'll be sailing to prove him wrong and twist the knife tomorrow by not showing up for the last race. Mark my words." He walked over to the rest of his crew. "Gather round. You saw what just happened. It has nothing to do with us. Y'all sailed a great race. I'm going up to see if the committee has posted the results and I'll let you know. I want you to keep your heads in the game. We have another race today and it's the main event. Get something to eat and get back here. Starting gun is at two so you don't have much time."

As he walked up to the club building, the crew got back to work or wandered away to the picnic packed for them. All, but one. The man with the shaved head. He stood frozen to the spot, his eyes glued on Jack as he talked to people around the dock. I noticed with a chill that the cop curled his hands into fists.

"Hey, O.T., are you okay?" Charlie asked him.

But the man just stared, took one step backward, then another as if he was in shock.

An older man in the crowd of sailors moved toward O.T. "Hey, man. Are you okay?" There was no response, so he called out again. "O.T.?"

Then, as if someone threw a switch, he was looked at the man and said, "Sorry, Uncle Morris. I'm fine. Just remembered I've got to go. There's something I have to do."

"But the Governor's Cup—"

"I'll be back in time," said the boardman on *Island Memory*. "Not to worry." O.T. turned and took long strides to the parking lot.

People started milling around in a clash of emotions—excitement, confusion, resentment, hurt. It was all there, and more.

I decided to follow my race companion's advice and get out of Jack's line of fire. The safest thing to do was to leave the club during the break between races rather than risk getting involved in a scene. I dropped the top on my car and headed for the Fair Winds.

As I drove through St. Michaels at a snail's pace, I thought about stopping by Mrs. Clark's kitchen to sneak away some of her delicious leftovers from the night before. Then I remembered that first, I had to release Simon from his prison in the cottage. Thoughts of his bladder bursting quickened my step. He was a growing boy. Those little accidents he had as a puppy were more like a deluge now.

At Fair Winds, I breathed a sigh of relief that the politician visitors hadn't found my usual parking space. I left the sunscreen and other things I might need on the boat in the car and sprinted to the cottage. Simon wasn't used to being locked up inside for several hours, alone. I tried to explain to him that it was a busy weekend at Fair Winds with strangers driving around the property and that he had to stay in the cottage for his own safety. All he did was cock his head to the side in that cute way of his then licked my nose. Now, after an all-important pit stop near the bushes, he chased the ball several times before we made our way into Mrs. Clark's kitchen. He was looking for one of his cookies. I was hoping for a morsel left over from last night's buffet for the politicians. I was surprised to find Mrs. Clark reading the comic page of the newspaper and having a cup of coffee.

"Did Lorraine cancel everything and I'm the last to know?" I asked.

"No, no such luck. We've done all we can to prepare dinner.

We just have to wait for them to bring in the fish the politicians caught or talked to death." We laughed at her little joke.

"What if they don't catch anything, or don't have enough for dinner?" I asked, as I poured a mug of coffee for myself.

She snickered. "There's always peanut butter and jelly."

I wasn't sure if she was serious. Before I could ask, she shrugged her shoulders and continued.

"It's hasn't happened... yet. When the boat comes in, we'll spring into action to clean and fillet the fish then bake or broil the beauties. All the last-minute preparation will happen while they change and go to the yacht club for the presentation of the Governor's Cup. Did you know the governor himself is coming? Flying in by helicopter. Should be impressive, but I won't see much from the kitchen." She wiped her hands on the towel that always hung from the tied apron at her ample waistline. "That's okay. I didn't vote for him. Anyway, they'll come back for cocktails and if I've timed it right, they'll sit down to the feast just as everything is ready."

I opened the fridge to start foraging. "There's no question in my mind that you'll have the timing right down to the minute. You always do. And it's always delicious."

"You're sweet, but you don't have to say nice things like that. I'll still feed you from *my* refrigerator." She waved me over to the island and started pulling out wrapped packages and covered bowls of leftovers.

Before I knew it, a sampler plate of goodies sat in front of me. The bite-size crab cakes were delicious cold. The coleslaw added a little tang and the potato salad flavors melted in my mouth.

She scooped a warm chocolate chip cookie off a cooling rack, popped it on a paper napkin and put it down in front of me. "Will you be there this evening?"

"No, I found a way to avoid all that stogy political conversation full of posturing."

"It really doesn't happen that way when they come to Fair Winds. Often, they leave with some kind of consensus."

My eyes grew big. "When did you become a political analyst?"

"I spend a lot of time here in the kitchen with the radio and TV pundits running their mouths in the background. Besides, I hear things."

I wondered if there were ever late night conversations when guests tiptoed down to the kitchen for another cookie or something. The way she pursed her lips, I didn't think I'd get anything more out of her now, but I'd check back with her after everyone left.

"So, how are you getting out of tonight's debate?" she asked.

I licked the melted chocolate off my fingers. "I've been invited to another log canoe crew dinner and party at the club tonight."

"That crowd sure knows how to party." She laughed. "Almost as much as the politicians."

"Yes, I was staggered by how much they ate and drank last night. Then they got up this morning, hopped on the canoes and went sailing. Truly amazing."

"Well, they say that sailors are cut from a different cloth. And speaking of sailors isn't there a race going on right now and aren't you supposed to be on board the chase boat?"

I looked up at the clock and slid off the chair. "Yes, on both counts. I don't want to miss my chance to go out on the chase boat. The captain of *Flying Wing* changed his mind this morning and wouldn't let me go out. He said he didn't want his crew distracted by another pretty face." I gave her a wide grin and cleared my dishes. "I hope he thinks I'm ugly this afternoon so I can go."

Simon padded into the kitchen, his nose madly twitching above the tile floor as he searched the floor in the corners for a forgotten morsel that escaped from the counters above. Mrs. Clark ran her hand down the length of his body. "He's growing some muscle."

"Yes, he is and eating me out of house and home, as they say. I kept him in the cottage this morning. These strangers aren't used to watching out for a dog streaking across the driveway."

She stopped him from licking something off her floor by offering a dog cookie instead. "Miss Lorraine locked up her dogs in the kennel. Maybe Simon would like to spend the afternoon with them instead of alone in the cottage."

"That's a good idea."

"You're late," she said as she grabbed another cookie from the jar reserved for the dogs. "I'll take care of him. You should get going."

"Thank you, Mrs. Clark. And thank you for lunch. I feel like I can face anything these sailors can throw at me."

She beamed as she stood at the sink with her hands on her hips. I ran for the door so I wouldn't be left at the dock, literally.

I tucked my convertible into the last parking spaces in the field. I had thought the place was busy this morning, but now it was insane. The Governor's Cup race had drawn a huge crowd. As I got closer to the main club building, I saw Charlie madly waving at me and I hurried.

"You're just in time." He put his hand on my elbow and navigated our way through the crush of people. "I want to get you on the chase boat. Jack wouldn't hesitate to leave without you."

I slowed my step. "Maybe I should—"

"Absolutely not. I promised you a view of the race up close." He picked up our pace again. "When you're on board, remember you can put on a life jacket. Not everybody is comfortable being out on the water."

"I'll be all right." I promised, but there must have been something in my voice.

He looked at me and raised one eyebrow. "Are you sure? There's no shame…"

"No, I'll be fine."

He shrugged. "Okay, then. Elliot is a good, responsible captain.

He'll have life jackets tucked around in places on the boat. Check it out when you get aboard so you can grab one fast, if you need it."

I felt my lips tighten.

"Not that I anticipate an emergency," he added. "It will be fine."

"Scope out a life jacket. Got it." Hopefully, I sounded like I knew what I was doing.

The girl with the crazy hairstyle from this morning danced her way through the crowd down to the dock, singing out, "I'm here, I'm here." She held Jack's high-tech water high in the air. "I've got it," she announced and stepped aboard *Flying Wing*. She stowed the water bottle at the captain's place by the tiller and scampered to her position on the outrigger.

Charlie hustled me along. "I've got to get you aboard, so I can get to my canoe. Ready to do this?"

I took a deep breath. "Yes." After all, it was a beautiful day. What could go wrong?

CHAPTER 11

In the finer Houses, the practice of applying any kind of a thin coating meant to protect the silver surface is not held in high regard. It is a lazy approach to the preservation of the valued item. Attend to the preservation of silver pieces in a correct, consistent and proper fashion.

"The Butler's Guide to Fine Silver"
Mr. Hollister, 1898

CHARLIE STOPPED next to a blindingly-white power boat idling close to *Flying Wing*. A black burgee flapped at her bow. I glanced over at the boat's name on the stern. There was no question that this was Jack's chase boat. He called it *Fixed Wing*.

Charlie had only a half-minute to introduce me to Elliot, the captain, who flashed me a smile then dropped his eyes to check out my shoes. Fortunately, I'd invested in pair of good boat shoes last year when I was going out on the water with Ryan. But this wasn't the time to think about him.

"Come on," Elliot ordered in a friendly tone. "It's time to come board." He didn't say it, but I got his message that he was in charge as clearly as if he'd said, *This is my boat. You're a guest. Do as I say.*

"Nice boat," I said, as I followed his steps from the dock to the transom to the deck.

In a whirl of activity, he checked gauges, hit switches and something rumbled under my feet. I scooted into a corner to be out of the way and, of course, that's the one spot he needed to be.

He unwound the line from the cleat. "Yes, she's okay. Nothing fancy, just reliable and big enough to handle the canoe and take the crew on board if need be, but that's not likely to happen. Sammy!" he called out to the skinny teenage boy on the bow. "When you're ready, cast off and give us a push from the dock."

Sammy moved efficiently and as our bow pointed out to the channel which led to the river, Elliot adjusted his ball cap and put on the polarized sunglasses that hung around his neck. The tow line gently tightened and I could feel the drag of the log canoe on our boat. Elliot bumped up the speed a little and we were on our way toward the racecourse.

I pulled the tube of sunscreen from my bag and turned toward the water before I applied it. Somehow I had the feeling that *real* sailors didn't use protection, but I already had enough freckles on my face. There was just enough redhead in me to give my brown hair an auburn look and make my skin pale. A smart person with my coloring would live in Minnesota or Montana, not in the mid-Atlantic where life revolved around boats, crabbing and sunshine. But I hated the cold and was truly falling in love with this area So, I'd use some sunscreen to protect my skin. I popped open the barrette, smoothed back my curly hair and anchored it in place again. Who knew how long the stray ends would stay in place.

Finished with my preparations, I turned and saw Elliot looking at me. I braced for a sarcastic comment from the sailing veteran at the wheel, but got a smile instead.

"That's a good idea. I'm always telling my kids to put on more sunscreen. They don't need all the problems caused by skin cancers. You're smart. Even though you stand in the shade, the sun's reflection off the water can be brutal." He kept an eye on the canoe behind us, and the starting line ahead, as he talked. "People are always surprised when they see the burn on their face." He nodded toward me. "Your shoulders are vulnerable, too. You might want slather some that stuff there, too."

"Great idea. Thanks." I reached for the tube again and followed his advice. "I watched the morning race from land using these binoculars Charlie loaned me." I touched the glasses hanging around my neck. "It was very dramatic."

Elliot frowned. "Oh, you can always count on Jack for high drama." He swung his head around, always on the lookout for canoes, other chase boats and random spectator boats. "Sorry, I have to keep a lookout. Some of these weekend warriors think it's cool to come out and watch a log canoe race up close. They have no idea what they're doing. They're always getting in the way."

I sat down on a cushion and tried to be very small. I wondered Captain Elliot was as volatile as Black Jack. I looked back toward the club with a growing sense of yearning for terra firma.

"I'm sorry, I keep interrupting our conversation." His smile was so friendly that I forgot about returning to the club. "You mentioned the drama from this morning. The nice part about sailing is another race means a fresh start. Another chance. Anything can happen. You could still lose… or you could win!" He leaned toward me and lowered his voice. "I happen to know that Jack took TWO bottles of champagne on board for this race. The Governor's Cup is really important to him."

I looked back at the people on the canoe attached by a tow line. "They're very quiet. Just sitting there."

Elliot smiled. "Don't be fooled. He's talking to them softly. Encouraging them. Motivating them. Molding them into a crew that can win."

Jack? It was hard to believe. I looked back and now I could see that every member of the crew had their eyes glued on their captain. Jack took a long swig from his water bottle and continued talking to his crew. Then someone waved to us. Elliot called out to Sam to release the tow line. Though he was at that awkward age when a teenager is all arms and legs, the boy moved quickly and confidently around the power boat. Free of the canoe, Elliot moved the chase boat off the race course, but stayed close with an eye always on *Flying Wing*.

"I'm sorry," Elliot said. "We should have done this before we left the dock. Don't tell anybody." He pointed out the places where he'd stowed the life jackets. "You can wear one if you want. Charlie said you're kind of new to the water." He held one out to me. "It's okay, like using sunscreen."

"No, I'm good, as long as I know where they are." I surprised myself at how confidant I sounded.

"Cool." He offered me some cold water and pointed at the ice chest. "Remember to stay hydrated. You can get hot out here and feel sick pretty fast if you're not careful. And there are potato chips and stuff in the galley. You should be able to find something you like."

I looked inside the cabin and he wasn't kidding. Bags of snacks and cookies covered the counter in the galley and the table. He was going out of his way to make me feel at ease.

"Help yourself," he said. Elliott was a real contrast to the Black Jack.

When I was fortified with a bottle of water and two Oreo cookies, I sat on a bench in the stern and took in the scene. The afternoon sun was brilliant and the blue sky was so clear, I could see almost the edge of space. It was hot, but the warmth wasn't just coming from the sun. The air crackled with the heat of competition between two boats with billowing snowy white sails. After all, this race was for the Governor's Cup Trophy. I remembered the man's commentary from the morning race and wondered which team would be more intense, more determined to bring home the win?

"There it is," Elliot said, pointing to an inflatable orange mark set across from the committee boat. "That's the starting line."

From land, in the moments before the starting gun, the canoes looked all bunched up. Now, I was up close and could see the furious action and reaction as each canoe jockeyed for position. Captains yelled at their crews and each other. I almost couldn't watch. As they moved around, I kept cringing. It felt like a pileup of wood, sails and people was only a moment away. All of a sudden, everything seemed to go into slow motion. Each canoe had a position.

Someone on the committee boat raised the shotgun and fired. And they were off, calling to their crews with instructions that seemed to change every minute. But once they all crossed the starting line on the tack that each thought was the best, the air quieted so the creak of wood, the shush and splash of a canoe cutting through the water and the sigh of the breeze could be heard.

"At least he got a great start this time," Elliot said with a sigh of relief. "He'll be glad he's in front of *Island Memory*." He glanced at me when I didn't respond. "That's Dominick's boat."

Of course, his arch rival. I remembered the confrontation of the two captains at the seafood feast... was it only last night? I remembered the look on Nina's face as Jack pummeled her with his words and body language. I also had to remember whose boat I had to rely on to take me back to shore.

"What about the handicaps? How do they play into the race?" It seemed like a safe question.

"A handicap doesn't mean a thing. These two boats are equals. This is a battle between their captains. It is a question of who is smarter at reading the wind and the water. Who has the courage to make The Call? And who will blink first. Their stately ladies are built to race. It's as if they're all alone out there, racing to see who is the fastest, who is the queen."

I stared at Elliot. When he caught me, he shrugged. "I was an English major in college with a concentration in poetry. Can't make a living rhyming words, but the talent comes in handy at a moment like this."

I smiled and turned my attention back to the race. Elliot was right. Forget the handicaps. This was a race between only two log canoes, *Island Memory* and *Flying Wing*. The rest of the boats were far behind.

Elliot pointed at *Island Memory*. "She's coming about."

The boardmen were acrobats, sliding down the board and clambering out on the other side just to keep the boat upright. The two competing log canoes were headed to the first mark, a tall wooden pole with a navigation number posted just below the osprey's nest. *Flying Wing* took a direct course to the mark, *Island Memory* went wide, a tactic that didn't make sense to me.

"Elliot, what they're doing? Why aren't they racing side by side?"

"It's a little complicated. The easy answer is they need the wind to keep up their momentum, but it's coming from only one direction. If one boat gets between the source of the wind and the other boat, it's called covering and the other boat loses speed."

"It should be called stealing. Is it legal?" I asked.

"Yes, if it's done right and these skippers know how to do it well. By approaching the mark from different directions, they prevent the competition from stealing their wind, as you say."

"What happens if they both get to the turn first?"

"Oh, to answer that question, I need the rule book. They know what they're doing. Watch and learn."

I did and I learned what a catastrophe looked like.

CHAPTER 12

Perform your responsibilities in an honest way. Only use the most prudent and recommended approach when working with silver.

"The Butler's Guide to Fine Silver"
Mr. Hollister, 1898

THE LOG CANOES readied to execute the first turn on the course. The sails stretched tight to squeeze out every bit of speed. Looking through the binoculars, I could see the tense faces of the boardmen. This was no time for joking around as they sat with their legs dangling over the water beneath. The canoes made subtle adjustments to maintain the balance of their boats.

"It's hard for a captain to have a clear view of the action," Elliot pointed out. "The sails are in the way so he relies on his crew to call out information about what's happening. Listen, as they get closer to the mark. We may be able to hear them."

Flying Wing and *Island Memory* bore down on the mark from different angles. My eyes jumped back and forth, anticipating the upcoming maneuvers. When Elliot sucked in a breath, he caught my attention. His reaction wasn't from anticipation. It was from fear. I searched the area, but everything looked fine. Neither boat was in danger of capsizing. I couldn't tell what alarmed Elliot.

Softly, he said, "*Island Memory* has the right of way."

"What does that mean?" The two boats weren't near each other.

"It means that *Flying Wing* has to allow *Island Memory* to go around the mark first. Jack gambled and it didn't pay off. He's gotta be hot."

"Maybe they can make it up on the next leg of the race," I said, trying to sound upbeat.

"Maybe, but—" He leaned forward. "They see it too. Can you hear them?"

The crew of *Flying Wing* was calling out to Captain Black Jack. *She's got the right-of-way.* Then Dominick of *Island Memory* started yelling at *Flying Wing. Give way! Give way!*

"Jack's letting it ride. He's playing chicken with Dominick," Elliot said in growing horror. "If he doesn't change course, it won't matter if he gets to the mark first. He'll be disqualified for breaking the rules." Under his breath, he said over and over, "Come on, Jack. Give way, give way, give way."

From *Island Memory*, Dominick screamed at *Flying Wing*, "Give way!" His crew added to the noise, urgently trying to get the other crew to respond. There was no change in course. What was Jack doing? A maneuver like this could cost *Flying Wing* the race and the Governor's Cup.

Elliot lurched forward and grabbed a rail. He breathed, "Oh no." Then screamed, "NO!" Frantic, he spun his head around like radar noting the positions of the other boats. Seeing he was in the clear, his movements became controlled as he stepped to the wheel. He swung it around and nudged the throttle. We turned toward the mark.

"Abby, keep an eye out. Let me know if we're getting in the way of an oncoming canoe or any other boat."

Reluctantly, I dragged my eyes away from the clash of the two rivals and scanned the scene. "Nothing right now."

"Good. Keep watching."

I glanced back to the screaming crews and the two log canoes on a collision course.

"I don't know what's going to happen, but we have to be prepared. Pull out all the life jackets so they're ready if we have to throw them to the crew."

"Look," I pointed to a power boat flying a red pennant. "Over there."

"That's *Island Memory*'s chase boat." A cruiser with classic lines in rich wood approached the area. "He sees what's happening, too. We've both got to get into position in case we have to pick up the crews and tow the boats out of the way." His head turned this way and that, looking out for boats. "Keep an eye on her, too."

He turned his focus on *Flying Wing* and yelled, "Dammit, Jack. Bear off!" His words didn't make a difference.

I grabbed the binoculars and trained them on our canoe. "There's something happening on *Flying Wing*."

"Tell me what you see," he ordered, peering in the direction of the log canoe.

"I'm not sure." I didn't know the terminology. "Somebody's moving his arms around. A big sail is going limp."

"That's the foresail. Kevin is the foresail tender. He's letting it luff to slow the boat down."

Commands reached us a moment later from across the water. "Fall off! FALL OFF!"

"Kevin is giving the orders. Something is wrong." Elliot corrected for drift and moved us closer. "Very wrong."

"Now, somebody's moving around in the boat."

"The boardmen?" Elliot kept an eye on other boats.

"No, somebody in the middle of the boat. He's standing up... moving to the back."

"Stern," Elliot said automatically. "It must be Kevin."

A shout reached us from *Flying Wing*: "Head off! Head off!" A big sail shifted suddenly.

"Kevin's moving the mainsail."

Then everything went into slow motion. *Flying Wing* leaned to one side as if she'd caught the wind and was making a run. But she wasn't moving forward. She was leaning farther and farther. I reached out as if I could stop what was happening. The boardmen scooted out to the very ends of their boards on the opposite side, hoping to bring her back up again. But it was too late.

"She's going over!" Elliot yelled.

KER-RACK!

The sound sent shards of wood everywhere. "What's happening?" I was screaming now, too.

"Dear Lord! A mast broke."

Yards of canvas slapped the water. Lines hung loose. The splintered mast stabbed the water while the other mast settled into it like a child who was too tired to keep her head up. The movement pitched the crew into the water. Other sailboats in the race bearing down on them quickly steered around to avoid a collision. Teams on the other chase boats stood frozen in surprise, but for only a moment. Engines roared to life. Crews prepared to help prevent further problems and keep people safe.

"Hold on, Abby," Elliot cried as he spun the wheel.

I grabbed for the handrail so the quick change in direction didn't toss me overboard. We headed over to the wounded canoe. Using the binoculars, I scanned the white sails now slowly filling with water. They took on the look of a ghost under the water's sheen.

"Get ready, Abby."

Get ready? To do what? Nobody had prepared me for this. I dropped the binoculars to my chest. It was so hard to look at

Flying Wing. Adrenaline pumped through my body. I wanted, needed something to do. But what? *Grab the life jackets,* I thought. I gathered them into an orange pile, ready … for what?

"People are in the water," I cried out to Elliot. "What do we do?"

"Stay calm, Abby. We're going to come around and get them. Sammy!" He called out to the teenager watching from the bow. "Get the lines ready so we can keep her from drifting away. Then get back here to help with the crew." Sam waved and started working the lines.

Elliot pulled down on his ball cap. "Okay, we need to get to our people, but we have to stay out of the way of the other boats," he said, talking himself through the actions he'd have to follow.

"Why don't they stop the race?" I demanded.

Elliot chuckled, more from nerves than humor. "They won't stop the race for something as minor as a capsize."

"Minor?" I squealed.

He shrugged his shoulders. "Sure, it happens all the time."

The tangled mess was sinking just below the surface. People were in the water, holding on to the canoe or swimming around. "Count heads! Count heads!" people commanded. And the count began: *One, Two, Three, Four, Five, Six, Seven, Eight, Nine, Ten, Eleven.*

Elliot breathed, "That's not enough."

"Again!" Kevin's voice was tinged with dread. "Count heads! ONE!"

Two, Three, Four, Five, Six, Seven, Eight, Nine, Ten, Eleven.

"Elliott, how many—"

"Twelve." He pushed the throttle forward. The boat lurched. "Somebody's missing. Somebody's hurt." He was staring at *Flying Wing*.

The crew waved frantically. They were screaming, "Help! Help!" Something was terribly wrong.

CHAPTER 13

Use the proper equipment when polishing silver. It is vital to the condition of the piece. If you use a finely powdered form of the rouge used by silversmiths and jewelers, choose carefully.

"The Butler's Guide to Fine Silver"
Mr. Hollister, 1898

No one cared about the race anymore. Now, it was about taking care of people and then the canoe. Elliot pushed our boat forward. *Island Memory* was around the mark and safely out of our way. The other boats had time to see what was happening and steered around the canoe with her sails in the water.

"Somebody's missing." Elliot yelled up to the bow. "Sammy, what do you see?'

The boy stood up gingerly and studied the wreck. "It's what I don't see. I don't see Jack."

Jack was the twelfth man and he was missing. Elliot slowed the boat as we neared the capsized canoe.

"Okay, everybody," he called out to the crew. "Calm down. I've got you. Get the line from Sammy and tie it off." The response was immediate.

As if in a trance, my eyes stared as ruby-red tendrils snaked over the snowy white sailcloth submerged in the water. They broadened into a stream and then billowed like crimson sails. *Crimson? River water isn't red.*

"Kevin, is it Jack?"

"Yeah." His eyes kept moving, searching, while he reported to Elliot. "I can't find him."

Then someone screamed. It was high, sharp, ear-splitting. She screamed and didn't stop. Tiffani, the girl with the water bottle, held on to the stern of the canoe and pointed. "Blood!" She screeched.

Reining in his fear, Kevin announced with a quiver in his voice, "Elliot, we've got blood. A lot of it."

Bear moved closer by pulling his mountain of a body along the hull. "He's under the sail." Bear dove down and in a fraction of a minute, popped up. "Help!" He dove under the sail again. Several men followed him under. I was dizzy from holding my breath.

"Abby, get the First Aid kit," Elliot ordered. "It's under the cushion."

Which one? I wanted to yell. There were cushions all around the boat.

Elliot was on the radio. "This is *Fixed Wing*, chase boat at the Governor's Cup log canoe race on the Miles River, requesting assistance."

Just find it, I told myself, *and do it now.*

Some man responded to Elliot on the radio, but I didn't pay attention to his words. I watched as the big men of *Flying Wing* tugged Jack's body out from under the sail. Blood gushed all over his face and flowed freely in the water, turning the submerged white sail scarlet. They pulled Jack toward our boat as they gasped for breath. Jack wasn't doing anything to help them.

Elliot hung up the mike. "Sammy, drop the anchor." The teenager did a double-take. "Do it now!" A moment later, a splash signaled the anchor was down.

"ELLIOT! He's alive!" Bear was almost to the breaking point, gasping for breath from the exertion.

Kevin sputtered as he fought to keep his face out of the water. "It's his head."

Dutch pull off his T-shirt and held it against the wound to help staunch the blood.

"Got it!" He started shouting instructions. "Abby, call 911. My cell's on the console, if you need it," he directed, as he tossed life jackets to the crew in the water. "Sammy, help me! Guys, we've got to get Jack out of the water."

I reached for my cell phone tucked deep in my pocket and fumbled with it, almost dropping it on the deck. I managed to open the phone app. I was shaking so badly that I could barely touch the simple 911 sequence in order. I stepped away from the action at the stern of the boat where they were trying to haul Jack's body aboard. I touched the green button, took a deep breath and made the call.

The dispatcher answered. "911, what is your emergency?"

"We need an ambulance. Someone's been injured." *No, that's not right. We're in the middle of the Miles River!* I remembered what Elliot said when he made the distress call on the radio. "Ma'am, I'm calling from the Governor's Cup Log Canoe Race on the Miles River. One of the boats capsized and the captain has a head wound that won't stop bleeding." She requested our exact location and I yelled to Elliot.

"Tell them we're at the Deep Water Point mark and we're having trouble getting him aboard."

I relayed the information and felt better when she said she was alerting an emergency response boat and other medical responders as well as the Coast Guard. I confirmed what information I had. In just moments, I saw a bright red boat roaring toward us.

"Elliot, I think they're here."

Quickly, he gathered the crew members who were still in the water to the other side of the boat so they were safely out of the way of the incoming rescue boat. The red boat emblazoned with "ST. MICHAELS FIRE/RESCUE 40" on the side in big white letters pulled up neatly and took charge of the rescue.

Her captain called out to Elliot, "Take care of the crew. We will take care of the injured." He turned to his own crew. "Get the dive door down. Get the backboard. Greg, you're going in the water."

The men moved quickly and calmly. A sliding section of the red hull called the dive door slipped down so the rescue boat's deck was just above the water. After pulling on life vests, Greg and his partner slipped in the water holding on to a floating backboard. They moved to Jack's body where Bear and Kevin were keeping his head above water.

"It's okay, guys," Greg told the men. We're paramedics. We'll take him from here."

Reluctantly, the men of *Flying Wing* backed away and swam to the other side where they were helped aboard the chase boat. They positioned the backboard underneath Jack's body and strapped him in place. They floated Jack to the rescue boat and their team lifted him to the deck through the dive door. Meanwhile, a man with white hair, who had an air of command about him, went inside the cabin and picked up the microphone. "Talbot Center. This is Boat 40."

Talbot Center responded immediately, loud enough for us all to hear. "Boat 40. Go ahead."

"Talbot Center, we have recovered an unresponsive patient from a log canoe accident in the Miles River. We will proceed to the Miles River Yacht Club. Requesting ambulance with medical assist."

"Roger." And tones sounded to dispatch equipment and personnel.

Someone aboard the rescue boat grabbed a medical bag and started setting up equipment.

"That's a nasty head wound," Greg said as he checked the collar around Jack's neck used to protect his head and back. "Pupils pinpoint. Checking vitals."

I held my breath as I watched, trying to stay out of the way as the rest of *Flying Wing*'s crew secured the canoe to the chase boat. Tiffani was sobbing, curled up on a bench in the cabin. Somebody grabbed a bottle of water and thrust it in her direction. People had a few bumps and scraps, but there were no real injuries from the accident. Only Jack. Jack was the only one hurt.

"I've barely got a pulse." Greg spoke with authority. "Start rescue breathing." The others followed his orders. One took out a mask and put it on Jack's face to create a seal. He attached a bag for ventilation and began to squeeze in a steady rhythm.

"Beginning CPR," announced his partner. "Starting compressions."

"Ellie, we're losing him. Get the paddles."

I hadn't noticed that one of the responders was a woman. She took charge. "His shirt. It's got to come off."

I watched as someone grabbed a pair of scissors, cut the shirt and pulled it away. Then he used a towel to dry off dry chest.

I jumped when someone whispered in my ear, "Why are they taking off his shirt?" It was young Sammy. Evidently, the older crew members had taken over and he was lost without something to do.

"They have to attach the leads to his chest and it has to be dry or they'll electrocute him when they give him a jolt."

"CLEAR!" Ellie ordered.

Jack's body tensed.

We could hear the thump as his body fell back on the deck.

"No pulse."

CHAPTER 14

ifferent types of rouge used in the polishing process create different looks. Red rouge produces a high color and lustre. If you polish a silver piece with black rouge, it will create a dark appearance. Once it is used, it is difficult to reverse its effect.

"The Butler's Guide to Fine Silver"
Mr. Hollister, 1898

"Greg, ready to go," said the white-haired man at the wheel of the rescue boat.

"Hold on!" Greg turned to our chase boat now with the damaged log canoe lashed to its side and crammed with crew members, all but one. "Who knows this man well?" The men looked at each other. "Come on, we've got to go. One of you, come aboard. We need information."

"Kevin. Go!" yelled Dutch.

In a moment, Kevin moved with lots of hands reaching out to help him make the shift to the red rescue boat. Her captain revved the twin 300 HP Evinrude engines, moved away with care then headed to the docks at the Miles River Yacht Club at full throttle.

Elliot called out to get everyone's attention. "Okay, everybody, find a spot and hold on. We're heading in, too."

We followed in the wake of the rescue boat, but at a slower speed because of the canoe. As we came up the channel to the yacht club, we could see emergency lights flashing. A fire truck marked 'Engine 49' and an ambulance with a red stripe were parked on the grass where, less than twenty-four hours earlier, people enjoyed an incredible seafood feast. A feast sponsored by the man suffering chest-crushing compressions by a woman trying to save his life.

The dark blue SUVs of the St. Michaels police department were there, too. Officers spread out to control the growing number of onlookers. We watched as the firemen took the lines to tie up the red rescue boat. Two paramedics ran down to the boat from the ambulance. They dropped their gear and stepped aboard to assess the patient and move him to the dock. The paramedic never stopped doing compressions.

Elliot pulled up to the dock and Sammy jumped off to secure her lines. People didn't wait. They crowded off the boat and went to watch as Jack was wired to machines to monitor his vitals like heart rate and oxygen saturation.

"Continue CPR," ordered the blonde paramedic.

"No pulse," reported her partner. "No breathing. Asystole."

"Continue chest compressions." The paramedic tore open a small package, checked the syringe and stuck it in his arm. "Administering Epi."

They were quiet, waiting, hoping for some response. We all were.

She leaned over and checked Jack again. "Asystole."

"Ok, we need to transport now." She stuffed the medical gear back in the bag and stood. She looked at the firemen standing by to help. "Let's get him on a stretcher." Two men were rolling the stretcher over the grass. They lowered it next to the body still strapped to the backboard. As they moved to lift it, four boardmen stepped away from the group and took up places around Jack.

Bear said to them, "It's okay. We've got this."

A fireman looked at the hefty young men. His partner gave him a small nod and they stepped back. The boardmen of the *Flying Wing* with solemn faces reached down to get a grip on the board.

The blonde paramedic straddling Jack's body told the men, "You have to do this quick so I can continue compressions."

They nodded. When she shifted off the backboard, Bear said, "On a count of three, men. One, two, three."

Like they were moving a precious baby, they hefted the backboard that held their captain onto the stretcher, then they stepped back. As the firemen strapped him down, the paramedic jumped on top again and continued compressions. They hustled the stretcher to the ambulance, moved it inside and slammed the doors. With sirens blaring and lights flashing, the emergency vehicle roared up the hill to the road.

We surged forward and stood as group surrounding Kevin, desperate for information.

"Why did they want you on the rescue boat?" asked Bear.

Kevin kept his eyes on the ground. "They thought I could give them information about Jack." His voice caught when he spoke his name.

"Like what?"

"Basic stuff." But Kevin wasn't giving enough information. Everyone wanted details.

"Like what?" Dutch pressed.

Kevin sighed. "Like his name, age, if he has any medical problems, if he is taking any medication." He paused for a moment. "If he is using." His eyes scanned the group. "He isn't, is he?"

Someone in the back gave him a quiet *no* for an answer.

"Come on, guys," Kevin insisted. "It's important. Is he using?"

Dutch took a step forward. "Definitely not."

"What caused the gash on his head?" someone asked.

Sammy started to speak, but his words came out more like a squeak. He stopped, cleared his throat and started again. "I think the sprit got him when the mast snapped. I looked at the canoe and the sprit looks like it exploded." His voice cracked with tears when he said the words, "There's blood on the splintered wood."

"What happened on the rescue boat when you were coming in?" someone else wanted to know.

Kevin looked down at his feet and shook his head. "It was rough. They shocked him again. It was awful to watch. They got him back, so they stopped CPR. Then she said there was no pulse. That he was in cardiac arrest so they started it again." He looked at the faces surrounding him, hoping someone would say it would be all right. But no one did. "The grunts as they worked his chest and the counting..." Kevin looked down again and shook his head slowly. "I don't think I'll ever forget it."

No one knew what to say so we all just stood together on the dock close to *Flying Wing*. There were only quiet murmurs between a few people as each one of us tried to process what had happened.

Kevin moved away from the group in a daze and stared down the channel toward the river, rubbing the palms of his hands over his face. He might have been there all afternoon if Elliot hadn't gone to talk to him. I know, because I had an inkling of how Kevin felt. It wasn't real. Maybe a person could make sense of what happened by just looking out at the water. But what was a person to do now, right now, when there was nothing that could be done?

Kevin looked at Elliot with eyes wide, searching for answers. Elliot steeled himself from the pain. He squeezed Kevin's shoulder. "I know, I know." But he didn't let Kevin all apart. There was work to do and he was going to make sure it was done, but with compassion. "Come on, man. You've got to hold it together a little longer. We still have to take care of her." He gestured to *Flying Wing* gently rocking with the movement of waves from the river. "We can't leave her tied up here. We've got to get her home, safe."

Kevin shifted his eyes and stared at the log canoe that had outlasted several captains in her almost 100-year history. She'd endured and Elliot was going to make sure she survived to race another day.

"Let's get her on the trailer while everyone's still here so we can get her back to her slip." Kevin didn't move. "Come on Kev, I need your help." Kevin still didn't move, so Elliot said what everyone needed to hear. "It's what Jack would want."

That got Kevin and the crew moving. I stepped back, out of the way, as they prepared to move the canoe out of the water. Teary-eyed Tiffani came and leaned against me. There wasn't much her petite body could contribute. At least I could offer her some comfort, so I put my arm around her shoulders. She was still wet from being in the water, but I didn't care.

The crew was about to move *Flying Wing* around to the ramp when Kevin yelled out for everyone to stop. He ran to the stern and reached under the bench where Captain Jack had stowed the fresh bottles of champagne meant to celebrate winning of the Governor's Cup. Seeing them made Tiffani sob and she buried her face in my neck, her drenched blonde hair sent rivulets of water down my back.

The crew took up their positions again and was about to lift the canoe when a thundering bass voice ordered them to STOP! The uniformed police lieutenant from St. Michaels stepped forward with an officer from Natural Resources Police. "Can I have your attention? We need to keep the boat here and secure the property," he told the group. "It's procedure."

Not one person moved. They stared at him in disbelief. An officer wearing gloves walked over to Kevin and tried to take the bottles of champagne from him, but Kevin didn't want to let them go. First, their captain was taken away, barely alive. Now, the police wanted to take away the champagne as well as the boat. And the crew of *Flying Wing* was having none of it.

They all started talking and shouting at once. The big men moved into a position that put their bodies between the boat and the police.

Elliot put two fingers in his mouth and let loose a bone-rattling whistle that froze everyone in place. "Listen up!" he roared. "Everyone step away from the boat!" He glared at the police lieutenant. "EVERYONE. Until we get this worked out."

The lieutenant signaled his men with a small jerk of his head and they stepped back.

Elliot gave the lieutenant a subtle nod in thanks and scanned the group. "Okay, crew of *Flying Wing*. We've had a terrible accident. I'm not sure why the police are treating this as a crime scene, but..." A rumble started to grow from the group. Elliot held up his hand and yelled even louder. "BUT we want to help in any way we can. It's what Jack would want. So, Kevin, give the officer the champagne bottles." Elliot swung his head over to the police lieutenant. "We will get them back, won't we?"

"Absolutely!" His answer was loud enough for all to hear and that went a long way to defusing the situation.

"Kevin, the bottles," Elliot said quietly.

Reluctantly, Kevin handed over the bottles and they went into an evidence bag.

The officer relaxed his shoulders. "Thank you, sir." He joined the others.

The lieutenant walked over to Kevin. "Can you back up your trailer and haul the canoe?"

Dutch looked like he was ready to spit bullets. "And do what with it? Keep it in some police impound lot?" He didn't give the police a chance to respond. "You can't just haul her out and leave her exposed to whoever or whatever might come by."

Bear added his opinion. "You can't do that. She'll dry out! Don't you know anything about wood boats? "

The lieutenant took a deep breath. He didn't want the situation to escalate again. "Okay, okay. We'll try to arrange to put her in a slip here at the club, just until we get the report back." He turned to Elliot. "Does that work for you?"

When Elliot nodded, the lieutenant pointed to a uniformed officer, pointed to the building and the man took off to make arrangement.

"What's going to happen to her when she's released from custody, if Jack doesn't make it," asked Kevin.

The officer shook his head and shrugged. "I suppose she'll go to the next of kin."

"That's a good plan," Nina called out, sarcasm dripping from every word. "His dad lives in Arizona now. Not a lot of opportunity for sailing there."

There were some challenging gestures, but most people looked at the log canoe with concern. Her captain was on his way to the emergency room. They didn't want to lose *Flying Wing*, too.

The uniformed officer returned at a trot followed by a gentleman with a mane of white hair and two dock attendants. "He says we can use a slip around on the other side."

"It's a transient slip for guests. The boys will show you where it is. They can move it—"

Dutch stepped up, shaking his head. "Oh, no. We'll take care of our boat, thank you."

Elliot roused the crew to action. "Kevin, get her ready for a tow. Sammy, we're on the chase boat. Come on, guys. Let's tuck her in for the night."

O.T. walked over to Kevin and put a hand on his shoulder. "I'd like to help."

"Sure, thanks, O.T." Kevin started calling out assignments. There was a lot to salvage and store: sails, lines and more.

"Thanks to all of you for your help," said the lieutenant. "You'll have your boat back as soon as we get confirmation."

I noted that he didn't say confirmation of what.

It wasn't long before the call came from the hospital. The emergency room doctor in Easton had made the pronouncement. Jack was dead. The official cause of death was cardiac arrest as a result of a severe gash on head.

The news rippled through the crowd. Some people didn't move, as if their feet were stuck to the ground. One woman covered her mouth and ran toward the club building. Others turned to each other for solace, crying on a shoulder, holding hands or just leaning against one another for support. Soft voices exchanged private thoughts.

Then the police moved into the crowd. Quietly, they took people's names and organized them into groups. Why? Because no one could leave. Everyone had to give a statement about what each might have seen or heard, anything out of the ordinary. I knew they would ask if there was bad blood between the crews, if someone held a grudge, if anyone wanted to hurt Jack. The kinds of questions meant to uncover hidden tensions and secrets. Questions asked in a serious investigation.

People believed it was a tragic accident, but it could be a case of murder. After all, the mast could have been sabotaged. In the chaos, someone could have bashed his head in or held his head underwater. The possibilities triggered the police response and made me shudder.

The lieutenant, assisted by the other officers, worked to calm the group's concerns and keep the situation under control. No, he promised, it wouldn't take long for them to take the statements. I looked at the size of the crowd and stifled a laugh. I sat on a bench and resigned myself to a long wait. It wasn't long before my head started pounding. Maybe it was the heat. Maybe it was the flashing lights and blinding strobes of police cars from different jurisdictions, the fire truck sent to support the St. Michaels response boat, the SUVs from the Natural Resources Police. Maybe it was the horror of what I had seen on the water. There was so much blood.

My eyes wandered over the crowd and locked on one man, standing alone in the crowd milling around on the lawn of the yacht club. He was the one man who always materialized when there was a suspicious death. And now he was here, sipping coffee. I pushed myself up from the bench and walked over.

"Detective Ingram, what are you doing here?" He looked the same as he did when he worked the murders at the Plein Air Art Festival in Easton. All the way down to his suit. A suit in this heat made me perspire.

"I seem to be the go-to guy here in Talbot County, even though I'm State Police," he said with a long-suffering sigh.

"I guess you're just lucky," I said, trying to get us off on the right foot since we were sort of adversaries during the other investigation.

He took a sip from the paper cup and kept his eye on the activities in front of us. "And what, may I ask, brings you to this shindig?" His tone was casual, but it was a serious question. The one thing I knew about this man was he was deliberate about everything he did. And now, I was going to put myself directly in his crosshairs.

"Funny you should ask," I began, as I too surveyed the crowd. "I was on the chase boat for *Flying Wing*, the log canoe that capsized, not far from where it happened." I didn't have to look. I could feel his almost pitch-black eyes boring into me. "I saw a lot of what happened through binoculars. I picked a great day for a boat ride, didn't I?" My little attempt at humor didn't work.

"Come with me, Ms. Strickland." He turned toward the club building, pausing only a moment to ask an officer to tell the lieutenant that he would be inside. I followed him to a table in the corner of the formal dining room and we sat down in relative quiet.

He asked me to start at the beginning and I did. I gave him as much detail as possible to save time, because he would hound me about every little thing if I didn't. That's probably what made him such a good detective.

"Talbot Center said a woman made the 911 call. That wasn't you, was it?" I nodded and he sighed. "Of course, it was. Why am I surprised that you're right in the middle of this?"

"It's bad timing on my part." I leaned closer. "Seriously, this was an accident, a terrible accident. We don't need a homicide detective."

"You could be right, but it's not your call. This incident falls under the jurisdiction of the Natural Resources Police, because it happened on the water. They wanted me here, just in case."

I nodded. "That makes sense, but why are so many other departments here?"

"Dispatch contacted NRP and, at their request, Maryland State Police was alerted. St. Michaels Fire & EMS responded with their boat, fire truck and ambulance. St. Michaels police got here first to control the scene. EMS on Tilghman Island and Easton were alerted. The Sheriff sent a car. And there's the Coast Guard, of course."

"Wow, it's great how you all work together."

"Thanks to all kinds of Memos of Understanding to keep the lawyers happy." He took a sip from the coffee cup and grimaced. "Frankly, I hope they don't get in my way."

"If it's a homicide."

"If it's a homicide," he agreed as he got up from the chair. "Now, I think it's time for you to give your statement."

"But I—"

"Gave me some background. I appreciate that." He waved an officer into the room. "Will you see that Ms. Strickland gives her statement now?"

"Yes, sir. If you'll come this way, miss."

"Thank you, detective." I wasn't sure if Ingram noticed my sarcasm.

I followed the officer into the ballroom where people were huddled in pairs. There was a low din of conversation as they talked and filled out paperwork. It all made me a little nervous, even though I hadn't done anything. Except witness a tragic accident. Surely, it was an accident.

CHAPTER 15

here are many forks available for the place setting. The number of forks placed to the left of the plate is limited to three. The only exception is the seafood fork. Its proper position to the far right of the plate.

"The Butler's Guide to Fine Silver"
Mr. Hollister, 1898

THEY MADE space for me at a table and I told the officer what I knew. He questioned me about certain details, but I didn't really see anything worthwhile that could add to his investigation. At least I didn't think so. He wanted to know about my call to 911. Why was he asking me about that? It was recorded live at the dispatch center and if they needed it, they could just listen to it.

I felt sorry that my officer got a little frustrated, but he stood to thank me and was ready to moved on to someone else. I left only after I filled out a witness statement that included my name, date of birth, address and contact information and a narrative which repeated everything I'd just told him and Detective Ingram. I was free to go, but all the activity held me like a magnet. Okay, I admit it, I was curious what other people were saying, so I took my time leaving the ballroom, trying to pick up snippets of conversations.

"Honestly Officer, I didn't see anything."

"We were all too busy with our canoe. You see, our…"

I made a little detour toward the table where Elliot sat. His body language told me what was going on there without hearing his words. Elliot sat on the edge of his chair, leaning toward the officer. He jabbed his index finger into the table to emphasize key points. He even stretched his neck out to read the man's notes and gestured to the pad to correct something written there. Elliot was being meticulous about the facts as he saw them. No wonder Jack picked him to handle the chase boat. His attention to detail and proper procedure would be valuable in an emergency. They were today, even though Jack died.

Kevin was talking with an officer close to the door people were using to leave. I headed that way, dragged my feet and listened hard. After all, if anyone knew anything, it was Kevin. He was sitting right in front of Jack on the canoe. He saw it all.

Kevin ran his palms over his head as if trying to keep his brain from exploding. "I don't know, officer. There was so much going on." His shoulders sagged. "Jack was very slow to respond. I mean, we were in the middle of a race and he barely knew where he was. His speech was getting sloppy. His breathing was slowing down, too."

The officer asked, "Was this unusual?"

Kevin barked out a laugh. "Are you kidding? Jack is always…" He stopped and looked away. After taking a deep breath to steady himself, he continued. "He was always yelling orders and looking everywhere. He had to know exactly where every boat was and what they were doing. It was as if his head was on a swivel. But not today. He just kinda sagged against the tiller and held on to it with an iron grip. And then, just before we started to go over, to capsize, his eyes flew open. I mean, they were really wide. It freaked me out. His blue eyes were like the deep blue marbles we used to play with as kids."

"What do you mean?" The officer was making a note.

"I mean there wasn't any of that black part. His pupils had all but disappeared so there was only this deep blue color. Then his skin turned kind of blue-gray. Then he went limp."

The officer looked up from the paper. "What did you do then?"

"I grabbed the tiller. We had to avoid hitting the other boat. I had a bad time getting control of the tiller." Kevin put his heads in his hands. "That might be why we went over. Maybe this was all my fault."

"Why do you say that?" The officer asked, his attention riveted on the poor man.

"Well, these boats are touchy. They don't like the tiller yanked around. In a breeze like the one today, a canoe could go over just like that, if you're not careful. I had to tug on the tiller to get it out of Jack's hand." He raised his head. "So, is it my fault that Jack is dead?"

The officer examined Kevin's face, filled with anguish, then shook his head. "I wouldn't be thinking about it like that, not at this point. We're early in our investigation."

If the officer wasn't going to offer him some comfort, Kevin needed some answers. "Was it the mast that hit him in the head?"

The officer cleared his throat. "Why do you think the mast broke?"

"I don't know. Could have been several things. There might have been a crack or split in it somewhere and the strain of going over could have made it break." Kevin ran his hand through his hair again.

The officer shifted his attention to me. He pointed to the door inviting me to leave and I hustled out to the lobby and right into trouble.

"Abby!" The voice stopped me cold. It belonged to Harriet Snow, World Class Busybody, about the size of a garden gnome. "Oh, Abby. Isn't this awful? I came as soon as I heard." Her words flooded out of her mouth, as usual. "And to have such an awful thing happen to a log canoe captain. Why, log canoes are part of the foundation, part of the fabric of our way of life here on the Eastern Shore."

I had to stifle a sharp comeback. She and her husband had moved here less than five years ago from Pennsylvania. I looked around to see if she'd dragged Ben with her, poor man. "Ben is in the Grill to see how he can make things easier for the staff. I'm out here to find out how we can make things easier for the police."

At that moment, two uniformed officers rounded the corner. "Ladies, we need to ask you to move along. We're trying to keep this area clear."

I pointed down the hall. "I'm just on my way to the ladies room."

The taller man stepped aside and looked at Harriet with pursed lips.

She fumbled, but only for a moment. "Oh, and I'm Mrs. Bennett Snow and—"

"Did you give your statement?" asked the younger man.

"Ah, no. My husband and I were at home when—"

"Then we have to ask you to return home," the officer said.

"But I—" Harriet tried again.

"I need you to return home, now. This is an active police investigation. Only people directly involved should be on the property." His thin lips pulled into a small smile that barely blunted the edge of his message.

Harriet was speechless. Almost. "My husband is in the Grill—"

"Then you need to get Mr. Bennett Snow and..." He pronounced the next two words very carefully. "Go home."

I stifled a giggle as Harriet took one step backward and then another. The officer added a curt *Good-Bye* that sent her scurrying off to find Ben.

My cell phone buzzed in my pocket and I moved close to the wall to take Lorraine's call. "Hi, I'm okay."

"Thank goodness. Oh, Abby. What happened? I've heard the most awful reports on the news. Friends have been calling. I've been so worried." Her questions and comments came so fast that she had to stop for a breath before I had a chance to respond.

"I'm fine." While I gave her the short version of events, I admired the watercolor painting on the wall. It was of the ill-fated *Flying Wing*. "How do you hear?" I asked, always amazed at how fast news traveled in this small part of the world.

"First, I received a call that the governor wasn't coming. Then a security man said something had happened at the club. The phone has been ringing non-stop. This is the first moment I've been able to call you. Are you sure you're all right?"

"I'm fine, really. I'll be home in a little while. Please don't worry." I tried to sound reassuring though I did feel rattled by the events. Who wouldn't? The thought of someone dying right in front of my eyes sent a chill down my back. "How is it going on your end?"

"Right now, I'm up to my ears in political chatter. It's exhausting, but I think it's doing some good. We'll have to wait and see. At least I'm learning a lot. Let's catch up tomorrow after all these people leave."

We agreed and I tucked my phone away.

I wandered around the club. I didn't know where to put myself. I wasn't ready to rejoin the regular world where the feelings and events of the last few hours would be a curiosity. I wanted to stay here a little longer with people who'd shared the experience. For only a short time this day, I'd been part of the crew of *Flying Wing*, part of their world of sun and wind and sailing. Now, their world was filled with sadness and tears.

Outside, people were putting their gear away. One by one or

in small groups, they were getting in their cars to go home. Inside the building, the noise level had dropped to low murmurs. In the Grill, a few people sat at tables and spoke quietly about what had happened. They were almost eager to tell people who were just coming to the club for happy hour or dinner.

Everyone was part of a group, except one.

I recognized the young woman from the *Flying Wing* crew sitting at the bar hunched over a drink, alone. Her hairstyle with the black bows had not survived the boat's capsize and the traumatic events that followed. A few ponytails were still in place, but all the bows were either untied or missing. She looked like she needed company so I went and sat down next to her.

"Tiffani, isn't it?" I asked softly.

She looked up and gazed at me as if I'd awakened her from a bad dream. "Yeah." She paused for a minute and stared at my face. "I know you. You're…"

"Abby. I was a guest on the chase boat this afternoon."

"Yeah and…." She slurred her words a little. But who could blame her after what she'd been through in the past few hours.

"And I was sitting with Nina this morning when you were taking the water bottle to the canoe."

"That's right." She shook her index finger at me weakly. "I remember now."

"I'm really sorry." I didn't know what else to say. Fortunately, the bartender appeared and I ordered a light gin and tonic. Not that I really wanted it, but it was an excuse to keep her company. We sat in silence until my drink arrived. Then she picked up her glass and held it toward me.

"To Jack," she said.

"To Jack," I repeated and we clinked glasses.

After we sipped, we sat in silence again until she blurted out words that she couldn't hold inside any longer.

"I should have known." She leaned back against the bar chair and squeezed her eyes shut. "I should have known," she said again in a voice just above a whisper.

Her pain hit me like a wave. To ease whatever guilt she was feeling, I put my hand over hers. "There probably was nothing you could do," I said.

She opened her eyes and stared straight in front of her, not seeing the rows of fine liquor bottles on display. She was on board *Flying Wing* again. "We started to lean. I thought she was going to right herself, but she just kept leaning. I know it only took seconds, but it was happening in slow motion. When I knew she was going over, I scrambled out of my seat on the outrigger. Then..." She remembered her drink and took a sip from the glass. "I don't know what happened. I heard a crack and the sprit came apart. Wood was flying everywhere. The sail was flapping. I think I put my arms up to protect my face. Somebody yelled, she's sinking!"

She frowned and shook her head. "That wasn't right. Log canoes don't sink. They flip over, but they don't sink." Tears started welling up in her eyes. "That's when I should have heard it."

I waited, but she just sat and stared, lost in the memory. "What should you have heard?" I asked as gently as I could.

"I should have heard Jack screaming." She took a long swallow to empty her glass as the bartender arrived with fresh drink. He swapped out her glass and turned to me.

"A Dark & Stormy for you, miss?" he asked.

"I'm sorry, I should know this, but what is a Dark & Stormy?"

He grinned, eager to share his knowledge. "It's the sailor's drink. The best Dark & Stormy is made with Gosling's Black Seal Rum. The ginger beer should be Barrett's, though Gosling's would not approve." He lowered his voice as if the manufacturer might be listening. "Frankly, I think they just want to monopolize the Dark & Stormy market, because they make a ginger beer, too."

I remembered I still had to drive home and with all the cops around, I decided to play it safe. "I think I'll just have an iced tea, please."

He scooped up my watered-down drink, poured my tea and left to tend to his other customers. I turned my attention back to Tiffani who sat, staring into space. A tiny line of perspiration glistened above her lips.

"Tiffani?" I laid my hand on her arm. "Are you okay?"

"Huh? What?" She dragged her attention back to me. "Oh."

"You were a hundred miles away."

"No, not really." She stared deep into her glass. "I was back in the boat."

"Did you hear or see something unusual?" Maybe she remembered something that could help the police.

"Huh?" She scratched her head and swatted at the end of a black ribbon.

I tried again. "What did you see or hear?"

"Um, it's what I didn't hear. I should have heard him screaming." Her body straightened. "'Save my boat! Save my boat!' That's what I should have heard. But I didn't. That's when I should have known." She scratched an itch on her arm. "Ow, guess I got too much sun."

I couldn't figure it out, so I asked. "What should you have known?"

"I should have known Jack was hurt or dead. He wouldn't tolerate losing his *Flying Wing*." Then the tears spilled down her cheeks. "Maybe if I had realized…" She wiped at those tears, but they kept coming. "This isn't working. I have to go." She downed her drink, slipped off the stool and was gone.

I'd never felt comfortable sitting at a bar, alone. Even at this nice bar at a private club. So, I went and found my car in the dark parking lot and drove back to Fair Winds. First, I had to go to the main house to retrieve Simon from the kennel. Lorraine thought all the dogs should spend the weekend there to keep them safe from all the visitors' cars traveling in and out. It was a good plan.

Simon could be with his buddies and I didn't have to worry about him. I was surprised to see the kitchen lights on. It seemed that I wasn't the only one planning a raid on the kitchen for a midnight snack. I just didn't expect to see Lorraine.

"What are you doing up? You're usually sound asleep at this late hour," I said.

"I know, I know. I just kept tossing and turning. I figured some warm milk might help. Do you want some?" She took one look at the expression on my face. "Oh, I guess not."

"It's not one of my favorite things," I explained for fear that I'd offended her. "In fact, just the thought of it makes my tummy—"

She held up her hands. "No, don't tell me." She came over and rubbed my arm, a way that she often showed concern. "Tell me, how are you?"

"Oh, I'm okay. Still a little rattled by Jack's sudden death and all. It wasn't a great way to spend a summer afternoon."

She dropped her eyes. "Sorry I got you involved."

"It's not your fault. I wanted to go and sometimes things happen. And now I'm hungry." I went over to the refrigerator and yanked open the heavy door. "What's got you all riled up?" I checked out the leftovers there. There were enough to feed an army. Some foil packages had names on them. It was all more than I could handle. I settled for a slice of Smith Island Cake and reached for a cake knife.

Lorraine poured her warm milk into a mug and plopped down on one of the kitchen chairs at the counter with a deep sigh. "I don't know. I think it was all the talk at the dinner table tonight got me riled up."

"The dinner didn't go well? I can't imagine something going wrong at a dinner prepared by Mrs. Clark and overseen by Dawkins." Even though Dawkins was a little strange at times, I had to admit that he knew what he was doing and could manage just about any situation. "What happened?"

"Oh, it wasn't the dinner. They did a beautiful job, as usual. I can always count on them to make me look good. It was the conversation around the table. I swear that whenever politicians and community leaders come together, I get a bad case of heartburn."

"But I thought that you were following your daddy's tradition of conciliation and compromise at the dinner. At least that's the way I thought it was supposed to happen. Are you saying that approach doesn't work anymore?"

"No, they made some real progress on developing a better understanding of some issues and even coming up with some possible solutions to explore," she said, with a spark of satisfaction.

"So the dinner was a success, right?"

"Yes, it was."

"So, what's the problem?" I was confused.

"The problem is me. I haven't been active in the community for a while. Tonight, I realized that I'm really out of touch with what's going on. We're facing some serious problems and I feel like I was slapped in the face with them tonight." I started to react, but she shook her head. "No, no. Nobody was out of line, except me. Tonight, I was drawn into conversation about situations and facts that I should have known about already." She dabbed her lips with a napkin. "Oh, I think I covered my reactions so no one else at the table knew how I felt, but I was... Oh, I don't know, deeply disappointed in myself."

I sat down at the island next to her. "Rather than beating yourself up, why don't you tell me what upset you so much and what you're going to do about it."

She patted my arm. "This is one of the reasons why I like having you here, Abby. You don't let me wallow. Over the past months, I certainly have had good reason to do just that, but you haven't let me get away with it, thankfully." She got up and went to the counter. "Do you want a cookie?"

Simon appeared at her feet in a nanosecond, his tail wagging at high speed. She looked down and said in a sweet voice that she reserved for the dogs, "I didn't mean a cookie for you." Simon's ears sagged in that cute little way that tugs on the heartstrings. "Oh, all right. But just this once." Simon happily devoured his treats while she returned to her seat with Chocolate Oatmeal Raisin cookies for us.

Between bites, she said, "I guess the first thing that got my blood boiling was a broken promise. You're familiar with Tilghman Island, Abby. There's that little stretch of water that runs between the Island and the mainland."

I nodded. "Of course. There's a drawbridge there."

"That's right. All kinds of boats use that stretch of water known as Knapps Narrows. It's a direct route from the Chesapeake Bay to the Choptank River. The only other option is for a boat to go around Tilghman Island and that adds twenty-five miles to the trip."

"That's a long way," I said in surprise.

"I agree. It makes a big difference in time and money. Gasoline is expensive and waterman want to spend their time pulling crabs and oysters from the water, not taking a cruise."

"So, what's the problem?"

"Knapps Narrows is useless if boats run aground. Work boats have a shallow draft so they can go just about anywhere and even they are having trouble. The authorities are moving buoys around and the watermen are timing their passage for high tide to avoid problems and damage to their boats."

I recalled some of the news reports from coverage about hurricanes. "Silt doesn't build up overnight unless there is a big storm. Fortunately, we've dodged those lately. Didn't they see this problem coming?"

Lorraine nodded. "Yes, the men and women who work the water know what's needed and stay in close contact with the Army Corps of Engineers. A plan for the Narrows was approved and funded. It was supposed to be dredged four years ago. It didn't happen."

"Why not?" I asked.

"The answer is one word: politics. And now the seafood industry, the tourist industry and emergency response are all threatened." Lorraine was indignant and her voice was getting louder. "If the watermen can't get to the crabs or the oyster beds or can't get their catch to the buyers, they lose money. If their boats run aground, fixing the damage becomes an unexpected expense. The tourist trade is falling off, because the big sailboats and power boats can't get through and now the marinas there are hurting. And you'll understand this, when you called 911 this afternoon, a lot of responders came to the accident." I nodded, remembering the wide array of trucks and boats. "One of those was the new Tilghman Island Fire Department boat."

"Yes, it was there. It came flying in, barely skimming the water."

"That's one of the things I learned about at dinner tonight. That boat can do 54 miles an hour so it can be on the scene to fight a fire or rescue people from the water in a matter of minutes. But it can't do that if it can't go through Knapps Narrows." Lorraine got up and put her empty mug and plate in the sink. "It was good that our Congressional representative and state representatives were here tonight. The politicians were made to realize the magnitude of the problem and I think they're going to come up with a way to get that little stretch of water cleared out."

I gave her a big smile. "Then you should be happy that you put together this weekend."

"Oh, I am. Except it shouldn't have gotten to this point. I see now that I can still make a little bit of a difference by bringing people together. I've been shirking my responsibility, but that's over now." She patted my hand. "Thank you for letting me vent. I think I can go upstairs now and fall asleep." She yawned. "Good night."

I was glad that Lorraine wanted to make a difference and that she could go to bed and rest. But the tragic accident I'd witnessed was still right in front of my eyes. Was there something I should've done? Charlie said there was nothing. So did Elliott. But the question nagged at me as Simon and I made our way to the cottage and bed. It wasn't a restful night for me.

CHAPTER 16

*I*t is the responsibility of the Butler, with the assistance of his staff, to keep an inventory of the House silver. The silver cupboard and chest must be inspected on a regular basis to be sure that the pieces are safe and in pristine condition.

"The Butler's Guide to Fine Silver"
Mr. Hollister, 1898

"ABBY, ABBY! HELP ME!" *Jack's voice tugged at me as the red tendrils blossomed into a scarlet wave of blood.*

"Abby! Help me!"

His hand, scratched and cut, rose out of the water, his bloody fingers searching for me.

"Abby!"

They grabbed me like a vise and pulled me into the sea of blood.

"Help me!"

I SCREAMED. I shot up in bed and gasped for air. Was Jack was haunting me? The thought gave me chills. I threw off the tangled covers and scrambled down the stairs in my bare feet. Somehow the world felt safer than my bed.

If warm milk worked for Lorraine, maybe it would work for me. I headed to my refrigerator and stopped short. Maybe there was a better way. I took out my box of magnets and sat on the floor in front of the refrigerator door. I started playing this game when I was five. At the accident scene where the police discovered my mother dead in the front, they heard whimpering coming from the back seat. It's where they found me, covered in her blood. That was the day I stopped talking. Dad thought it was better for me to stay with Gran and her sister Agnes while he went back to sea.

Gran shuttled me to doctor and therapy appointments, but the one thing that worked was the game she created on the refrigerator door. It all started with the ice cream magnet, a scoop of ice cream on a cone. I loved ice cream and she said if I wanted some, I had to put the magnet in the center of the door. The day she saw that magnet in place, she couldn't hide her tears. It was the first time I had communicated with anybody since the accident. Over time, she changed the rules of the game and said if I wanted ice cream, I should move the magnet and say the word *please*. It took a couple of days, but my hunger for ice cream overcame the trauma and I was soon talking a mile a minute. Over the years, I continued to use magnets to organize my day or clarify my thoughts. They were always a lovely reminder of my dear Gran.

Now, it was time for them to work their magic again. I made some space on the door, sorted through my collection of magnets and started setting up my version of a incident board. This technique had helped me identify a killer many months earlier. Maybe it would work again.

The first thing I needed was a magnet to represent each suspect. I was about to reach into the box when I stopped. I didn't want to think of the log canoe sailors as suspects. They were becoming my friends. But I had been in this position before. I had to think of this little exercise as eliminating them as the killer, instead of accusing them. That idea made me feel better.

I started with Nina. I found a stethoscope that I thought might work, but opted instead for the heart magnet I found at the bottom of the box. Yes, the heart was a better choice. Nina was both a cardiologist and romantically involved with both Jack and Dominick.

Now, what would be a good magnet to represent for Dominick? I found a sailboat, but that could represent so many people. This was going to take some thought. I got a little help from Simon. Since I was sitting on the floor, I was fair game for a wrestling match. We tussled and rolled around with a little more energy than was probably wise. My puppy was no longer a puppy. At our last visit, the vet was pleased with his progress, but sixty pounds was still a lot of weight slamming into the cabinets or sitting on my chest. Plus Lorraine, my dog whisperer and trainer, would probably not approve of such unrestrained play. Realizing that one of us could get hurt, I pulled myself up and reached into his cookie jar. When I turned around to offer him one, he was sitting so perfectly and looking so cute that I grabbed two more. The vet could put him on a diet some other time.

I wanted to pick out magnets for the main players before I went to meet with Dawkins and time was short. I pulled a chair over to the refrigerator and put the box on my lap. Simon realized that playtime was over and trotted over to the corner where his second favorite pillow bed lay. I went back to the question: what would be a good magnet for Dom? I dug around in the box and came up with an old simple addition magnet Gran had once used to quiz me. It was worn around the edges, but the 2+2 would work for a man who studied the physics of the wind and sails.

The police wanted to talk with Tiffani so she should be included. It took me a few minutes to settle on a ribbon tied in a bow. It was red, not black, but it would still remind me of the black bows she wore on her ponytails the day the boat capsized. And then there was Charlie. He was mad at Jack for changing his mind about letting me go out on his chase boat, but was he mad enough to kill him? I didn't think so, but he still belonged on the board. I chose a purple flower since he did landscaping work and was involved in Project Purple.

I was about to put the box away when I remembered two more people. Kevin developed software for Jack as well as sailed with him. Charlie had mentioned that Kevin and his wife had recently adopted a baby, so the baby doll magnet went up on the refrigerator door. And then there was Dutch. I'd forgotten about the conversation I'd overheard outside the ladies room door. I'd have to mention it to the detective. Dutch was scary. His big body was naturally intimidating and he was arrogant. I found the magnet of a gorilla that I always thought was cute and cuddly, but this time, it would represent a bully.

What about Jack's involvement with drugs mentioned in that conversation with Dutch? Did a vengeful drug dealer or disgruntled user kill him? There wasn't a magnet in my box that could represent illegal drugs, but, after what I'd learned from Charlie about Project Purple, a little prescription bottle seemed appropriate. I put it at the edge of the door. The box could go back in the pantry now. Magnets representing seven suspects hung on my refrigerator door. It was time to go back to bed, hopefully to sleep.

The next morning, while walking over to Mrs. Clark's kitchen, I threw the ball for Simon again and again until he stretched out on the grass panting. I couldn't believe it. This was the first time Simon quit our game of ball before I did. It seemed like everything normal had gone out of my life. As soon as I opened the door, the incredible aroma of biscuits and cinnamon buns picked me up and carried me down the hall into a scene of orderly confusion. Mrs. Clark was like an iceberg moving around her kitchen, cool and calm. Without missing a beat, she handed me a plate and pointed to the baked goods fresh from the oven. I took several with the hopes that they'd raise my spirits then I retraced my steps back to the cottage.

Yesterday's events had definitely knocked me off center. I couldn't seem to settle. I kept thinking about the accident. Those blood-red tendrils snaking through the water over the submerged sails kept appearing in my mind's eye. Maybe doing some research about the silver would distract me. I pulled out some reference books and lugged them to the porch. I marked a few pages, but I couldn't concentrate. I kept staring at the river. My cell phone vibrated and almost walked off the wicker table. The caller ID said it was Charlie and I answered it with a silent prayer, Please no more bad news.

"Abby, how ya doing?" He sounded wrung out. The enthusiasm I'd always heard in his voice was absent.

My antenna went up, looking for trouble. "More importantly, how are you?"

He sighed. "I'm okay, I guess. I keep thinking about what happened yesterday."

"I know what you mean." I felt badly for Charlie. He knew all the people involved.

Charlie gasped. "Abby, you were right there. You saw it all. First, in the binoculars and then… and then…"

"I know, but I …" My voice trailed off. I really didn't know what to say.

"Look, I called, because everybody is feeling the same way. We're hot competitors on the water, but on land, we're really good friends. Even though Jack was nasty and obnoxious, he was still part of our little community."

"Your group is very tight," I said.

"Yeah, I guess we are. That's why we're all gonna meet up at the club this afternoon. Kinda be together. I don't know what we're gonna do, but the club is opening the Grill and bar to us.

They're going to let us pay for food and drinks. Usually members sign their checks and the charge is put on their monthly bill."

"So they're opening the club so you all can be together? That's nice." I felt a little jealous.

"Frankly, I think they need the business today. I heard a lot of members are staying away. Superstitious, I guess, thinking an accident might be catching." He sighed. "Look, the reason I called, do you want to come? You were part of all this. You should come so we can all be together. Will you?"

I thanked him for thinking of me and we made a plan to meet on the little porch by the front door. With cups of ice water to counteract the broiling temperature, we strolled around the grounds together.

I felt so comfortable with him and wanting to talk about anything but the accident, I said, "Superstitions. You said people weren't coming to the club today because they are superstitious. The other night, we talked about ballplayers' superstitions."

Charlie held up his hand to stop me. A smile played on his lips. "Please don't remind me about the unwashed underwear." The tension in his shoulders seemed to ease. It felt good not to talk about death.

I touched his arm. "No, I won't. Promise."

He gave me a crooked smile. I took his arm, hoping the contact would bring us both comfort.

"Charlie, are sailors superstitious about clothing, too?"

"Well, I remember a story that one captain was wearing a brown and yellow striped shirt when he won his first log canoe race." He shook his head. "He wore that shirt from then on until it almost fell off his body in tatters. I think his crew found him a new one."

"And did he wear that one to tatters as well?" I asked.

"Yes, he did. Jimmy was one of the winningest captains in log canoe racing history." Our footsteps crunched on the gravel. "And sailors have problems with the starting line and fouls. If you cross too early or approach it the wrong way, the race committee will send around to start again. That's the kiss of death." He scanned the fluffy clouds backlit by the sun as it sank to the horizon. "Superstitions held by watermen and sailors are more logical than the ones those baseball players have."

"Oh, really? Maybe I should be the judge of that." I said with a stern look that was meant to be funny.

"Okay, you decide. Let's start with this one: bananas are not allowed on a boat," he declared.

I stopped and looked at him to see if he was kidding, but he was serious. "No bananas?"

"No bananas," he repeated.

I paused for a minute, ransacking my brain for a reason, but could come up with nothing. "Okay, I give. Why no bananas?"

"Bananas come some very big spiders and that's trouble in a confined space."

I shook my head. "Come on, that's not true. "

"About the spiders? Oh yes, spiders used to hitch a ride with banana shipments and could find their way into a grocery bag. People were very careful not bring those spiders home, because they were tarantulas."

A shudder ran through me as I thought of the bunch of bananas on my kitchen counter. "But that doesn't happen anymore."

"It wasn't that unusual years ago. Why take a chance today?"

"So, no bananas?"

"No bananas."

I peeked at his face and saw a bit of a smile. My ploy was working. We were both feeling better. "Okay, tell me another superstition."

He looked up at the sky for inspiration and said, "If a boat has a blue bottom, it's bad luck."

I stopped and put my hands on my hips. "I thought you were going to be serious."

He gave me a very dramatic shrug. "I am. Judge for yourself. It's a bright, sunny day. The sky is blue. You're on a sailboat and it goes over for some reason. You can't right it and you need help. A boat comes by at a distance. You yell and scream, but it's a power boat and the people aboard don't hear you."

"If they're close enough, they'll see my boat has capsized and—"

"Will they? Remember, it's a sunny day. The sky is blue. Water reflects the color of the sky so the water is blue. If the bottom of your boat is blue, it blends in and rescuers can't see you. So, a boat with a blue bottom…"

"Is bad luck." I took his arm again. "Okay, I'll give you that one. Anything else?"

"One more," he said with a smirk. "No women aboard!"

I gave him a little jab in the arm for making fun of me. "That's not true."

"It is true and it's very smart. The rule doesn't apply to wives, mothers or daughters, but every other female is off-limits. If a man, especially a married man, takes a female out on a boat, there's no telling what happened while they were out. A wife can have a very active imagination. I think it's a talent she gets on her wedding day. She can make his life miserable so if a man is smart, he'll take his wife or mother out with him if there's going to be another female on board."

"Okay, your superstitions make more sense."

We were ambling back toward the club now when someone called out. "Charlie! They need you down at the boat."

He patted my hand. "I've got to go. Thanks, Abby." And he ran off to attend to the love that would always come first in his life, a sailboat.

CHAPTER 17

A knife is set to the right of the plate and must never lie hidden under the rim. Always position the edge of the sharp edge of the knife edge toward the plate. If it is facing out, it conveys a hostile message and considered bad form.

"The Butler's Guide to Fine Silver"
Mr. Hollister, 1898

AFTER THE CHAOS and calamity of the weekend, I was grateful to return to the world of silver on Monday . When I walked into the Fair Winds formal dining room, I found Dawkins was true to his word and had left all the silver pieces related to fish on the table.

Magically, he appeared a moment later, as usual. "Ah, Miss Abigail, your arrival is auspicious. I find I have time to discuss the fish implements with you."

"Thank you, Dawkins. I appreciate the fact that you didn't bundle them away after the dinner on Saturday night. I don't know why the fish sets have never been a priority for me."

"Perhaps because they are so specialized. These forks and knives are never used for anything other than serving and eating of the fish. And speaking of putting them away…" He opened a cabinet door and brought a stack of boxes to the table. "We'll need these."

As he was about to set them down, my cell phone rang. "I'm sorry, I need to answer this call." I turned aside. "Charlie?

"Abby." He was breathless.

"Charlie, what's going on? Are you alright?"

"Abby, they want the crews… *Flying Wing*…and our boat, *Island Memory,* at the club right now. You need to come."

I took a deep breath and tried to sound calm. "Charlie, let's slow down. Who is *they?*"

"The police. The detective is here. And the dog. And everybody. Can you come?"

"Do they want me there, because I was on Jack's chase boat?"

"Yes, yes. I said I'd call you. They want everyone here like now."

I glanced at Dawkins who was returning the boxes to the cabinet. "I'm on my way." I put my phone back in my pocket. "Dawkins, could we leave everything just the way it is? The police are asking people to come back to the yacht club, though I'm not exactly sure why."

He didn't react to my request, just proceeded to arrange the boxes and close the cabinet door.

"I'll be back as soon as I can and help you put everything away. I promise." I didn't know what else to say to make him understand.

He turned toward me and stood straight and still. "You were the one who wanted to learn about the fish sets, Miss Abigail."

He always used my formal name. "And I still do," I said. Please, will you wait for me?" I knew I was pleading and normally I won't do such a thing with Dawkins, but working with the silver was a normal thing for me to do. And I needed something normal in my life right now.

Dawkins must have read my mood. His blue-gray eyes softened. "I'll leave everything as you see it and we can continue our work and discussion upon your return."

"Thank you," I said, with more appreciation and relief than I'd ever shown Dawkins before. Whenever I thought I knew the man, he'd surprise me.

I flew out of the house, jumped in my car and made it to the club in quick time, mainly because it was a Monday morning. Most tourists had made their trek home on Sunday. Those who stayed were sleeping late probably. The sidewalks in town were empty and traffic was sparse.

At the yacht club, I was able to find a parking space close to the building where I saw Charlie pacing on the porch. Before I reached him, I was surprised to see that the parking lot and grassy area that ran down to the water were overflowing with police vehicles of all descriptions. This wasn't good.

Charlie looked so worried. As I walked up to him, I mentioned that I'd found a nearby parking space, hoping to make him laugh.

Instead, he barked at me. "Of course you did. The club is closed on Mondays." Before I could react, he gave my arm a little squeeze. "I'm sorry. I'm so sorry, Abby." His hazel eyes were filling with tears. "I can't forgive myself for putting you in harm's way. I'm so sorry."

I was very confused. "Why are you so upset, Charlie? What's happened?"

"They're saying that Jack died from a drug overdose." His voice was strained. "I didn't even know he was a user."

"Wait, what?" Things were moving fast and I had to catch up.

"They're saying that the medical examiner said the doctor in Easton got it wrong. Jack didn't die from a gash on the head from the capsize. He died of an overdose of heroin and fentanyl.

FENTANYL! Do you know how dangerous that stuff is? You don't have to snort it or put it in your mouth. You can overdose by *just touching it.* Do you know that two police officers almost died, because they weren't wearing gloves when they were cleaning a little white dust off a table after a drug bust? Someone saw them go down and gave them Narcan. It reversed the effects. It's the only thing that can. It saved their lives." Charlie's voice was getting higher and higher. "And I put you on Jack's boat. You could have—"

I threw my arms around the poor man and held on tight.

People walked by, glanced at us standing there in an embrace, then they went on their way without saying a word. Everyone, except Ryan.

"Abby?"

Charlie pulled away from me and turned his tear-streaked face to his friend. "Man, I'm so sorry. I can't believe—"

I reached out quickly and put my finger against his lips. "You did nothing wrong. You didn't know. Don't worry about it." Ryan gave me a quizzical look and I gave my head a little shake. "Ryan, Charlie is upset about everything that's happened."

"I think we all are," Ryan responded, trying to read the meaning behind my words.

"And I think he could use a cold glass of water and a few quiet minutes with a friend."

Ryan put his hand on Charlie's shoulder. "Come on, you're with me."

"I didn't know what was going on." Charlie was starting to babble. "I don't know what to think about—"

"Let's go inside, my friend." Ryan was calm and comforting. "We'll go inside, get you something to drink and see if we can make sense out of anything."

"B-But the club is closed," Charlie stammered.

"Not for you, my friend. Not today. Come on."

I mouthed the words *Thank you* as Ryan led him to the door.

Charlie said that he didn't know what was going on and that

really unsettled him. I thought I might be able to do something about that. I moved between the knots of people standing around, waiting for something to happen. Then, I headed toward a group of law enforcement personnel clustered together. That's where Detective Ingram would be.

Weary of trying to keep the crowd back, a young uniformed officer pleaded with the civilians. "People, this is a restricted area. You have to move back." He wasn't having any luck getting them to budge.

Most of the people raced log canoes. This was a case about one of their own. They might be fierce competitors on the water, but here on land, they stood together as one. They'd lost one of their captains and an owner of a canoe. It seemed like a tragic accident, but the police were here at the club in force. They wanted to know what the police knew.

There were cars from the St. Michaels Police, the County Police, Easton Police, the Sheriff's department and the State Police. Even the St. Michaels K-9 unit was in attendance. Max, the yellow Labrador retriever, sat quietly at the feet of his handler, ready to go to work. His ears perked up. I heard it, too. A siren was approaching. I looked up to the main road as the big red truck with lights flashing made the turn, came partway down the hill and stopped. Why was the hazmat unit here?

We all watched as the team put on white Tyvek suits that completely enclosed their bodies to block exposure to hazardous substances. But this was a yacht club, for heaven's sake. Probably the most harmful materials around were in the boats' gas tanks and maybe the frying tubs in the kitchen. This was a place for recreation, fine dining, and a little friendly competition. Until there was a suspicious death.

The team checked their suits, gathered their equipment and headed down to the boat slips. I gasped when I realized that they were going to the log canoe *Flying Wing*. Maybe Charlie was right. Maybe I was closer to the danger than I thought. I had no idea what they would find now. Had they forgotten that the boat capsized? Any trace of a hazardous material would have washed away, wouldn't it? Or were they looking for something else? It was time to get some answers.

The hazmat team had ordered everyone to stay off the dock so Detective Ingram would be standing here on the hill where we'd enjoyed a seafood feast only days ago. I scanned the crowd. The man didn't stand out. There really wasn't anything remarkable about him. His medium height, slight build, thinning hair and the dark brown suit he often wore made him blend in. Maybe that was one reason why he was so effective as a homicide detective. He was non-threatening, until he needed to be. I scanned the people again and found him leaning against a marked police car, waiting. Quietly, I worked my way to his side.

"Good morning, detective. Nice day for a hazmat incident." He slid his eyes over to look at me, but didn't smile at my little joke. "Can we talk for a minute?"

He glanced my way again and sighed as he pushed himself off the car fender. "I guess I'd better talk to you now or you won't go away." He touched my elbow and steered me toward a line of trees that we followed to the water, far away from attentive ears. "I swear you remind me of a terrier who gets a bone in her teeth and won't let go."

"I guess I'll take that as a compliment," I said brightly. He harrumphed.

We stood on a strip of sandy beach by the gently lapping water and admired the tranquil river scene. Then he spoke. "Okay, you want to know what changed, right?"

"You are very perceptive, detective. The doctor who declared Jack dead said the cause of death was a gash to the head, right?"

"That's what we all thought would be the final determination."

"That doctor…" I thought for a moment. "Oh wait, I remember now. Any unattended or suspicious death has to be evaluated by the medical examiner in Baltimore."

"That's right and that happened yesterday morning at 8:15."

"On a Sunday?" I asked in surprise.

"Death doesn't wait. Neither does an investigation. Let me tell you it was a great way to spend my day off." He stared at the water again, lost in thought.

I meant to respect his space, but the words burst out of my mouth. "What happened?"

He took a deep breath and launched into the story. "As the investigating detective, it was my job to stand by the body and brief the medical examiner, answer questions and so on. Keep in mind, it's not just me and the M.E. in a small room with the body of the deceased. It's a big room with bodies covered with two sheets from all over the state of Maryland all lined up, most with a law enforcement officer present."

"Why two sheets?"

"One is used to only expose the face. The other is used to uncover the body if the doc needs to look at something." He frowned at the memory of what he'd seen.

I gave my head a shake to clear my brain. "I'm sorry, I don't know why I asked you that. That's a visual I won't soon forget. So, what happened?"

"During the whole ride up to Baltimore, I reviewed the case in my head, because, as I said, it was my job to summarize everything for the doc. Something in one of the statements kept bothering me. One of the men on Jack's log canoe said that just before he passed out, Jack opened his eyes wide. He said they looked like deep blue marbles."

I wasn't getting the importance of the comment. "Okay…and?"

"Well, one of the signs of opioid overdose is pinpoint pupils," he said.

I spoke slowly as the significance hit me. "And if there is almost no black showing, the eyes look like marbles. So, you're saying he died of a drug overdose?" I was having trouble with this sudden turn of events.

"Hold your horses. Haven't I told you not to jump to conclusions?"

I remembered how he'd investigated the murders at the recent Plein Air Easton Art Festival. Slow and methodical. It almost drove me crazy, but, in the end, he found the killer, uncovered the motive and secured a confession. Admirable work. So, I pressed my lips together, trying to be patient.

He took a slow breath and continued. "The doctor pointed out that a gash on the head can have the same effect on the eyes. Then he ordered a rush tox screen to see if drugs were involved." Detective Ingram ran his right hand over his thinning brown hair now flecked with graying strands. "The report came back this morning, positive for opioids. Jack had high levels of heroin and fentanyl in his system. Very high. Fentanyl is 100 times stronger than heroin. That gives you an idea of how deadly it was."

I drew in a long breath and tried to figure out what we had here. I almost didn't want to ask, but I had to know. "Was it enough to kill him?"

The detective nodded. "This was not an unfortunate accident. It's either an accidental overdose or…"

"Murder," I whispered.

CHAPTER 18

complete silver serving collection includes many types of spoons designed for specific purposes. These include the pea spoon, the pierced olive spoon and the tiny caper spoon.

"The Butler's Guide to Fine Silver"
Mr. Hollister, 1898

"And this is when you ask me for my opinion, right?" I nodded silently like a child. "First, you have to remember that we've just started our investigation." I waited for him to continue. "If he was using drugs, he would have been an idiot to take that much, especially being a long way from shore if something went wrong." He gave his head a little shake. "An accidental overdose? No. My money is on murder, pure premeditated murder."

I turned my head slowly, looking at all the people sitting on the lawn, talking in hushed tones on the dock, working on boats. One of them could be the killer.

"But," he said with a lighter tone. "It's still early in the investigation. We have to interview people again, but now, we can focus our questions. We need to find out how the drugs got into his system. The M.E. didn't find any needle marks. There were traces of heroin and fentanyl on the tongue, esophagus, and in the stomach. The question is, did he take the drugs on purpose?"

"You think he was poisoned during the race?"

"It's all possible. We have to explore every possibility." Ingram folded his arms.

"But why are you using the hazmat team when you have a drug dog here?"

He glanced at the dog and smiled. "Max, he's a good one. I would never use him or any of his fellow service animals."

"Why? Wouldn't it be easier to find the drugs?"

He gave me an incredulous look and shook his head a little. "You don't get it, do you? You really have no idea how serious this is."

I bit my tongue so I wouldn't snap at him. "Sorry, I guess I don't, detective. Tell me."

"Fentanyl is dangerous for humans *and* dogs. As the investigating officer, I could go over to the K-9 handler and order him to *run his dog* for the drugs and he could refuse to follow orders. In the state of Maryland, the K-9 handler is the expert and has the final word. He knows that exposure to even a minute amount of fentanyl can be fatal to the dog."

"Should the dog be here at all?" Worried, I looked as Max lay down on the cool grass by his officer.

"The handler carries a first-aid kit for the dog that includes Narcan in case of exposure." He closed his eyes and sighed. "We thought the fight against drugs was tough before. These opiates make it so much worse. People get hooked after using a painkiller prescribed by a doctor. Then they doctor-shop to get new prescription. When that source dries up and they learn that the opiates are synthetic heroin, they go looking for the real thing on the streets. They find it's cheaper than the prescription drugs so it's easy for them to up the dose, initially. And fentanyl, don't get me started. The dealers cut the heroin with it which makes it more potent at a fraction of the cost to them."

He touched my arm. "Of course, all this is between us." His ebony black eyes bore into mine. "Do you understand?"

The words *Yes, Sir* sprung from my lips.

A small smile played at the corners of his mouth. "You're not to say anything...unless you have an idea who wanted Black Jack Spalding dead?"

I gazed at the crowd again. "So many. So many."

CHAPTER 19

Use great care. It is easy to mar the luster of silver. An undercooked egg yolk can turn a silver spoon black. Even water can leave spots that dull the finish.

"The Butler's Guide to Fine Silver"
Mr. Hollister, 1898

DETECTIVE INGRAM and I watched without a word as the hazmat team scoured the canoe. Something was niggling at my brain, but it wasn't coming clear. I turned my attention to the dog, but he wasn't there nor was his handler. After the scary information the detective had told me about the danger, I quickly scanned the docks, hoping he wasn't there. With a little sigh of relief, I searched for him on the lawn and saw them by the K-9 unit vehicle. Max was slurping up the water from a bowl. His handler added more.

And that's when it hit me.

"Were the drugs in his water bottle?" I asked.

Ingram rolled up and back on his toes. "We confiscated all the water bottles on board."

I turned around and stared at the detective, certain I was on to something. "No, I mean Jack's water bottle."

"We're testing them all—"

"No, Jack only used a high-tech bottle." I had his attention now.

"I have to check, but that doesn't sound familiar. I thought—"

"Jack insisted on his own bottle. After all, he was the captain. Everything had to be better."

Ingram's eyes narrowed as he studied my face. "And you know this, how?"

"I know his water girl. She is… was responsible for filling the water bottle and securing it to the canoe right under his seat so it was within easy reach during a race."

"I don't suppose you know the name of this water girl?"

I ignored his sarcasm "Tiffani. Her name is Tiffani. I'm afraid I don't know her last name." I realized that last names didn't matter in log canoe racing. It was all about your first name, your boat and your position.

"Thank you. That's good information, Abby." He started toward the dock and doubled back. "Where did Jack sit?"

"By the tiller at the stern of the boat." Then I added another piece of good information. "That's the back of the boat."

He scrunched his eyes closed, then sighed. "Yes, thank you, Abby." Without another word, Detective Ingram walked toward the dock with long, determined strides.

I watched as he called someone over from the hazmat team. They consulted for a moment and the team still on the boat was alerted. Attention turned to the back of the boat, underneath, all around. But the only thing the search yielded was a group of shaking heads. There was no water bottle in or around the boat.

The detective returned, the spring in his step was gone. He resumed his position next to me and crossed his arms. "Well, it was a good idea while it lasted. I have a feeling nothing is going to come easy with the case. Nothing is what it seems. Log canoes are not little wood boats you paddle. No, they're great big sailboats." He gestured to the river where the Governor's Cup ended in death. "Now, you tell me about a water bottle that doesn't just keep water cold. It could be a murder weapon." He walked around so he could direct his attention to the knots of people watching the hazmat investigation. "Add the people to this crazy mix. I've always heard that sailors are a special breed. They're not content to compete on land using engines to go fast. They have to harness the wind with acres of canvas attached to a boat that barely sticks out of the water trying to stay dry at the same time. I don't know."

His expression changed as he examined the people. "They look normal, but I bet someone is lying. Somebody looked us right in the eye and lied. I think I'm looking at the killer right now. I just have to figure out who it is." He paused, still scanning them. "And I have to remember that nothing here is what it appears to be."

I followed his gaze, taking in the dozens of people standing around who loved sailing, loved being outdoors, loved to compete and loved to win. We stood there together, watching until the spell was broken by the tall man with an unusual name.

"Detective, I'm Lieutenant O.T. Smith, Maryland State Police. Sir, I may have some information for you."

"Abby, if you could—"

"No, she doesn't have to leave. I understand she helped in your investigation of the Plein Air murders. I wanted to introduce myself. I'm an administrative property officer." I made myself small so Ingram would let me stay. "You may know we're making inroads into the drug supply from Baltimore to the Eastern Shore. We've seized some sizable shipments at a dock north of the Bay Bridge. We think the suppliers are looking for a new way into the Shore, because of all the attention they're getting farther north." O.T. leaned closer to Ingram, but I could still hear every word.

"There's scuttlebutt about a new facilitator on the Shore, one with his own runners."

O.T. took a step back. "We know Jack's been spending time in Baltimore with some high rollers at games, parties and all. We know that some guys on the fringes tend to dabble in drug running. Lord knows they don't need the money. Guess they're in it for the thrill. They just …" He used his fingers to make air quotes. "Make the connections and take a little on the side for their efforts."

Ingram scowled. "Are you saying Jack was the connection, the new facilitator?"

O.T. raised his shoulders and dropped them dramatically. "I'm just saying there might be something there. Maybe Jack was getting greedy or worse, wanted out? If these guys are responsible for Jack's demise, I wish you luck connecting the dots." He took a step back. "Thought you should know since the murder weapon was a heroin and fentanyl cocktail? Thought you should know, sir." O.T. walked away leaving us with a whole new line of investigation to think about.

Silently, Ingram watched the man walk away, with only a *hmm-m-m* in response to the information. Then he reached into a pocket and pulled out his keys. "Well, I guess I'd better get something going along that line of inquiry, too. See you later."

Again, I was left standing alone in the midst of a lot of activity. The drug angle sounded plausible, but I still wanted to know what happened to the water bottle. I couldn't imagine how they would find it two days after the boat capsized. That bottle could be anywhere by now. Well, I felt it was time for me to do something else, anything else, as long as it was far away from death.

I turned to go to the parking lot and slammed right into Harriet Snow, literally. I grabbed her arms to keep herself upright.

"Are you okay?" I asked, hoping for a quick answer so I could escape.

She ran her hands over her chest to straighten her blouse. "No, I am *not* okay."

My thoughts ran to calling an ambulance, sitting in the emergency room and/or calling a lawyer to defend me. But there was no need to worry. Harriet was her normal self.

"I am not okay, young lady. Just look around us. Police cars, fire trucks, an ambulance and men running around in white moon suits."

"They're protective suits for the hazardous materials team, Harriet. I have a friend who did that kind of work and he called it his bunny suit."

She stared right down her nose at me as if I'd used some four-letter word. "This is no laughing matter, young lady."

The easiest way to relieve the tension was to apologize, which I did quickly.

"I should hope you're sorry. I mean, this sort of thing doesn't happen here. And certainly not at the yacht club, for heaven's sake." She rubbed her arms as if there was a chill in the air on this hot July day. "It's terrible, just terrible."

"Yes, it is, especially for Jack," I said and traipsed up the hill before I used a four-letter word with that woman who only saw the world as it affected her. I passed close to two officers who were talking while they watched the activities on the dock.

"It's really weird that Jack should be killed by an overdose."

"Yeah, he's one of the sponsors of 'Talbot Goes Purple.'"

Yes, I thought, that is really ironic.

CHAPTER 20

Be ever vigilant. A piece of silver, whether it is silverware or a service piece, may be scratched by accident during normal use.

"The Butler's Guide to Fine Silver"
Mr. Hollister, 1898

As I CLIMBED the hill to find my car in the parking lot, I caught sight of a petite, blonde woman with wide black streaks in her hair, slipping through the front door of the club. Tiffani. Seeing her alone, I thought I'd follow her in case... in case, what? I had hoped, but wasn't surprised when I saw her slip into her usual place at the bar. She looked so lonely and sad.

As I moved closer, I noticed that her skin was pasty and her hand shook so much that the ice clattered in her glass. A sheen of perspiration lay on her forehead. Maybe she needed more than a friend. Maybe she needed help. I went over to the bar.

"Are you okay?" I asked her.

"Think I may be coming down with the flu," she moaned.

I leaned away. I didn't mean to be rude, but I didn't want to get sick.

"Don't worry." Gently, she scratched her scalp underneath a barrette with a big plastic sunflower on it. "I don't think you can catch it." She patted the bar stool next to her. "Sit down, take a load off."

I slipped onto the seat and ordered an iced tea.

"That's not very exciting," she teased.

"I know. I don't feel like anything stronger right now." The thought of dulling the pain with alcohol was tempting, but I was in no mood for a headache or hangover. "Are you really getting sick?"

She slouched over her drink on the bar as if she didn't have any energy. "No, I just said that. It keeps most people away." She shot up straight and said quickly, "Not you. I don't want you to go away." Then she slouched again. "I think it's just everything that's happened." She slipped off her stool. "I'll be right back. Don't leave." She was gone in a hurry, leaving her purse open on the bar.

I reached over to close the flap so people walking past couldn't peek inside. That's when I saw a prescription bottle on top. Curious, I thought. Maybe she was taking an antibiotic for her flu symptoms, but I thought an antibiotic was useless against a virus.

She was back. "I forgot something." She grabbed the pill bottle, turned away as she checked inside. A little groan escaped her lips. "Got to go to the ladies room." And she was off again.

I wondered how the hazmat team was doing outside so I went over to the big windows overlooking the boat slips. But my attention was drawn to two people talking outside. Tiffani and Dutch.

I didn't notice the tiny woman with milky-white hair enter the Grill, but she certainly saw me. "ABBY!" barked Harriet Snow. She was on the warpath with her poor husband shrinking along behind her. "Is it true what I'm hearing? Was it murder? And it's all related to drugs?" Her indignation made her voice more and more strident. "I mean, really! This kind of thing doesn't happen here. We left the big city to get away from all those horrible goings-on, didn't we, dear?" She didn't leave a second of open air for Ben to answer.

I looked away to still my urge to snap at her and caught sight of Tiffani outside again. Her head was tilted up as Dutch towered over her. Her lips were pulled tight as she seemed to plead with him.

"Abby!" Harriet yanked me back. "I'm talking to you. Don't you dare ignore me!"

"I'm not ignoring you, Harriet." I wanted to scream at her, but kept my voice low. "I'm as appalled as you are by what's happened ."

I glanced outside again and caught a glimpse of Dutch as he reached into his pocket and passed Tiffani something. Like a shot, she raced back inside the building.

Harriet waved her hand right in front of my face. I looked down at the little woman, her soft curls framing her stone-hard face. "I do not think you are as appalled as I am." She thrust her chin out at me. The deep lines and wrinkles on her face distracted me. I wondered if I connected them if I might get the outline of Ohio."

"Abby!" Harriet stamped her foot.

"Look, Harriet." My words now had an edge. "I'm not the one you should yell at. I haven't done anything wrong. In fact, I wouldn't be here at all if Lorraine hadn't sent me." Oh, to my surprise, hearing Lorraine's name had a magical effect on the irate woman.

Harriet's voice took on an ethereal quality, "She sent you?"

"Yes, she did. You don't think Lorraine Andrews would condone anything to do with drugs and murder, do you? She wants to find out the truth."

As if in a trance, Harriet murmured "Of course."

I hurried on while I still had the upper hand. "Then I think you should express your concerns in a letter to the president or commodore of this club." Standing behind his wife, Ben gave me a little nod. "But tonight, I think you should go home, put your feet up and have a nice little toddy to relax." Ben winked at me. "Now, let Ben take you home and forget all this." Ben steered his pacified wife out the door.

I got back to my seat at the bar as Tiffani reappeared. She sprinted across the room and leapt onto the stool. Her hands fluttered around like butterflies as she talked. Nonstop. I couldn't have gotten a word in, even if I'd tried. Instead, I sat and watched as if she was the entertainment for the evening. And I started noticing little details. A fingernail gnawed down to the quick. A torn cuticle. Little beads of sweat on her brow. The hair around the barrette tangled into a mess. When she reached for her glass, her hand was steady now, but the words still flowed in a torrent.

"STOP!" I said. This manic behavior was wearing me out. "What's with you, Tiffani?"

She grunted. "Abby, maybe I have a dirty little secret." She gave me a shifty look.

"Are you on something? You know, I saw you outside with Dutch and—"

"Dutch is a good friend and he's very sad about what happened to Jack. We were commiserating. We're all very sad."

But Tiffani seemed anything but sad. She seemed exuberant.

"You just seem so different from a few minutes ago. Are you—" I couldn't bring myself to say it. I had almost no experience with drugs. If I was wrong, she might haul off and hit me.

Suddenly serious, Tiffani turned to me, her eyes boring holes in me. "Wait a minute. Do you think I'm doing drugs?" Threw her head back and roared. "I am not doing drugs. That's stupid." She picked up her glass. "I'm trying to manage this awful experience, that's all. Some people cry. I…" She held up her glass and drained it.

I couldn't take it anymore so I used the standard getaway line. "Oh, is that the time? I've got to run. See ya."

Free of the manic behavior and depressing atmosphere, I cruised through St. Michaels, feeling good. Except, I was starving. Of course, Mrs. Clark would have something, probably lots of somethings for me to eat. But I wasn't ready to talk about the turn in the investigation of Jack's death. No, now it was murder.

I had someplace else to go where people didn't care or preferred to talk the latest gossip, other than murder. I hit my turn signal and headed for the parking lot by the Cove, the little restaurant in the back corner of the local drug store. Walking into the eating area, a challenge stopped me in my tracks. A challenge that made me want to turn around and leave.

"Are you following me, Ms. Strickland?" demanded Detective Ingram who was sitting in the corner at the round table meant for eight people. He had only a mountain of papers for company. The strain around his eyes relaxed a little as if he was thankful for the interruption.

If a little playful conversation would give him a little relief from this confusing case of homicide, I was happy to play along. ""It looks like you're staking out my favorite haunts. Fair Winds is private property, so I'm not surprised to find you lying in wait here in a public place." Actually, I was surprised, but I wasn't going to let him know it.

His eyes lit up. "I guess it's hard to hide in a small town, Ms. Strickland."

"That it is, Detective Ingram." I stepped closer, hoping to see what he was reading. "Didn't anyone tell you that paperwork can kill you?"

He frowned. "You're telling me, especially when it's all about murder." He pulled out an empty chair. "Since you're here, why don't you sit down?"

"I'm happy to sit at the counter."

"Don't bother. We'd just spend the whole time trying to ignore each other."

He was right, of course. I sat down and tried to read the hand-written pages without him noticing. It didn't work.

A girl in a yellow uniform that was a size or two too large approached the table like a timid mouse. Not the usual attitude of the servers who regaled her customers with a barrage of opinions and abuse. It was the main attraction at The Cove along with fresh soups and heavenly pies. No, this was a newbie who peered at her order pad like it was a hot love scene from a romance novel. I ordered a grilled cheese sandwich and Ingram asked for the meat loaf dinner. Comfort food.

He shook his head slightly. "Don't know when I'll get to eat again. Candy bars and chips are starting to get to me." He patted his stomach that still looked flat and toned. Ever alert to details and nuance, that was Detective Ingram.

Alone again, I gestured to the papers. "Should you leave the statements out like this for anyone to see?"

He tensed. "How do you—"

I patted his arm. "Relax, it's easy to see that each page is hand-written by a different person. I jumped to the conclusion that these are the statements from Saturday night."

"You're good at jumping to conclusions." I started to react, then realized he wasn't kidding and stayed quiet. "But this time, you're right. These are the dozens and dozens of statements we took after Jack died."

"I've always wondered about witness statements. Does the guilty party ever write, 'I killed the guy!'?"

Ingram gave me a small smile and shrugged. "It would certainly make my job easier." He picked up one of the papers. "The killer might not write those words, but he…or she tells us a lot by what is said and how it's written." He leaned back in his chair. "Let's say someone on the crew is meticulous about the time line and writes, 'It was almost time to board the canoe. Stored my cell phone in the trunk of my car. I went to the club and used the bathroom. Put sunscreen on my nose. Cleaned my sunglasses. Stepped on the boat. Helped attached the jib." He stopped, waiting.

"What?"

"Did you catch it?"

Uneasy, I answered, "No, was there something...?"

"Yes, you missed a big clue." He raised his eyebrows, disappointed. "The writer was meticulous about small details, the cell phone, sunscreen, sunglasses and so forth, but his time line jumps from cleaning his sunglasses to stepping on the boat."

Feeling defensive, I stated, "Maybe he was cleaning his glasses while he walked to the boat. That's possible."

"Yes, but he didn't say that. He was very specific about the other things. Here, he left a gap, a little space of time when he could have poisoned the water bottle, if you're right about it holding the poison. Gaps are very important. If I find a gap in someone's statement, it gives me a line of questioning to follow. It helps me identify who should be interviewed again and to go into it prepared. I need to read every statement, analyze each one for clues like that."

"Analyze them? Wouldn't it be better to put them on computer? You could scan them and..." My words dwindled away as he shook his head sharply.

"That would defeat the whole purpose," he declared.

"Maybe the state could invest in some iPads and people could type in their statements."

"Wrong again. A statement can tell me more than what the words convey." He picked up a statement handwritten on one side of a piece of paper, turned it face down and slid it over to me. I reached over to turn it right side up. "No, leave it like that. What does it tell you?" He folded his hands on the table and sat with a professor's blank expression, waiting.

I felt like a student who hadn't studied for an exam. I looked down at the blank page. There must be something there, but what? "Well, it doesn't say much since the writing is on the other side and I don't have x-ray vision." I glanced at him. He didn't even crack a smile. I looked at the paper again. Yes, there was something there. I reached out and ran my fingers over the blank page. "Wow, this person really pressed down hard. I bet a trained person could read the words by running a finger across these ridges. What does it mean?"

He leaned back in his chair, pleased. "Good, good. This witness might have been angry when writing the statement … or trying hard to write down a credible lie. The words are formed deliberately."

I was so tempted to flip over the sheet, but he took it and replaced it on the pile.

"What can you do with that assumption? You can't indict a person by how much pressure was used to write a statement."

"No, that would make my job too easy and the smart criminals would try to use light, feathery strokes." His face relaxed into its normal expression that gave away nothing. Inscrutable, again. "It's a little clue that could lead to a bigger one and another and another and then an arrest and conviction."

I pointed to the pile. "What about that statement? It's a short one." The statement didn't fill even half the page. "Was it written by the killer?"

"There you go, jumping to conclusions again. No, I don't think so. The person might have arrived during the race and didn't have much to add or he was trying to hide something from the police by being vague. But murder, I don't think so. It would be worth following up with that person, but it's not my day to go trolling. I have enough on my hands at the moment." He picked up some of the statements and started pushing it into his briefcase. "Now you know why statements are handwritten. They can tell us a lot."

I was fascinated by his techniques. "What else do you see when you look at these pages?"

He raised his chin. "Oh, I can't reveal all my secrets."

Our lunch arrived and we ate in silence. It felt good to sit quietly and enjoy a simple hot meal for a change. My eyes strayed to the pile of statements. "Is Dominick's statement here?"

He raised his eyebrows. "It should be. Why?"

"Well, I was just wondering," I said, trying to sound innocent. "I wanted to see how hard he pressed and…" I paused as Ingram shook his head. "Hmm, you're not going to let me see it, right?"

"Right. Besides he has a rock solid alibi. People swore they were with him from the time he arrived at the club to the time of Jack's death."

"And you believe them?"

"Yes, he was observed by more than one person the whole day. Besides, he strikes me as a man who wouldn't leave something important to chance. He's always figuring the angle of the sails, effects of water currents and such. No, I think he would handle a murder in a way that left little to chance." He quickly added, "IF he was going to commit a murder." He put away the rest of the statements and closed his briefcase. "And I don't think he did."

"Even though he's the logical suspect?"

"Even though he's a great suspect." He finished his coffee. "By the way, I saw your girlfriend this morning."

"My girlfriend?" He'd confused me by switching gears.

"Nina."

"She's not my—"

"Believe me, you want her as your friend," he stated with certainty.

What a curious thing to say. "Why?"

"Because she gave you an alibi."

I was taking a last sip of my iced tea and almost spewed it across the table. "Me?"

"Yes, you. You were there, weren't you?." He narrowed his eyes, trying to look sinister then relaxed his face back to its inscrutable expression. "But I'm satisfied that you weren't involved in the murder."

The feeling of relief distracted me, though I wasn't guilty of anything criminal. I had to catch up with what Ingram was saying.

"...is Jack's former lover and now the girlfriend of his arch rival."

I asked, "Since Dominick is off the hook, did she say anything interesting about Jack?"

"Yes, as a matter of fact, something very relevant. She was sure Jack wasn't using drugs, that he treated his body like a temple."

"To be adored by every female within a radius of—"

"Abby, it's not polite to speak ill of the dead." He paused just long enough to make me feel a little ashamed. "But I've heard the same thing. Nina thought maybe he ate something, but then she remembered how upset he was by the results of the morning race. She said our Romeo had a sensitive stomach that reacted to stress. When they were together, he insisted she carry some heartburn medicine. She wasn't sure, but thought he only drank water at lunch and on the boat."

"So, we're back to the water bottle," I said with some satisfaction.

He rolled his shoulders. "Which was not on the boat."

I heaved a sigh. "It's probably long gone."

"Maybe not. We're doing a grid search along the shoreline. The diver is checking the area where the boat capsized and nosing around the river bottom around the yacht club."

"That won't be easy. How do you find a black water bottle in mud?"

He lifted one shoulder. "I don't know, but we have to try. We may get lucky." He stood and lifted his bulging briefcase. "And with that, I'm going back to work."

"You never stopped working, detective."

"Somebody has to." He picked up both lunch checks.

"And thank you for lunch." I grabbed my things and headed back to Fair Winds and the fish sets. My meeting with Dawkins had slipped my mind and I had to hurry.

CHAPTER 21

hen the Family acquires a new silver piece or collection, it is important to assess its condition and learn its proper use so that it can become a valued part of the silver service of the House.

"The Butler's Guide to Fine Silver"
Mr. Hollister, 1898

I RUSHED into the main house to the formal dining room. The fish forks, knives and sets were still laid out on the table. The room was empty, but not for long. I was sure Dawkins was standing behind me.

"Thank you for leaving the silver out," I said.

He moved to the head of the table. "I told you I would, Miss Abigail." And we picked up right where we'd left off.

I ran my hand over the boxes. "I'd forgotten that serving and flatware fish sets usually come in a fine storage box." These boxes were covered in velvet, silk and leather.

"Some older sets were covered in hides like suede, snakeskin, even alligator, before the ban, of course."

I opened some of the boxes and spread them out on the table. They were lined in elegant velvet or watered silk over forms to cradle each piece. "They remind me of jewelry boxes."

"To a hostess who prided herself on a varied seafood menu, they were gems. Each piece of fine sterling, each has a specific use."

I beamed with delight. He'd touched the chord that made me enjoy working with silver so much. "That's an aspect of silver design I find fascinating. Imagine having a spoon just for bonbons or a choice of three different types of asparagus servers. One of my favorites is the serving spoon for peas. I still can't get over the fact that it's hard to find a pea spoon for less than six or seven hundred dollars. I don't think any other serving piece is priced so dearly, except maybe a carving set, but that's three pieces. Not one spoon."

Dawkins straightened his tie, a signal that it was time for business. It was his custom to wear a coat and tie every day, as part of his work attire even though Lorraine didn't require her staff to wear uniforms. He cleared his throat. "Shall we proceed with the fish sets?"

I cleared my throat and tried to look serious. "Yes, of course."

He missed my mimicry… or chose to ignore it. He pointed to pairs of large fish knives and forks. "These are some examples of the serving pieces. The blade of the knife is wider than those used for meat or fowl. The serving fork is also wider than other serving forks, often having five tines."

I was sure I could puzzle out the reason why, but why make the effort when an expert stood in front of me. "Why is that?"

He paused for a moment and pursed his lips. "I believe it's because fish is often flaky and can fall apart during the transfer from platter to plate. The width of the silver pieces gives the server better control."

"And the knife has an unusual pointy end."

"Yes." He picked one up and examined it. "It allows the server to get into small spaces when boning the fish. Also, notice that the edge of the blade is dull because fish is usually delicate. One doesn't have to saw through the fibers of meat or poultry."

I held up another knife and touched the tip. "And the notch on the end?"

"It's used to separate and lift away the bones when filleting a fish."

I pointed to a set with matching mother-of-pearl handles. "These are beautiful."

"Not all sterling silver pieces are all silver. A fish set gave the silver designer the opportunity to be a little more creative, to use materials too rare or expensive for sets to entertain twelve or twenty people. Since fish sets weren't always used every day, the handles could be made of a less durable material than silver, like those of mother-of-pearl or nacre. Another favorites of mine are bone, tusk or antler. They have a more rustic look that reminds one of the excursions to catch the fish."

He showed me another knife. "The wide blade gave the designer another opportunity to be creative. Sometimes it was plain and shiny or etched with an intricate design."

"What about the pieces used in a place setting?"

"Again, there is some latitude. The fish knife and fork may match the pattern of the set or they may match the serving knife and fork. It is up to the hostess."

I examined a knife. "This is like a baby version of the serving knife with the same pointy tip."

"There are times that a whole fish is served that has not been filleted in the kitchen or by the server at table. The diner needs to be able to navigate around the bones, something that is difficult to do with a blunt or modern tip of a dinner knife."

I noticed that the fish fork for the place setting was wider than a dinner fork, probably to keep a piece from coming apart on the trip from plate to mouth and dropping bits of fish on the table-cloth or the lap. *How uncouth!* I thought, but didn't say aloud in fear that Dawkins would think I was making fun of him. Normally, I wasn't so obnoxious, but for some reason, this man brought it out in me.

"One of the fork tines is wider than the others. And the reason is…?" I looked to my ever-present font of knowledge.

"It's used to cut and separate the meat of the fish from the bones. You'll notice it is always the tine on the left that is wider."

I quickly survey the array of forks on the table and found he was right. "Why is that?"

"Society favored the right hand." He picked up a fork and demonstrated. "If someone who is right-handed cuts something with the fork, the fork is turned and pressure is applied to that tine. It is designed to handle the extra stress."

Dawkins was good at presenting logical answers. Quickly, I moved down the table and picked up a unique-looking spoon. Most of it was similar to a large serving spoon, but along one edge was a series of serious pointed teeth.

"This looks like a lethal weapon." I froze at my words. It hadn't been that long ago that a fine silver serving piece, an angel food cake server, was used to commit murder in the kitchen, right on the other side of that wall. Dawkins and I exchanged looks and, by mutual agreement, decided to ignore my comment and continue our conversation.

"Oh, that's one of my favorites," he said with some energy. "It's so unusual. Mrs. Clark added a particular dish to the menu just so we could use it."

"What is it?"

His eyes twinkled. "Care to hazard a guess?"

I examined it and shook my head.

"It's a fried oyster lifter. I guess a hundred or more years ago, someone decided that this popular delicacy deserved its own serving piece."

As I put it down on the table, I was almost sorry I'd missed the Saturday night feast. It would have been a treat to see these pieces in use. We put the silver away and as we closed the door to the silver closet, my phone rang.

Dawkins murmured. "Thank goodness your adoring public waited until we completed our work." And he walked away, apparently done with my life's frivolous interruptions. I had to laugh. Talking about the silver fish sets had settled me, made me forget the horrors of the last couple of days. And it helped that Dawkins was back to his normal self.

I answered the phone and a distraught voice breathed a deep sigh of relief. "Oh, thank goodness." Dr. Phillips words cracked with age. "Abby, are you all right?" He didn't wait for a reply. "I heard the news about what happened during the Governor's Cup Race. Were you there?"

"Yes, I was on the chase boat and saw it all, unfortunately." I tried to sound like it was sad, but not as unnerving as it was. He was perceptive and saw right through me.

"How awful for you. Are you traumatized?"

"No, I don't think so, but it was very upsetting. You know, they're saying it's murder."

"Yes, I heard." He paused and took a deep breath. "Abby, I'm sorry I got you into all this."

"Oh, it's not your fault. I blame it on that little silver bowl engraved, *Governor's Cup.*"

"Be that as it may, I wanted to check in with you. Is there anything I can do for you? If there is, you must not hesitate to let me know. I mean it."

"Yes, Dr. Phillips. I can't imagine what it would be. The police are dealing with the case now, but I'll let you know if I think of anything."

"You must let me know if you do," he insisted. "Pass along my regards to Charlie. Please take care of yourself, my girl."

"I will and thank you." I ended the call and thought about what a caring person he was and an expert in so many things. I'd keep his offer in mind, but right now, I couldn't think of thing he could do. We had to wait for the police to find the water bottle.

I poked my head in the library door and sure enough, Lorraine was at her desk and on the phone again. Ever since she held what I called the Governor's Cup weekend, she'd been having conversations with more people on the phone then here at the house. She must have seen me, because she madly waved her left arm that I should come in.

She crooned, "Thank you so much, Mary. I'll be in touch." Then she hung up the phone and fell back against her chair. There was a look of utter frustration on her face. "I can't believe it. They're trying to close the elementary school on Tilghman Island."

"And that's a problem because?" I was taken aback that such a simple question would launch Lorraine right out of her chair and send her pacing around the room.

"A problem? Oh yes, I think it's a big problem. The powers that be are talking about busing elementary school children eleven or twelve miles each way every day. I know the speed limit is 50, but still, that makes the day pretty long for little kids, especially when you add the time it takes to drive around the Island to drop them off at home. Will they have time to go to the school library or club meetings before their bus leaves? They'll be in class with kids who won't be part of their scout troops or on the same baseball teams. They won't see when they're out riding their bikes, *because they live so far away*."

Lorraine paused at the big windows overlooking the river and caught her breath. But her tirade wasn't over. "Birthday parties! What about birthday parties? They're big social events at that age. Their parents will have to drive miles and miles to drop them off and show up a few hours later to pick them up. A waste of time for everybody. It's ridiculous."

"I can understand what you're saying. Don't count today's

parents short. They're very good at arranging carpools and play dates."

"Of course they are, but doesn't a round trip of twenty miles or more sound excessive?" She sat down on the arm of the chair by the fireplace and let out a long sigh. "But those are details, really. What's important is that the school they want to close was ranked the sixth best school in the state and the number one school in the county. And I think someone said that one of the teachers is in the running for Best Teacher in the State. Here's a school that's working, doing the job we want it to do and politicians want to close it. It doesn't make sense and makes me angry."

"There aren't any children here at Fair Winds, are there?"

"No, not anymore. The point is it's about the quality of life in the county and the Shore."

"So, who told you about the school?" I asked, happy she was quieting down.

"The subject came up during my political weekend party. I knew that event was going to get me into trouble," she groaned.

"The event wasn't the problem. It's you. You're caring person." I sat down in the other chair by the fireplace. "You care about people and this community. I bet you've kept silent and watched while something happened that you thought was wrong."

Lorraine took a deep breath and let her body slip into the chair, tired and upset. "I guess you're right. My sense of justice has gotten me into trouble more than once. But, Abby, this issue and the one about the dredging project have certainly dragged me off my comfy perch. The people who live on the Island are getting hit with a double whammy. A waterway becoming unusable that threatens the livelihood of the watermen, the marinas and the whole seafood industry there while busing their children to a school, miles away. It's just not right."

I could barely control my smile as I lay down the challenge. "What are you going to do about it?"

"Well, smarty, I'm talking to people. I've been on the phone so much these last few days I feel like a phone is growing out of my head. Meetings are coming up. People will testify. Documentation has to get into the hands of the right people. There's a lot of work to do."

Grinning now, I said, "And you're going to be one of those people who gets the work done."

She looked at me with a very serious expression on her face. "Abby, I can't sit by and do nothing when a way of life is under siege. I just can't do it."

Serious now, I went over, took her hand and gave it a squeeze. "Of course you can't. You're not built that way and that's one of the things I like about you."

"Thank you for that." She gave me a weak smile. "I'm glad you understand."

"Of course, I do. In fact, I hope you'll let me know how I can help. I did my share of rabble-rousing when I was in college. I'll do anything I can."

Lorraine beamed as she put her arms around me and gave me a hug. I wasn't sure which stars to come into alignment that brought this woman into my life, but I said a silent prayer of thanks. And not for the first time.

Moments later, I was walking down the hall and she called me back. I found her running her hands through her hair.

"Abby, I'm sorry. My mind is going in fifteen different directions with all the political talk that I forgot to ask, what's happened about that poor man who died during the log canoe race?" She led me back into the library. "Tell me everything. I can't imagine a canoe capsizing and killing someone. What an awful accident."

I didn't want to add to her concerns, but she asked. "I'm afraid it wasn't an accident. The medical examiner ran a tox screen and the results showed Jack died of an overdose."

"Don't people overdose all the time?" She paused and looked away. "Oh dear, that sounded flippant. The whole opioid situation is tragic. What I meant to say was, sadly, it's not an unusual situation for a person to overdose."

"True," I agreed. "But the amount of drugs was off the chart."

"Yes, that does sound bizarre. Therefore, the police think it is murder?" I nodded.

She closed her eyes. I was sure she was reliving that moment when she'd heard a woman on her staff standing right here, screaming. Moments later, she found her closest friend dead in a pool of blood on the kitchen floor. Lorraine's eyes opened and a look of determination came over her face. She would control those memories and deal with what was happening now. "Who do they think this?"

"The investigation seems to have hit a wall, but the detective in charge is methodical.

Lorraine hesitated. "That could mean he's drowning in the details or he knows what he's doing. Which is it?

A little smile crossed my lips. "This detective is good. He'll find out."

"I hope you're right." She paused for a moment. "Keep me in the loop and Abby, be careful."

CHAPTER 22

he Butler is in charge of the staff. It is his responsibility to select the proper choices of silverware and serving pieces determined by the foods listed on the menu.

"The Butler's Guide to Fine Silver"
Mr. Hollister, 1898

ON MY WAY back to the cottage, my phone rang again. This time it was Charlie. I was cheerful as I answered. "I was just talking about you."

"Not with the police, I hope." He sounded afraid, almost despondent. "I've haven't done anything wrong."

"Why would you say that?"

"I don't know." There was sheer misery in his voice. "I don't know. This whole situation has got everybody on edge. Rumors are buzzing like black flies. I don't know how much more I can take of this."

"What are people saying?" I stopped walking and listened closely.

"They're saying Dominick did it. That he had had enough of Jack's needling and obnoxious accusations. But I don't believe it. Not Dom. Now, if Dom had been murdered, I would have made a citizen's arrest on the spot. Jack would have been guilty as— but he's the one who is dead." There was a little catch in his voice. "And everybody is looking at everybody else with suspicion." There was a strained silence. "Even me, I'm guilty of suspecting someone."

I perked up. "Charlie, if there's something you know—"

"That's it. There's nothing I know for sure. It's just—"

"Do you want to come over and talk about it? We can sit on the porch without anyone listening and watch the river. A little quiet reflection might help you sort things out."

"Now? Can I come now?"

I was a little surprised at his eagerness. "Um, sure, if you want to. I'll meet you at the main house where you picked me up."

"I'm on my way, and Abby, thank you."

Simon came over and rubbed against my leg. "We're going to have a visitor," I told him. "He's not coming to play, but to talk. Can you sit and listen?"

Simon glanced at the kitchen as if to say, I'll do anything if we can visit the cookie jar. So, we did. I put a few extras in my pocket, just in case I had to distract Simon during what promised to be an interesting conversation.

It felt like minutes before Charlie and I sat down on the fluffy cushions that made the white wicker chairs so comfortable. If I thought the setting might cheer him up, I was wrong. I settled back, but Charlie sat on the edge of his chair. I could have told him to relax, but it wouldn't have done any good. Maybe a neutral subject would be better.

"I wanted you to know that our mutual friend, Dr. Phillips, asked about you."

"Was he complaining about his grass?" Charlie was really jumpy.

"No, not at all. He's thinking about you… and is a little worried about you."

"I'm worried about me, too. I'm not sure whom to trust. I mean a man I admire and respect is a prime suspects in a murder investigation. He's the obvious choice. Jack was always on him, teasing him about *playing with his sails,* he called it. Always making adjustments, even little ones that didn't seem to make a difference, but they did. Dom took us out on practice runs early in the season so we could learn to work as a team. And once he picked his crew, he stuck with it." Charlie got up and started pacing. "He takes care of us, makes sure we show up for each race. He even has our families and girlfriends over for barbecues and swim parties at his house so they feel part of it and we have their support. He believes that if we train and trust each other, we'll race as a unit. It's paid off. We won a lot of races last year and this season has been good."

"That a solid approach to take. Dom sounds like a good leader," I said.

"He's a good guy and great captain, but Jack was all over him about it. He was always aggravating Dom. Last week, he called him a Gestapo captain, claimed Dom didn't let his crew breathe or be themselves. It wasn't true. We feel like a family."

"Didn't he say something at the seafood feast?" I closed my eyes and visualized the feast on the lawn of the club. "Jack was talking to two of your crew, remember? He said they should come over to his boat where they could a say in the strategy of a race."

Charlie opened his eyes wide. "Yes, I remember that." Then his whole body sagged and he threw his head back. "That doesn't help. It's just another reason for Dom to kill Jack. It's kind of an unwritten rule that you don't raid another canoe's crew during the season."

"Oh, sorry. Guess that didn't help." I tried to give him a little smile.

"I don't know what does help." Charlie paced like an electric current was running through him. "And then there's Kevin."

"What about Kevin?" Had I missed something? I couldn't remember if I'd put a magnet on my refrigerator door to represent Kevin . The refrigerator door! I had to make sure Charlie didn't go inside the cottage.

"Abby, you can't say a word." The man was babbling. "You have to promise you won't say anything. I told Kevin he should tell the police right away. That if he doesn't, I will." He stopped and looked down. "No, I-I-I should give Kevin a chance to do the right thing."

I sat up straight in my chair. "Charlie, you have to tell the police if you know anything about Jack's murder."

He dropped his head in his hands. "No, it's nothing like that." He groaned and raised his head slowly. "It's what Jack did."

Charlie was heading down a dangerous path. I spoke sharply to help him focus. "Charlie, what is this all about?"

He plopped into the chair and let out a sigh that started the bottom of his feet. "You know the story about Jack being this great entrepreneur, making lots of money and how he was getting ready to do it again?"

"Yes." I slipped Simon a cookie so he wouldn't interrupt the revelation that was coming.

Charlie turned his red-rimmed eyes toward me and in a small voice said, "It was all a lie."

I almost burst out with a slew of questions, but somehow kept quiet.

It took Charlie a long time, but he finally continued. "Jack knew this guy in college who wrote software. They'd sit up late at night, drinking and dreaming about how they would hit it big. A couple of years later, this guy got in touch with Jack later. Said he was on to something and wanted Jack to look at it. Evidently, Jack thought it was brilliant, showed it to some people and was offered funding."

"FOR SOMEBODY ELSE'S PROJECT? So, they went into business together." It didn't sound so bad. People in tech did that all the time. "That's great."

But it wasn't. Charlie was shaking his head.

I leaned forward and asked, "What? What's wrong?"

"Jack told the investors it was *his* project."

"No," I breathed. "He stole the code?"

"And that's not all. He changed a little something – I don't understand the details, but he knew enough about how to break it. He told the guy that the idea wasn't so great and the code didn't work when stressed."

I leaned my head against the back of my chair and closed my eyes. "Then what happened?"

"Jack took it to Kevin—the version that wasn't broken-- and with a couple of other guys, developed it into a viable piece of software. He sold the code and the company."

I delivered the punch line, the punch in the gut. "And didn't give the original developer a dime." Charlie squeezed his eyes shut and nodded. "So, Jack really was a pirate. Did Kevin know the code belonged to someone else?"

His eyes popped open and stared at me with great intensity. "No, he told me he never knew… and I believe him."

"How did he find out?" I felt like an interrogator, but this was important.

His belief changed into sadness for his friend. "Jack told him last week. Then he told Kevin that he was out of money and was going to shut down this new venture."

My skin felt chilly. It could be a motive for murder. "Kevin was going to lose his job?"

"Yes." He dropped his eyes. "And right after he and his wife adopted a baby."

"That's tough." I licked my lips and tried to frame my next

question as gently as possible. "Charlie, do you think that Kevin hurt Jack?"

"I thought about that, but no. I don't want to think that Kevin did anything to hurt Jack. I've known him since elementary school. He's such a good guy. I think he should say something before the investigation goes any farther. He needs to get ahead of this. Without Jack and the influx of cash, the company will go under and the truth will come out. I told Kevin to volunteer the information about the company and the theft of the software."

He slumped in the chair again. "Abby, do you think I did the right thing? Or do you think the cops will jump to conclusions and—" Before I could say anything, Charlie continued. "I hope Jack doesn't tarnish Kevin from the grave. He could go on and do some amazing work for someone else who runs an honest company. I hope the cops and the lawyers leave him alone."

I put my hand on his arm and spoke softly. "I think you gave him the right advice, but you can't make Kevin or anyone else do the right thing."

Simon's head popped up and he launched himself off the porch and soon came back prancing at Ryan's side. "Oh, am I interrupting something?" he asked almost embarrassed.

Charlie pushed himself up from the chair as if he'd aged decades in the last few minutes. "Nope, I was just leaving. I have to go talk with a friend."

It was obvious by the look on Ryan's face that he wanted to know more, but Charlie said good-bye without further explanation.

After Charlie disappeared around the corner, Ryan turned to me. "I'm sorry about that."

I didn't invite him to sit down. I only asked why he had come to my door.

He answered happily. "I wanted to invite you to dinner. Anytime, anyplace. Your choice."

"Is that why you came unannounced?"

Ryan looked away and his cheeks reddened a little. "Yes, I didn't want to give you a chance to ignore my call."

I bit my lip then said, "I never—"

He held up his hand. "I know. You're not tied to your phone the way I am. I wanted to make sure we connected in the middle of everything going on."

I felt like someone had stuck a pin me and I was deflating like a balloon. "I can't believe…" I didn't know what to say. I looked at the man who'd disappeared for months without a word and my heart wobbled. I couldn't deny I had feelings for him.

He continued to speak softly. "I can't imagine what it's been like for you. It's one thing to read about murder. But to see it happen right in front of your eyes? And to be surrounded by the people who knew him? To see how his death affects them. It's all so different from reading about it at a safe distance.

Could it be that the Ryan I knew was back? Seeing his sharp edge soften gave me a warm feeling. I decided he was worth taking a chance. "When would you like to have dinner?"

His head swung around toward me with a big smile. "Anytime you say."

"How about tonight?"

The old saying *his face lit up like a Christmas tree* came to mind and brought back the memories of the time we'd spent together at Christmas. It was magical. I'd had no inkling then, no warning that he would soon disappear. I needed to find out what happened and why. I was sure I'd made the right decision. "Yes, pick me up at 6:30?"

"Will do. Where would you like to go, the club?"

A shudder went through my body. "Oh, no! Please, no."

"Of course. What was I thinking? No problem. I'll make reservations someplace else. Not to worry. See you tonight."

Pleased with myself, I folded my arms and watched him walk away, . Yes, I had done the right thing. "Come on, Simon. We have things to do."

CHAPTER 23

When the Family acquires a new silver piece or collection, it is important to assess its condition and learn its proper use so that it can become a valued part of the silver service of the House.

"The Butler's Guide to Fine Silver"
Mr. Hollister, 1898

THAT EVENING, Ryan arrived right on time and admired my LBD —Little Black Dress. The peach print scarf I draped around my neck made my tanned skin glow. We drove through St. Michaels without stopping at any of the restaurants there. I tensed. Had he had ignored my request not to go to the yacht club? The phrase *Oh ye of little faith* sprang to mind as he turned into the long drive to the Inn at Perry Cabin.

"I don't know if you've eaten in the dining room here, but I can assure you, it's delicious and the service is impeccable. I snagged a reservation which will keep us away from most of the summer-time tourists."

They gave us a table near the windows overlooking a cozy cove. The blue heron and snowy egrets put on an impressive show and gave us something to talk about when the conversation slowed. As much as I loved seafood, the Rack of Lamb was a welcome change after the expansive seafood feast days earlier. We splurged on dessert. The Pear and Cranberry Tart with local goat cheese ice cream and honey sounded intriguing and didn't disappoint my taste buds. I was thrilled when Ryan gave me a bit of his Chocolate Pecan Pie, one of my all-time favorites and one of the few ways I like chocolate.

As we lingered over coffee, Ryan looked down at the white linen tablecloth and spoke without preamble. "It was business, Abby. That's all. They had me running from one time zone to another, from one crisis to the next. There were things they felt the boss should handle, but they should have had more faith in their own abilities. We'll work on that." He gave the maître d' a subtle nod. "I—I'm not used to keeping in touch when I'm away on business."

His voice fell so low that I had to lean forward to hear him, even though the dining room was elegantly quiet. "I haven't had someone I wanted to stay in close contact for a long time. I'm out of practice and that's something I'll work on."

Just as I opened my mouth to ask the first of many questions, a box arrived, beautifully-wrapped in silver paper and a huge bow. Ryan took it and presented it to me. I was so overwhelmed that all my questions evaporated.

"Go on, open it. I've been waiting a long time to see your expression when you unwrap it," Ryan said, looking very pleased.

I pulled off the bow without untying it. It was too pretty not to keep. The glittery paper sent sparkles all over the table. Inside the box, nestled in white tissue, was a strange piece of silver with a handle. I didn't know what to say.

"Do you like it?" he asked, like a little boy. When I held it in mid-air, he let out a laugh. "This is perfect! You don't know what it is! I'm so happy."

I didn't know quite how to react. Was he making fun of me or genuinely pleased by the uniqueness of his gift?

AS IF HE read my thoughts, he stifled another laugh and said, "I'm sorry. I'm not laughing at you. I can't tell you how hard I tried to find something special and now, to see that my efforts paid off… well, this is perfect. I found your gift in London at the Silver Vaults."

I looked up at him and tried to hide my envy. That was one place I dreamed of visiting someday. He gathered up the wrappings from the package and set them aside. "Now, shall I tell you what it is or do you want to guess?"

I was mystified. I'd never seen a silver piece like it. The slim silver handle fit comfortably in my hand. From the end of the handle, a wide piece of silver curved around like the end of the cane used in vaudeville shows to pull a performer from the stage. But it wasn't rounded like the cane. It was flat and thin with a short serrated edge on the outside of the curve. Not ready to give up, I asked for a hint.

He thought for a moment. "I hope you left some room for dessert."

I looked at him. "That's it? That's my hint?" He nodded. I looked at the piece again. "I guess it could be an instrument of torture." It was a logical idea. The curved part could almost fit around part of my neck. "But the cutting edge is on the outside. And I've never known a dessert to be torture so," I paused and sighed melodramatically. "I give up. Tell me what it is."

"Better than that, I'll show you." With a flurry, the maître d' presented us with an ice cream roll and two plates.

"It's an ice cream roll server?" I'd never heard of such a thing.

"Yes, it is." He reached for the dessert/torture device. "May I?"

He placed the interior curve over the top of the ice cream roll and pressed down and until the two ends on either side touched the plate. Carefully, he removed the serving piece and turned it over, serrated side down and gently sawed the bottom. With a slight move of his wrist, he moved the slice onto the flat side of the curved and transported it to my plate without a glitch.

It was my turn to be delighted, as I clapped my hands together softly. "That's wonderful! May I try?"

He talked me through the process and soon we both had a perfectly cut piece of ice cream roll in front of us. Smiling, we both took a bite and then one more. I didn't want to hurt his feelings, but I couldn't eat another thing. With a nod, he gave us permission to push our plates to the side and the server swooped in to remove them and refill our coffee cups. We sat silently, enjoying the feeling of being together again. My questions would have to wait for another time.

Later that evening, I curled up with an afghan on the sofa. It was July, for heaven's sake, but I was cold. Simon lay across my feet which helped in more ways than one. So many emotions were swirling around that it felt good to just stop. I think I was nodding off when Simon bolted off the sofa to the kitchen door, barking his head off. Had Ryan come back for some reason? No, Simon wouldn't be acting like a crazed animal.

I grabbed my phone, ready to call... who? Dawkins? The police? But I couldn't wait, because Simon was trying to claw his way through the wood door.

"Okay, boy. Settle down." I peeked out kitchen window and didn't see anyone or anything. There was no movement at all. I knew not to open the door, but it seemed safe to crack the window.

"Hello?" I called. "Who's out there?"

There was no response. I leaned closer to the window to listen. I thought I heard somebody crying. "Who's out there?"

A female voice barely escaped the darkness. "It's me."

"Tiffani? Is that you?"

She answered with a sob.

I turned to my furry roommate. "Simon, it's okay. You have to stay and be quiet. I'll handle this. Sit." His bottom hit the floor and his tail wagged madly. He glanced at the cookie jar. "No, not yet. You have to stay."

But as soon as I opened the kitchen door, he shot outside. Tiffani started screaming. "Go away! Get him away from me!" Her voice came from deep shadows at the corner of the cottage.

I flew after him and grabbed his collar. "Come on, boy." It took a few minutes to wrestle him into the kitchen.

I went out again and closed the door. "Tiffani? What are you doing here?"

"Oh Abby, I didn't know where else to go?" She wailed. "I knew I could trust you."

That comment put a heavy weight on my shoulders. "How did you know to come here?"

She sniffled. "Charlie told me about this neat place where you live." Her voice was filled with despair. "Maybe I should go."

I hesitated then suggested she come inside, but she refused. "I can't." She heard Simon whimpering at the door. "Oh, no. He's upset. I've hurt his feelings." She let out such a long breath that I wasn't sure there was any air left in her lungs. "I'm no good for anybody."

"That's not true." I really wasn't sure if it was or not, but what else could I say to this poor girl, full of despair, crying her eyes out by my kitchen door? "Why don't you come inside and tell me what's wrong?"

"I can't take it anymore," she sobbed in the dark. "It's not enough. It's never enough anymore and I can't let myself … not after what happened to Jack."

Was this grief or more? "What do you mean?"

"I can't take the ups and downs. They're wearing me out.

Dutch says there's an easy answer. Just take more, but I can't. I won't! I promised myself I'd stop, but now..." Her voice trailed off.

I finished her sentence for her. "Now, you can't stop taking the pills."

"I'm sorry. I'm so sorry," she wailed. "You were right. I'm using." Her voice quaked with tears. As she got control of herself, she asked, "Are you shocked?"

I wanted to say the right thing. To lie, would be unfair. The girl wasn't stupid. She'd know if I was lying. A gentle truth might keep things calm. "Am I shocked? Not really. I suspected when you went to the ladies room and left your purse on the bar. The prescription bottle was sitting right on top. You came right back and made a joke about forgetting something. Then you left again. Your purse was still on the bar. The bottle was gone."

Tiffani whined. "Oh, Abby, what am I going to do?"

My first reaction was *I have no idea*, then I remembered Project Purple. "I'll be right back. You stay here. Don't move."

I rushed inside, found the bright purple and white pamphlet, opened it to the list of names and numbers and grabbed my phone. I consulted with Tiffani, told her I wanted to call for help and she agreed. The man on the hotline was so nice. He referred me to a special mobile response unit. A counselor could come right away and would be driving an unmarked car. I agreed and gave her some basic information about Tiffani plus directions to bring her directly to my cottage. In minutes, Simon was scarfing down a pile of cookies and Tiffani was settled on my porch. She pulled her bare feet up on the chair cushion and curled in a ball. She was moaning.

"What's wrong?" Then realized that was a stupid thing to say.

"Turn them off the lights, please." Tears made her voice ragged.

I dashed inside and flipped the switch. I asked, "Is that better?"

She nodded and rocked gently back and forth. There was nothing else to do except wait.

Without warning, words started tumbling out of Tiffani's mouth. "It wasn't supposed to be like this. It wasn't. It just happened. It was all because of the surgery on my stupid knee."

I remembered seeing the big purple sign outside of St. Michaels when I drove to the yacht club. *4 out of 5 people who use heroin started with recreational use of prescription painkillers.* That couldn't be the whole story. I saw it as a good sign that she put her feet down on the floor and sat up when I asked her what happened.

"I love being outside. That's one reason why I love sailing, but I can only do that during the summer. Last February, I had cabin fever and decided to learn how to ski. I've never been able to take things slow and sure enough, I overdid it. I fell in some weird way. Tore my ACL and fractured a bone in my foot. The doctor gave me hydrocodone for the pain. It's good stuff. It took away the pain and made me feel good. I had so much energy. I got so much accomplished." She looked down at her hands then curled her fingers into a fist to hide the torn cuticles.

"I loved those pills. How bad could they be if the doctor prescribed them? They made me feel good about myself. So creative. I was teaching art classes all over the Shore and got an offer to add a few more in Annapolis. It was great. But it was a lot of driving and I needed a lot of patience to work with my students." She leaned over and grabbed my arm. "Don't get me wrong. I love my students." She sat back in the wicker chair. "But they can be draining. My own work was suffering."

"You're an artist?!" I had no idea. The outrageous hairstyles might have been a giveaway or was that idea lumping her into a stereotype? I chided myself and sat quietly to listen.

Her eyes grew wide. "Didn't you know?" I shook my head. "I thought you'd seen my watercolor of *Flying Wing*. It's hanging in the lobby of the yacht club. Usually that's the only time anybody talks to me. Most people don't notice me or take me seriously unless they see my work. I only seem to be myself when I'm working."

She drew up her legs to her chest again and planted her chin on her knees. "You see why that great feeling of strength and creativity was so important to me. I was even thinking about starting my Master's Degree in Fine Arts. But the feeling didn't last long. When a pill wore off, the feeling went away. I missed it. I've always had this little voice in the back of mind whispering that I'm not good enough. It's always been there. Until the pills shut it up." She turned toward me. "Can you blame me for wanting to feel good about myself?"

I suspected my response was crucial, so I quickly shook my head.

"When I needed more pills, the surgeon wouldn't renew my prescription. I found somebody else and told him my foot was killing me. I got really good at moaning. He wrote a prescription for oxycodone, 5 mg. When I wanted more, I found another doc on the Western Shore. Told him I worked close-by and I needed help for the pain or I'd lose my job. He wrote me prescriptions for 10 mg." She hung her head. That's when I knew I was hooked."

"But you were in pain, right?"

She chuckled, but there was no happiness in it. "I was only in pain when the drug wore off. I was fine, except for the need and I needed more and more. Dutch said I should up the strength and be done with it. But I got scared."

"I don't understand."

"I was taking oxycodone 5/325. That's 5 mg of oxycodone and 325 mg of Tylenol. Then it was upped to 10 mg of oxy. If I go up to the next level, I'll be taking 15 mg of oxycodone and there's no Tylenol in that pill. That's a huge jump. I don't want to do it."

"Good for you. We're going to get you some help so you don't have to handle this alone, Tiffani."

"My dad died when I was a kid." She started to cry again. "This will be the first time since then that I won't be alone."

My heart lurched. At least I'd had the love and attention of Gran and Aunt Agnes when I was growing up. And their love was with me still.

Simon barked. He was better than a doorbell when a stranger approached. "I'll be right back. I think your help has arrived."

I met the young counselor, who was about thirty years old with long brown hair scooped back into a ponytail, and led her to the porch. On her instruction, I went into the living room and turned on a lamp to cast some light on the porch. She sat down on the rocking chair, her briefcase on the floor beside her. When I returned to the porch, I could see Simon stretched out on the back of the sofa by the window, watching. It helped to see him there, my source of strength, support and love.

The counselor spoke directly to Tiffani with a voice that was soft and clear. "Tiffani, my name is Mandi. It ends with an 'i' just like your name. I'm very glad to meet you." She held out her hand. Tiffani stared at it for a moment then shifted her eyes to look up at her chestnut brown eyes framed with the dark lashes.

"I don't feel so good. I have a headache," Tiffani grumbled. Tiny beads of sweat were popping up all over her face as she began to nod off.

"Tiffani, hang in there," Brandi said, part plea, part instruction. "Stay with me."

"I don't know." Tiffani swung her feet to the floor. "Maybe I should go."

"I hope you'll stay with me." Brandi continued to hold out her hand to the young artist.

This was the moment that would affect the rest of her life. When Tiffani took Mandi's hand, I breathed again.

"Good," said Mandi. "Now, we can talk here or go someplace else."

Tiffani turned her head to me as the tears spilled over her long lashes and ran down her cheeks. "Can we stay here? I can't do this alone!"

"You don't have to do it alone," Mandi said gently. "I'm right here to help you."

"No, I don't know you. I need my friend. Can we stay here? Can she stay with me?"

"It's up to Abby," answered Mandi.

I hoped I was hiding my panic. What am I getting into? Somehow, this counselor read my mind. "Your friend can sit here with us right now while we talk for a little while. Then you and I will go from there."

I didn't know if Tiffani caught the subtle message—*you and I will go from there*—but I did and relaxed. "Of course you can sit here." I stood up. "Why don't I get some ice water?" As I was about to go inside, Tiffani grabbed my arm in her sweaty hand. I patted it and smiled. It seemed to give her strength.

"I know how you feel, Tiffani, because I was once where you are." Tiffani's eyes grew wide. "I can help you. You can beat this thing and get control of your life again. Are you ready to work with me?"

Tiffani's voice was strong when she said yes and began answering the assessment questions to determine the extent of her addiction and best course of treatment. Mandi was non-threatening, kind and very thorough.

When our water glasses were empty and the initial part of the evaluation was done, Brandi smiled at my young friend. "OK, Tiffani. You're doing great. Why don't we go to your house to go over your options and discuss some things. I'll wait for you by the cars." She turned to me and held out her hand. "It was good that you called, Abby. You're a true friend. Good-bye."

When we were alone, Tiffani looked out at the river. "Do you think I'm a terrible person?" Her lower lip trembled.

I took her hand and squeezed it. "I'm proud of you. You're doing the right thing. You are one brave lady."

Tiffani turned and looked at me. When I gave her a nod of encouragement, a small smile played over her chapped lips. She took her hand from mine. "I have to go now. Mandi's waiting for me."

She walked down the steps on a new path for her life, to meet the woman who would be her guide. In my mind and heart, I wished them well and closed my front door softly.

CHAPTER 24

If an undercooked egg yolk comes in contact with a silver spoon, the spoon can turn black.

"The Butler's Guide to Fine Silver"
Mr. Hollister, 1898

THE NEXT MORNING, I took Simon outside and tossed the ball again and again. It was just the two of us and before I knew it, I was having a serious conversation with him as he ran back and forth.

"Ryan and I were just getting to the point when I could have asked about his trip. I know he said it was work, but I don't know what he does. He doesn't go to an office or keep regular hours. He said the staff needed the boss to do certain things. *The Boss.* So, I learned he is the boss of something that operates all over the world. That's more than I knew before, but—"

I threw the ball harder. Simon was panting from all the running.

"I want to know more and there was my chance. We were sitting in this beautiful room, enjoying a beautiful view, eating a beautiful meal. So, did I ask about his business? No. Did I ask where he went? No. Did I say, Tell me, Ryan, didn't they have phones or the internet where you were?" I took a deep breath and wailed. "No-o-o." The ball sailed high and away.

"I SAT THERE like someone who doesn't have two brain cells to rub together. And then he does this whole big deal with the present and the ice cream roll." Simon dropped the ball at my feet and dashed over to the water bowl I kept outside. "I have to give him credit," I said as I watched Simon slurp until the bowl was empty. "The whole gift thing took planning and it showed he was thinking of me." Simon sat at my feet, waiting.

I scratched his silky ear. "Oh, why can't all men be more like you?" I moaned. His response was to nudge the ball with his nose. "You're right. I should stop fixating on him and get on with it." I picked up the ball and cleaned off some blades of grass and a gross-looking bug. "I should get on with what I love. I should tell him to go away!" And I hurled the ball as hard as I could.

"If you're talking about me, you should know that I'll do everything I can to change your mind."

As I whirled around, I stumbled. He caught my arm and kept me from falling. My heart skipped a beat, not from love. From shock. "What are you doing here, sneaking up on me like that?"

"Not the greeting I'd expected." He pointed over his shoulder. "I dropped off some Newhaus Belgian Chocolates for Lorraine that I brought from Europe. They are her absolute favorites."

I was burning for so many reasons. "She can get Belgian chocolates here in the United States or through the internet."

He gave me a small smile. "Ah, but the Belgian chocolates made in Europe are very different from the *Belgians* or even what they call fine chocolates made here in the States."

"How is that possible?"

"Different recipes. Different percentages of milk fat and… Oh, I don't know. She explained it to me once. Tasting is believing."

"Well," I sniffed. *Did I just sniff like Harriet?!* "I don't eat a lot of chocolate, but when I do, Godiva is pretty good."

He let out a hearty guffaw. "Don't let Lorraine hear you say that! Even Godiva's taste better in Europe, but on the scale of fine chocolate over there, Godiva is close to the bottom." The sparkle left his eyes. "Anyway, she said it was all right for me to wander over to say hello. And no, I wasn't sneaking up you."

He stood there in a white polo shirt and dark blue shorts with his hands in his pockets, looking like the most self-assured man in the world. His handsome face and casual manner made my frustration boil over.

I put my hands on my hips. "You think you can waltz over here, call me for a drink or dinner, *be there for me,* anytime you want and then disappear…" I snapped my fingers. "Just like that?"

"Whoa, I didn't mean to…"

"Well, I have news for you. The days of a woman waiting patiently for a man are over, long over. This is the age of the independent woman. I don't need a man to define my life."

He stood there with a stunned look on his face. "I know. That's one thing I like about you. One of many."

I was not going to let him sweet-talk his way out of this discussion. "That's nice," I sneered. *I sneered! What was I becoming?* I turned to look for Simon who should be galloping back with his ball. And to hide the tears prickling at my eyes.

"I like who you are. This is conservative county, but you didn't come over here to the Eastern Shore to strike a blow for your sisters. You're not obvious like that. You do things quietly and you make things happen. You walk the talk, as they say."

I swiped at the tears running down my face. Was it a delayed reaction to seeing Tiffani take action to save her life and that she came to me for help. And I delivered. I did the right thing at the right moment. That's what was triggering these tears. It had to be.

BUT RYAN WASN'T DONE. "You came to the Eastern Shore, because it's a unique place. Sure it has its problems, but the beauty and way of life make it a sanctuary in a chaotic and complicated world. A place you can feel safe and live your life the way you want. Here, you're surrounded by individuals. It could be a waterman and his wife who prefer to be on the water than anywhere else. Or a retired couple ready to do what they been saving and dreaming about for years. Except now what he's doing is hardly considered important and she's desperate to be involved anything to get out of the house."

I'd seen these women, well-dressed, with her hair done, chatting in the Cove about the pros and cons of a particular shrub as if the White House staff was awaiting their decision. Thank goodness Lorraine wasn't like that

Ryan still wasn't finished talking about this place he loved. "Think about those with money, real money. There was the person who made a donation with the caveat that his name not be made public. His gift to the Washington D.C. NPR station was based on its radio frequency."

My tears had stopped so it was safe to turn around. "I don't understand."

"The station's radio frequency is 88.5, so he contributed $88,500."

I was stunned. "A very generous donation."

"That's what I told my friend when he wrote that check. His response? 'Ryan, having money like this is a burden.'"

I didn't know what to say, no ever being in that position. But Ryan wasn't finished.

"And some are working to make ends meet month by month.

And what is important to them is to see their kids graduate and not get a GED while they serve a sentence in prison."

He had made his point and brought up a question I wanted to ask, so I did. "And what's important to you?"

"I want more, Abby. Not sure what that is or how to get it, but I'm willing to work for it."

I turned away, tears threatening to fall again. I didn't realize that I too wanted more, until I met Lorraine. Now, I wanted to bury my head in neck of my constant source of unconditional love. But Simon was nowhere to be seen.

I scanned the lawn. No black ball of fur. Fear gripped me and I started to run.

"Abby? What wrong?" It took Ryan only a moment to follow.

"Simon!" It was a response to Ryan, and a call to my pup. I ran all the way around the cottage and didn't see him.

"I'll look over this way," Ryan declared, trying to sound calm.

I ran to the kennel area. Simon wasn't with his buddies. I went to the kitchen and asked Mrs. Clark if she had seen him.

"Haven't seen him all morning." Mrs. Clark saw my face and lines of worry appeared on her forehead. "Is something wrong?"

Not wanting to frighten her, I said, "No, I'm sure he's around here somewhere. It's probably a new game of He Hides and I Seek." I laughed, but even to my ears, it sounded weak.

I scoured the lawns all the way to the farm fields, calling until I started coughing from the pollen. I'd trained not to go out there. And he hadn't. Where was my dog? What about the people at the house for the weekend? They weren't used to watching for dogs running free. I should check the pavement of the driveway, just in case… I couldn't make my feet go in that direction. I couldn't. I turned back to the cottage and met Ryan. Nothing. I paced around on the grass and tried to figure out where he'd gone.

"I shouldn't have spent so much time at the yacht club." I stomped around, not knowing where to look next. "Simon is spending too much time alone. He's still a puppy. He needs companionship and training. I shouldn't have gone to the log canoe race. I shouldn't have gone to any of them. Those races are silly. I mean, who put sails on a log canoe?"

Ryan caught my arms and held me in place. "Abby, stop it. It's going to be okay. We'll find him."

He leaned toward me and I peered over his shoulder at the river. Was he there? Had a goose attacked him? Was he bleeding? Drowning? I pulled myself out of Ryan's grip and took off running.

"Simon? Simon?"

There was no sign of him along the shore or in the water. It was time. I had to go back to the cottage and call the main house for help. I dragged myself up the hill, tired. So tired. I looked up at Ryan. He looked as scared as I felt. I shifted my eyes to the silent cottage. Tears burned my eyes again. *No, he can't be gone.* And I started to run.

The sounds of my huffing and puffing up the hill must have reached the porch. I couldn't believe what I saw. A furry black head popped up from the porch floor.

"SIMON!" Ryan and I screamed together and we ran toward him, ran harder than ever.

I threw my arms around him and buried my face in his neck. My tears made his fur wet. He wiggled, but I didn't let go. Simon planted his feet, broke my hug and madly licked my face. I didn't know whether to yell at him or hold him.

I grabbed his head and held it inches from my own. "What am I going to do with you?"

"You're going to love him, I hope."

I raised my head and saw Ryan kneeling next to us.

any pieces have been handed down through generations. They may be expensive or held in very high esteem. Treat all pieces with the utmost care.

"The Butler's Guide to Fine Silver"
Mr. Hollister, 1898

RYAN STAYED until I calmed down from the awful scare of losing Simon. We didn't talk about anything significant. We spent some quiet time together, the three of us. It was kind of him to offer to bring in a pizza or Chinese food or anything I wanted. His caring helped me recover so I was at peace when I said he could leave. I just wanted some time alone with my thoughts and my Simon.

I settled on my sofa with my big dog which didn't leave a lot of room for me. As I was playing with the idea of taking a little nap, my phone rang. I almost let it go to voicemail when the modern-day urge to check the caller ID overwhelmed me and I quickly accepted the call.

"Dr. Phillips! Hello."

"Abby! I'm so glad I caught you. How are you?" He sounded reserved, but I got the feeling that he was bursting with news.

"I'm fine, sir. Is everything all right?" I had to stop anticipating bad news every time the phone rang. That worry would drive me crazy.

"YES. Well—I've been following the story of that poor man on the log canoe. They're suggesting that the police investigation is stalled. Is that true? I thought it was an accident."

"The answers to your questions are yes and no." He deserved to know what was happening, but I hoped it wouldn't upset him. "Yes, the police are reorganizing the investigation. You see, they know the cause of death now. At first, they thought it was an accident. They thought the gash on his head killed him. That was wrong. It was really an overdose of heroin and fentanyl. They think he ingested it from his water bottle."

"Did he ingest it on purpose? To commit suicide?"

"No, the police are treating it as a murder."

"Do they know who did it? Surely, they should be able to tell something from the fingerprints on the bottle?"

"Well, that's the problem. Jack's water bottle has disappeared. They're doing a grid search along the shoreline of the Miles River, but my guess is it's bogged down on the river bottom or happily floating out to the Bay and beyond."

"Then maybe you should come and see me," he suggested.

"Oh, I'd like to sometime soon, but right now I'm exhausted by all this."

"No, not for a friendly visit, but you're always welcome. I found something interesting." The twinkle in his voice intrigued me.

"Is it about the case?" I asked.

"Yes. It is… or I should say, it might be."

"Would this afternoon be convenient? The police are stumped. You might be able to help."

"See you at five."

I arrived at the appointed hour and this time, I wore a summer print dress of white daisies against a black background for the occasion. The housekeeper ushered me into the library as before. Dr. Phillips was sitting in the same chair by the fireplace. The windows overlooking the river sparkled with the trails of raindrops on the glass. During my drive over to his house, the heavens had opened up to give us some desperately needed rain. Flashes of lightening and the muted rumble of thunder outside made the massive library feel cozy and rich with secrets waiting to be uncovered.

When the librarian saw me, he rose from his chair and greeted me with a muffled voice. We were the only people in the large room, but it must have been an old habit from years of working at the Library of Congress.

"I'm so glad you're here, Abby. Thank you for taking the time to come." Today, he was wearing a navy blue suit with a thin stripe. His tie was the robin's egg blue of the sky with accents of cloud white and lavender. I was glad I'd put on a dress.

"Let's work at the library table." He ushered me over to a heavily-carved table of dark wood near the bookshelves.

The table was different from a regular desk. It didn't have stacks of drawers, only an extra-large work surface that could handle stacks of books, reference books and maps. It was obvious that Dr. Phillips had prepared for our meeting. Neatly arranged on the table were a few books open to particular pages, some handwritten notes and copies of what appeared to be old newspaper articles, along with a few photographs.

Ever the gentleman, he held a chair for me on one side of the table and settled himself on the other. He rested his hands on the table and cleared his throat. "You're wondering what all this is about. The story of what happened during the Governor's Cup race has haunted me these last days. I've felt a bit responsible." He glanced at me, saw my concerned expression and hurried on. "Please don't fuss. I feel responsible. I sent you to watch the race."

I tried to interrupt, but he won't allow it.

"Please, let me finish. You were unharmed and that was a comfort. But for a man to die during a sailboat race," he looked down and shook his head slowly. "It was more than I could have imagined. When they let it be known that it was murder, that one word hounded me. Who would murder a man during a sailboat race … and why?"

I tried to soothe him. A man of his age and stature shouldn't be upset by events that didn't involve him. "Both you and the police want answers to those questions. I want you to know that the detective on the case is experienced, professional and intuitive. I saw him work through the situation at the recent Plan Air Art Festival." I reached my hand across the table toward him to offer comfort. He solved those cases. "I feel confident he will solve this one."

"I fear he will not, Abby, without the benefit of history. I believe the solution to this murder revolves around the boat."

That was the last thing I expected to hear. "Why do you say that?"

"Because I believe the answer lies in the past. It's all about the log canoe." He shook his aged head gently. "At least that's what my research leads me to believe." He put his hands flat on the documents in front of me and raised his eyes. "At least let me show you what I found. I will leave it up to you as to whether you tell your detective what you learn here or not. Do we have an agreement?"

I nodded. I didn't know if Detective Ingram would want to know any of this information, but I did. I was willing to sit and listen to what this highly-revered librarian had to say.

Eager now, Doctor Phillips moved up to the edge of his chair so he could be closer to his paper. "As you know the ill–fated log canoe carries the name *Flying Wing.* She is well over 100-years-old though I have not yet been able to ascertain the exact year she was built. At the end of the 19ᵗʰ century, she was owned by Captain Caulk of Saint Michaels. A copy of his portrait is here on the table."

Dr. Phillips handed me a sheet of paper with a faded picture of a man. He wore a suit with a stiff collar in a picture was taken long ago.

"Early in his career as a waterman, he used the log canoe to tong for oysters, a common practice in those days. He was successful and in time, he expanded his business by becoming a buyer. To do this, he bought a schooner so that he could transport oysters and other cargo to Baltimore Harbor. The schooner called *Dream* was fast and I guess, represented a dream of his coming true."

Suddenly, Doctor Phillips pushed back his chair and began to rise. "Oh Abby, I am so sorry. I'm a terrible host. Would you like some coffee or perhaps a cool drink?"

"No, really, I'm fine. Thank you. Please continue your story."

"All right." He settled back in his chair again. "Now where was I? Oh yes, Captain Caulk and his successful business. It was very successful, because he was a shrewd and honest man. It seems that he was highly respected by everyone who knew him. In fact, when they held his funeral at the Saint Luke's Methodist Church in Saint Michaels, it had the most highly attended funeral to date."

I sat back in my chair and crossed my legs. "That's certainly says a lot about a man and shows what his community thought of him."

"Yes, it does," he agreed. "It was a very sad occasion."

"A funeral usually is." I was hoping that Dr. Phillips would get to the information I could take to Ingram.

"It was a very sad occasion, because Captain Caulk's death was a result of a gruesome and shocking murder. Newspapers in the

St. Michaels, Easton, Annapolis and Baltimore reported the crime in horrifying detail. Even the *New York Times* published articles about it." He gestured to a stack of papers in the center of the table. "I've taken the liberty of making copies for you to read, if you wish. I think you will find the style of reporting reads more like a detailed fiction novel, then journalism about the crime, the trial and punishment."

"Then they found the person who did it?"

He nodded with a smile. "Oh yes, they did. They had him in custody within twenty-four hours of finding the decapitated body of Captain Caulk. They were able to try and convict the man without the benefit of DNA, fingerprint analysis or crime scene reenactment. The murderer was hung in Annapolis." He pointed to the copies of the news stories again. "All the facts are there, including the report that a great number of ladies wearing their better ensembles and hats were in attendance on the opening day of the trial. It would make for good reading if the details weren't so chilling."

He sat back in his chair and folded his hands over his vest. "But that's not the point of this conversation. As I read all these accounts and other historical background information about the log canoe, what stood out to me were the reports about Captain Caulk's family.

"The good captain was one of ten children. Even though he was in his late 30s, he lived with his widowed sister in their childhood home. Many of his siblings and their families lived on the Eastern Shore and worked on the water. Several of his male relatives were captains of steamboats. Many were waterman. All in all, it was a very tight-knit family.

"When the news arrived in St. Michaels that Captain Caulk's schooner *Dream* had been found aground and on fire close to the point where the Patapsco River enters the Chesapeake Bay, members of his family, including two captains, deviate from their courses and went to the scene. They offered assistance to the local police investigating the murder and conveyed the captain's remains to Baltimore with great respect. A local undertaker prepared the casket for transport to return his body to St. Michaels."

My eyes fell on the portrait of the captain. He had a serious, but not unkind face. It was a black-and-white photo so it was a little hard to tell if his hair was dark blonde or light brown. Either way, it was thin and his hairline had receded significantly. He would have been bald within a year or two, if he'd lived. His eyes were dark and his lips were thin.

Dr. Phillips continued his story. "He was very fortunate to have people who loved him. I'm afraid that the victim of this murder was not as fortunate. In many cases, Jack was merely tolerated. I only knew him during the last eighteen hours of his life, but I'm sad to say that, if he had lived, I would not have wanted him as a friend. I don't think he came from a large family. Someone said that his dad lives in Arizona somewhere. I can't imagine what he's going to do with the log canoe out there."

"Quite the opposite of Captain Caulk, who was greatly loved by his family. One of his nephews was serving as a member of the Baltimore City Police at the time. He was so concerned about the investigation into his uncle's murder that he took two days off from work and went to the site. During his own search, he discovered the severed head of the captain."

I shuddered. "I can't imagine what that was like."

"I agree. I choose not to ponder certain things. But the point is that a member of the family dedicated himself to finding the truth about what happened. Several days later, a contingent of family members, both men and women, traveled to Baltimore City and escorted the captain's casket home to the Eastern Shore. After arriving at the ferry landing in Claiborne, they boarded a train for the short trip to St. Michaels. After the service, Captain Caulk's body was interred in the Mt. Olivet Cemetery there. The family erected a monument, a large white marble obelisk inscribed with his name and dates. They added something unusual, a carving of his schooner on fire. It's really quite remarkable. I took the time to go and see it."

I picked up one of the photographs. "You've included a picture of the marker."

"It really doesn't do it justice. It's worth the time to go and look at it in person."

I set the picture of the marker on top of the newspaper articles. Without really considering it, I'd made a commitment to reading about the murder and this family who lived long ago.

"Where was *Flying Wing* when this happened?" He continued. "Rocking gently in her slip, waiting for her captain to return. She didn't fare very well in the coming years. Some of the men in the family used her to harvest various types of seafood, but she was never again an integral part of their business. Time took its toll on the wooden boat and she started to deteriorate. The family decided to sell her rather than do an extensive restoration.

"She bounced from owner to owner until she was bought by Lorraine's father. One could say that he restored her to her former glory, but that would be untrue. He made her better than she'd ever been and together they won the coveted Governor's Cup Trophy."

"Lorraine told me what happened following that race. After her daddy died, no one in the family was interested in log canoe racing so *Flying Wing* was sold to an avid sailor. Then something happened and the canoe was passed from owner to owner again."

DR. PHILLIPS LEANED FORWARD, his hands on the table tightened into fists. "And that brings us to the present day. The last time this boat went up for sale, there was some spirited competition between buyers. One of them, of course, was Jack Spalding. The other was a young man who desperately wanted to own the canoe. Jack got whiff that *Flying Wing* existed and decided he wanted to get involved in racing. He offered more than the young man could afford and he had to watch Mr. Spalding tow away his beloved log canoe."

"I'm confused," I said. "Why did he have to have that particular boat?"

Dr. Phillips beamed like a little boy with a pocketful of change in a candy store. "That's the whole reason why I wanted you to hear this story. The young man is related to one of Captain Caulk's sisters and was named for the man. I imagine he grew up with the family stories of the tragedy that befell his uncle a century before. That young man was at the Governor's Cup race when Mr. Spalding was murdered."

A shot of electricity ran through me and I almost jumped out of the chair. "Was he part of the crew on *Flying Wing*

"No, I believe he's part of *Island Memory's* crew."

"Dominick's boat? Is it Charlie?" I asked though I didn't want it to be him. The elderly gentleman shook his head. "Then who is it?"

"The young man was named for his uncle, Oliver T. Caulk. I believe he goes by the nickname O.T."

My jaw dropped. The police officer was a descendant of the original owner of *Flying Wing*.

We sat quietly together listening to the sounds of the rain splattering against the windows, each lost in our own thoughts. After going over the story again, I was almost afraid to raise the question that was obvious.

Dr. Phillips gazed at me with a kindly expression. I'll give voice to what I believe you are thinking. Did the descendant of Captain Caulk commit murder during the Governor's Cup race?"

I closed my eyes and massaged my temples. The possibility that a man who dedicated his life every day to enforcing the law could commit murder was a lot to take in. And to think that the man could justify such an act in his own mind, based on family tradition and loyalty, was more than I could accept.

"Abby, I'm sorry I brought this conflict and distress to you, but I think it deserves consideration."

I didn't want to be rude, but I had to leave. I needed a little time and space to process all of this new information. "I want to thank you—"

"You don't have to say anything more. The idea is fairly overwhelming. I know, I've been wrestling with it for days," he said as he gathered up all the papers and put them into a large file envelope. "I came to the conclusion that I would make my research available to you and you could decide what to do with it,"

"May I ask you one question?"

"Of course," he said as he stopped what he was doing to give me his full attention.

"Whatever made you look into the story?"

He smiled. "You can take a librarian out of the library, but you can't take away his curiosity, even if the librarian is retired. I started looking into Mr. Spalding's background and found it disheartening. The articles about his success in business were impressive. Some of the other things I learned about the man were not. I wanted to go no farther into that line of inquiry. I thought it would less upsetting to look at the history of the log canoe."

"But how did you identify O.T.?"

"I WAS STRUCK by the fact that the Caulk family really came together when the brother was murdered. It seemed to make an impression on the reporters at the time as well. I took a little trip to Easton and visited my good friend who is the research librarian of the Maryland Room at the Talbot County Free Library there. She showed me many of the articles you see here and, because she loves the hunt and likes to be thorough, she pulled out the Caulk family genealogy. I followed the line down to the present day and found the namesake." He handed me the thick envelope of information and I tucked it under my arm. "Abby, what you do with this information is up to you."

I left the librarian's home to face the driving rainstorm with a heavy burden.

CHAPTER 26

The Butler must keep a proper listing of silver pieces and the hallmarks of their makers. This information can help identify a fraudulent piece. A pretender does not belong in the Family's collection.

"The Butler's Guide to Fine Silver"
Mr. Hollister, 1898

I BELIEVED Dr. Phillips and his research. I wasn't sure I could accept his conclusion that O.T. was involved in the murder, at least not yet. If I couldn't convince myself, how could I convince Ingram? I headed home with the rain beating on the soft top and spent the next several hours poring over the treasure of information the librarian had given me. By the time the rain stopped, I picked up my cell phone and called the detective. I was ready to make the case to him. He didn't want to come to the cottage so we planned to meet at the Cove.

He found me sitting at the big round table in the corner, files and papers spread around. He signaled the server, the new girl, as he sank into a wooden captain's chair. "I'll have coffee and a piece of hot apple pie, please. Abby?"

I was fine with my mug of coffee. Before I could present the theory of how history played an important part in the case, he took control of the conversation.

"I thought you'd like to know that the case has taken a turn and it makes perfect sense to me." The waitress put a slice of steaming pie down in front of him, refilled my coffee and hustled back to the kitchen without a word.

Ingram cocked an eyebrow. "What, no pithy comment about sweets and a cop's waistline?"

"She's new. I think she prefers to stay in the kitchen and talk with people she knows. So, we're alone here, for all intent and purposes. Tell me what you've got."

Ingram dug into his pie. After a sip of coffee and a quick look around to confirm that we were indeed alone, he said, "With the help of investigators and undercover cops in Baltimore, I've been pulling on that thread about a drug supply highway to the Eastern Shore and it's paying off."

"Was Jack part of it?" For a moment, I wanted him to say no. I didn't want to imagine a successful software entrepreneur and leader of a sailboat racing team, who appeared to live a healthy life of exercise and good food, getting himself mixed up with the drug trade.

Ingram nodded with confidence. "Yes, ma'am, he was, up to his eyeballs. It seems that Black Jack's business wasn't in the black. Our erstwhile captain was pouring money into it and was beginning to scrap the bottom of the bank account." Ingram used his fork to pick up the last pie crumbs from this plate and leaned back. "It seems that Jack wasn't a stranger to nefarious undertakings."

"Nefarious? Have you been studying the dictionary, detective?" I said with a snicker.

"Thought you'd like that. He may have played fast and loose with some computer code several years ago. But that's for the fraud squad and his estate to work out."

Now, it was my turn to sit back with a smile of satisfaction on my face. "So, Kevin came to see you."

Ingram scowled. "You knew about this?" The accusation of *You didn't tell me* hung in the air.

"I overheard a little piece of something. It wasn't anything definitive. Really, it wasn't much to go on." He continued to scowl, unconvinced. "I can tell you that Kevin was encouraged to talk to you and I'm glad he did."

He scowled as he reached for his coffee mug. "Well, the proceeds from his business dealings with the guys in Baltimore were funding his company. Recently, things changed. They wanted to rollout a new product in the Eastern Shore market-place. What do these guys think they are, corporate moguls? Roll-out. Marketplace. Those are Madison Avenue terms. They were even talking about a demographic analysis for the product, like they are Procter & Gamble or something."

"It's big business now. You know that."

"Unfortunately." He sighed. "Anyway, this new product includes a dash of fentanyl that is a hundred times stronger than heroin, so it's more economical for their production line and gives a boost to their bottom line. But Jack didn't want any part of it. I guess his conscience finally caught up with him."

"Why do you think that happened?" I asked.

"Fentanyl was the drug was linked with the untimely deaths of Michael Jackson and Prince. It was pretty well publicized so Jack probably made the connection. He probably figured that if those wealthy and well-known men couldn't manage the drug and died as a result, people – normal people – would be more vulnerable than if they used the usual drugs like plain ole heroin and opioids. He doesn't want anything to do with the new plan. Even though he liked the money, the operation had gotten a lot bigger than he anticipated and he wanted out. Our brilliant sailing captain didn't understand a basic truth. Like the Mafia, you don't say bye-bye and walk away from a drug operation under any circumstances. If Jack told them he was uncomfortable, they would have laughed themselves silly."

I put my elbows on the table. "You think they tied up a loose end?" He nodded. "How do you know this?"

Ingram put his hand flat on his chest and pretended he was shocked. "What? You don't believe me?"

I didn't know what to say so I didn't utter a word.

He relaxed and said, "Good ole police work. We identified one of his runners who made the trip from Baltimore to the Shore and brought him in. He'd been away for a couple of weeks and demanded to see Jack. When we told him he was dead from an overdose of heroin and fentanyl, the guy went berserk, desperate to cut a deal. Our investigators went to work in Baltimore and we got the rest of the story. They're collecting evidence now and starting to make arrests. It's a good ending, I think." He smiled and straightened his body as if he was going to *bust his buttons* as Gran used to say.

"Tidy, I think is the word, detective. Maybe even a little too tidy," I suggested.

He gave me a wary look. "Why do you say that?"

"I had a conversation with a renowned librarian and researcher who retired to the Shore."

Ingram folded his arms and pursed his lips. "Now, I'm going to get a history lesson."

"Yes, and I think you'll find it interesting. He says the answer to this case is the boat."

Ingram brought his head forward as if to hear me better. "Did I hear you say, the boat?"

"That's right, the *Flying Wing* log canoe."

He suppressed a laugh. "Your librarian thinks the boat poisoned Jack?"

"Not exactly. As ridiculous as it sounds, you're not far off the mark." I pointed to the papers I'd laid out on the table. "It all goes back to 1899 and the murder of the Captain Caulk of *Flying Wing.*"

"Sounds like we have a cursed boat, if you ask me." He waved his mug at the waitress who had suddenly remembered we were there and reappeared.

I summarized the history of *Flying Wing.* Ingram's eyebrows flew up when I mentioned Lorraine's connection to the canoe, but moved alone to the present day.

His eyes started to stray around the little restaurant. "What's your point?"

"The original Caulk family was close-knit and loyal to one another. Their family tradition was strong. From what I understand, one of the descendants of the murdered captain tried to buy the boat, but Jack outbid him. Rumor has it, there were words. I think the quote was, *You didn't think I was going to let you win with your meager little salary, did you? How would that make me look? No way!*"

I had his interest again. "Those could be fighting words. Then what happened?"

"As you know, Jack restored the canoe, bought new sails that cost tens of thousands of dollars and started racing."

"And what happened to the disrespected descendant?" he said, eager for me to finish the story.

"He joined the crew of a different log canoe ..." I said these words slowly and distinctly. "That was racing for the Governor's Cup on Saturday."

"He was there? And you think he poisoned Jack? Who was it?"

I took a deep breath. "He was named after the captain murdered in 1899. Oliver T. Caulk."

Ingram stared at me for a moment then launched himself out of the chair and started pacing around. "There you go again. I don't know what your obsession is with painting this officer as a killer, but it's no longer annoying. It's getting serious. Come to me when you've got something concrete." He leaned over the table and glared at me. "Finding a murderer is all about evidence and good police work. Not genealogy." And he stomped out of the Cove, leaving me with his check.

Disheartened, but not surprised by Ingram's reaction, I wanted to do something that would make a difference. I guess I wasn't ready to take my frustration with Ingram home with me. I'd kept thinking about Charlie and how upset he was, so I went by the yacht club hoping to find him. Charlie wasn't anywhere around. In fact, the place was almost deserted, except for Tiffani, who was sitting in her usual place at the bar.

"Hey." I slid onto a bar stool next to her and ordered a club soda.

"Oh, big drinker, I see! You look like you've been put through the ringer. Your turn to talk."

She could tease me. She wasn't nasty like the detective, even if he had a point. I didn't want to go into details so I kept it simple. "I was talking to the detective investigating Jack's murder."

She sat up straight, eager to hear more. "What did he say? Have they found the man who killed him? Oh, I hope so. Please tell me they found him. Arrested him." Her words came out like bullets from a machine gun.

"Whoa, slow down."

"Tell me, tell me," she pleaded.

"Sorry to disappoint you. We just talked about the case a little bit. He didn't have anything new," I said and took a sip of my drink, the fizzy bubbles tickling my nose.

Tiffani put her arms on the bar and slumped. "Oh, I was hoping. If they found him, arrested him, I wouldn't have to—" She stopped abruptly and went quiet.

I waited, but finally my curiosity got the better of me. "You wouldn't have to do, what?"

"Nothing."

"Tiffani?"

"Never mind."

I felt my eyes narrow. The girl knew something. "Tiffani, if you can help the investigation—"

"I don't know anything," she said quickly.

"I don't think that's true," I countered gently. "It's important, Tiffani."

"What if I tell you? Then you can tell them." Her face was full of hope.

I shook my head. "It doesn't work like that."

"I can't go to the cops," she whined.

"Why not? What do you think is going to happen?"

"They won't take me seriously. Nobody ever does."

I tossed off her concern. "Is that all that's bothering you?"

"No." She looked around to make sure no one was listening to our conversation. "Well, just like everyone else, I might smoke a little weed once in a while or take a pill. If they knew, they could throw me in a cell."

"I don't think that's going to happen."

She didn't believe me. "I'm not going to take that chance. Good-bye Abby." With her purse in hand, she stormed out of the grill.

CHAPTER 27

I *t is recommended that the Butler count, and count again, the pieces of silverware at each place. Lack of only one fork or spoon would cause great embarrassment for the Hostess.*

"The Butler's Guide to Fine Silver"
Mr. Hollister, 1898

I WAS on a roller coaster ride and I was ready to get off. To ease my frazzled brain, I stayed close to home the next day. I worked on my research, did some cleaning and kept walking by the refrigerator door. The magnets seemed to be calling to me and I finally gave up and pulled a chair over to contemplate what I knew, or thought I knew.

The first thing I did was pull the little prescription bottle magnet to the center. If Ingram was right, the Baltimore connection had to be there. Then I looked if all the other magnets still belonged. I moved Tiffani's magnet with the red bow over to the side. I don't think she could have faked how upset she was about

Jack's death if she had poisoned him. I shifted Nina's heart magnet to the side as well. Yes, I guess she had a motive. She had taken a lot of abuse for shifting her feelings to Jack's arch rival, Dominick. A doctor probably could get her hands on any drug, but the idea didn't feel right to me. She was a doctor, after all. She'd sworn to do no harm. She didn't belong in the spotlight.

I was about to move Charlie's purple magnet to the side as well, but stopped. He seemed like a really good guy, but everyone had his limits. Charlie sailed for the fun and the excitement and the challenge. He was uncomfortable with Jack's sniping and underhanded shenanigans. Maybe Charlie had had enough and thought no one would suspect him of killing Jack with an overdose, because he was involved with a drug awareness program. No, though I really believed Charlie didn't do it, I decided to leave his magnet in the middle.

And what about O.T.? In my mind, he had earned a place on the refrigerator door based on Dr. Phillips' research. That's the only reason he was there. Ingram was convinced that he wasn't involved. But I wanted to be thorough. I found my sailboat magnet and O.T. went on the door with a click.

I stepped back and looked at the collection of magnets again. It felt good to move some of them to the side, but there were still too many suspects. Why couldn't I get a better read of the situation? As I was about to walk away, I remembered the conversation outside of the ladies room on Friday night between Jack and Dutch. I knew I should tell Ingram about it. It would add more weight to his argument that it was the Baltimore connection that ended Jack's life. Did that connection make Dutch their instrument of death?

"What are you thinking?" I said loud enough to wake Simon from his puppy dream. When his head popped up, I asked him, "Why would Dutch ask Jack for drugs to fight his hangover if he had access to heroin and fentanyl?" Simon stared at me, barely breathing. "Exactly," I said, as I started to pace. "He wouldn't.

Ohhhh, this is so frustrating. Usually I have no idea what the answer is. Now, I have too many answers, all of them good possibilities. What am I going to do, Simon?" My cell phone rang. "I know, answer my phone." Simon yawned.

The caller ID displayed an unknown number. I'd had it with unwanted calls from telemarketers. They didn't respect the No Call List and I was ready to tell one of them off.

"I want you to—"

"Abby, thank goodness." Tiffani sounded hysterical. "You have to help me!"

"Tiffani? What's wrong? Where are you?"

She took two quick breaths to fight back tears. "Abby, I'm in jail. I've been arrested. I need your help."

"Arrested? For what?"

"They found a drug bag in my car. I don't know, they called it a dime bag or something. It was empty. It wasn't mine, Abby. Honest."

I closed my eyes and willed myself to sound relaxed. Had Tiffani started using again? Was she trying to hide it by saying it wasn't hers? When I decided to help Tiffani, I promised myself that I wouldn't be dragged into her problem. Yet here she was calling me from jail. Things were definitely getting worse for her. I needed to gently remove myself from the situation.

"Tiffani, I'm sorry. I was happy to help you before, but now, I can't—"

She gasped and almost screamed at me, "Abby! NO! I'm clean. I've been clean since the night you took care of me. I promise."

I wondered how many friends and family members had heard that promise. "Tiffani, I can't—"

She took a deep breath to get her voice under control. "Okay, I get it. Just let me prove it to you, let me show you that this is about more than my addiction." Her words hissed as she whispered into the phone. "It's about Jack."

Jack? What does getting arrested for drugs have to do with Jack? Unless... "Tiffani, were you involved—"

"No, I wasn't." She lowered her voice again. "But I can't tell you on the phone. Can you come? Can you come now?"

I thought for a moment and then I wrote down the information where I could find her. As I grabbed my keys, I was tempted to call Detective Ingram. I wasn't on his list of favorites right now. It was better if I found out what Tiffani knew first. Simon whined as I flew out the door. "I'll be right back, big guy." And I hoped it was true.

I found a parking space right by the library which is a place I would've preferred to visit instead of the jail across the street. There, they ushered me into a room where Tiffani and I could talk. Her hair was pulled back in one long braid that was coming loose, probably because she kept pulling on it, a nervous reaction to the situation . I had to admit that it was the most conservative hairstyle I had ever seen on her. Her hands didn't shake. Her fingernails were still short, but nicely shaped. Was she telling the truth? Had she really stopped using? It wouldn't cost me anything to sit down and listen to what she had to say, so I did.

Tiffani gave me a weak smile and leaned towards me. "Abby, thank you so much for coming. I know it was a leap of faith on your part. I'm just glad you jumped."

I had to stifle a little laugh. My instinct said that she was a good kid and I suspected that she must have been very funny before she started using. "Okay, this isn't about me. It's about you. Tell me what happened."

She folded her hands primly in front of her and raised her chin to look me straight in the eye. "Last night, I went to a meeting, a twelve-step meeting, the same way I do every night. Then I went by the club. I've misplaced my sunglasses and thought I might have left them there. There was no one in the office and lost and found was locked up. I saw some of the log canoe racing crowd at a table in the corner, drinking and having a good time. They waved me over. I almost joined them, but decided the temptation would be too much for me right now, so I left. I drove through St. Michaels at the speed limit and then on the other side of town, I saw flashing blue lights in my rearview mirror. I pulled off to the side of the road."

She took a deep breath and let it out slowly. "The officer asked for my license and registration and I admit it, I was nervous. I'm still getting used to being drug-free and I still get a little, you know…" She held her hands out and shook them a little.

I gave her a quick nod to encourage her. "Then what happened?"

She looked down at her hands and squeezed them together. "Next thing I knew, he told me to get out of the car. I asked him what I had done wrong. He said he had gotten the call that a car had been seen driving erratically as if the driver was drunk. My car. He explained that he was going to give me a field sobriety test and I almost giggled. Where were they all the times I'd driven through St. Michaels drunk and high?

A car pulled up behind the officer's car and a man got out. They talked for a minute and the officer came back to me and said that he had another officer there who would move my car to a safer position off the road. I looked and saw that my car was straddling the line between the roadway and the shoulder. I told him I'd be happy to move it, but he said he couldn't let me do that until I passed the sobriety test. He led me to a safe place by his car and I saw the other man get in my car and move it over."

"Then what did they do?" I asked.

"The officer put me through my paces and I passed all his tests. I passed, because I was sober, Abby. I am clean."

"Okay, okay, I believe you. How did you end up in jail?"

"The officer who pulled me over was the K-9 unit. The next thing I knew, he was taking the dog out of the car. You know, the one that was at the club when they were searching the boat?"

A chill ran through me. "You mean Max, the yellow Lab? The

drug dog?" I really hoped she would say the dog was black or brown, but she didn't.

"Yes, that's the one. He's really cute." Then reality set in and Tiffani hunched her shoulders. "He walked around my car with the dog and when he got by the driver's door, Max sat down."

I was confused. "What did that mean?" I asked slowly.

"That's his way of alerting his handler to the presence of drugs, Abby. The officer put Max back in the car and started to take my car apart. It didn't take long for him to find something and show it to the other man. They came towards me and I could see the face of the other man in the headlights." Tiffani put her head down on her folded hands and started to cry softly.

"No, no, that won't help. You have to finish the story. Tell me what happened next."

She raised her head slowly and looked at me with a tear-streaked face. "I ran."

"You WHAT?" My response got the attention of the guard. "Sorry about that, sir. Everything is okay." I lowered my voice and began again. "Why did you run?"

"I ran because I knew he was going to hurt me," she wailed in a whisper.

"Why would he hurt you?"

"Because he wants to scare me, to keep me quiet. And now they've got me in here and I'm a sitting duck."

"Tiffani, I don't understand. You have to be clear if I'm going to help you."

"I don't know if I should tell you. If he knows that you know, he might go after you, too. I don't want anyone else to get hurt."

"Well, tell the police." That seems like the simplest solution to me.

"That's just it. I can't." She pleaded with me. "Don't' you understand?"

I sat back in my chair, frustrated. "This isn't making any sense. I don't think I can help you."

"Abby, don't say that." She started picking at her fingernail, a nervous habit she had when she was using. She must've realized it at the same time I did since she put her hands flat on the table took a deep breath and said carefully, "I'll tell you what I guess I should've told that detective days ago. "I didn't mean to do it." She pressed fist against her lips to stop the tears.

Had Tiffani done something? Deliberately? By accident? I tried not to react. "Tiffani, tell me what do you think did?"

"I gave him the overdose." Tears flowed down her cheeks.

"Did you put the fentanyl and heroin in the water?"

She gulped down the tears. "N-n-no. But I was the one who gave him the water bottle."

"Did you know the drugs were in the water?"

Her eyes grew wide. "No, I didn't. If I did, I would never have given it to Jack."

I relaxed in the metal chair. This was a false alarm. There was nothing here for Ingram. "I think you'll be fine. This is probably a misunderstanding, but if you know something, you need to tell the police. Somebody killed Jack and he or she shouldn't be allowed to get away with it."

"Oh, it's a *he.*"

"Tiffani…?"

She took a deep breath and let it out in a long sigh. "Okay, but you can't tell anybody, not yet. Not until I figure this out."

Against my better judgment, I agreed.

"Okay, you know how I was in charge of fixing his water bottle and taking it to the boat?" I nodded. "Well, before the Governor's Cup race, I went to get the water bottle from the ice machine as usual. I always fill it up with water and ice about an hour before the race and put it on ice so it's really cold."

I nodded so she would continue.

"When I went to get it, someone was standing there with the bottle in his hand. I think I surprised him."

"What did he do?"

"He handed it to me. Said he was getting some ice for his ankle." She shrugged. "I didn't think anything of it."

"Did you see him put something in the water?" I asked, almost holding my breath.

"No, it was full and had the cap on it. He said he saw it in the cooler when he went to get some ice and thought he'd save me some steps." She looked at me and frowned. "Why would he do that, Abby? He sails with another crew."

I wanted to scream, but stayed cool as I asked the all-important question. "Tiffani, who handed you the bottle?"

"It was the same man I saw in the headlights." She cast her eyes down at her hands again. It was O.T."

CHAPTER 28

*S*cratches destroy the look of silver. They are caused by lack of attention to what you're doing.

"The Butler's Guide to Fine Silver"
Mr. Hollister, 1898

THE IDEA that a member of the State Police was a murderer was still hard for me to process, even though it wasn't the first time I'd heard the accusation. Dr. Phillips had made a pretty compelling case, naming the same man. But Detective Ingram had dismissed the idea out of hand. He had the benefit of years of experience, so I chalked it up to an interesting coincidence.

Now, Tiffani named the same man, again, with what could be an important piece of evidence. If she was still using, I'd have written off her comment and gone home. But she said she was clean. She looked so much better than when I'd first met her. Maybe this was the time to give her the benefit of the doubt. And that meant that she had to be protected while she was in custody.

If O.T. really killed Jack, he could get to Tiffani right here in the jail. I had to act fast.

The guard said our time was up. Before I left, I told Tiffani to stay strong and not to worry. I believed her and I would do everything I could to keep her safe. And I did. She'd given me the name and number of her family's lawyer. I called and he was on the way to the jail. Then I asked an officer to get in touch with Detective Ingram and yes, it was an emergency.

Fortunately, the detective was awake and came right away. When I told him that we needed to talk, that I had something to tell him in confidence, he ushered me into a small office. I repeated what Tiffani told me about someone being at the ice machine, handling Jack's water bottle.

Ingram exploded. "I don't get it. She waits until she's arrested for possession before she says something? Do you know that if the tests show that the baggie found in her car contained the same heroin and fentanyl that killed Jack, she'll be charged with murder?" He leaned toward me. "And with this evidence building up against her, she tells that *you* someone else handled the bottle?" He brought his hand down hard on the table. "And you want me to believe her?"

This mild-mannered man was scaring me and I hadn't done anything wrong. No wonder Tiffani didn't want to talk to him.

He took a deep breath and said in a tone just above a whisper, "Are you going to tell me who it was?" Every word was icy with sarcasm.

"We're under surveillance, right?" He started to respond, but I waved him off. "Don't bother. You probably won't tell me the truth." I glanced around the walls and ceiling. A camera and microphone could be anywhere. "I have no idea who is listening. So…" I found a piece of paper, bent over it so no one could see what I was writing and moved it toward him with my hand covering the name.

"Games, now you're playing games with me. Show me." I

raised my palm so he could see it, but I didn't think anyone else could. And Ingram erupted.

"No! No way! He might have been there, but I'm sure it was for a very good reason and had nothing to do with what was in the bottle."

I don't know why I shot a glance over my shoulder at the door. I was afraid. "Shh-h-h, and he's probably here right now. I'm telling you. There's a connection."

He shot back, "I don't see it. He is an exemplary…"

I lowered my voice to a terse whisper. "I don't care. Even good cops go bad sometimes. Right now, you have a woman in lockup who is in danger. He can get to her in here. You don't want another death on your hands."

He took a quick breath and raised his chin as if I'd insulted him. I guess I had, but someone's life was in danger here. "I'll tell you exactly how it could go down. Tiffani is a recovering addict. She got addicted to prescription drugs and…" I waved my hand in the air to erase the distraction. "Never mind. The important thing is she's clean right now. It hasn't been very long, but she's in recovery. He could say she hurt herself, because she couldn't take the strain of being in jail, threatened with a charge of murder. I don't know, you can fill in the why. Be aware that the one witness you need to make your case would be dead." He sat in the chair as rigid as a sphinx. "Detective Ingram…" I wanted to scream to get a reaction out of him, but instead I kept calm. "You have to do something." My efforts didn't make a difference.

His face gave away nothing about what was going on inside his head, as usual. I'd made my case and now exhausted, I slumped in the chair. I looked for a hint of what his reaction would be. That's when I noticed that the lines there were a little deeper than before and his thumb was nervously rubbing his index finger, all signs of stress, but still, he sat still without saying a word. I had no clue if he was going to rant and rave again or ignore me. Or was he taking me seriously now? I closed my eyes and waited.

It seemed like forever before Ingram took a breath. He spoke as if we'd been talking about the weather. "I don't think there is an immediate threat." I opened my mouth, but he held up his hand for me to wait. "It is my understanding that the man you're worried about it on his way to Baltimore to help with the investigation."

I couldn't believe the wave of relief that rolled over me. He shared my concern about Tiffani, finally.

Ingram continued. "And, from what I understand, Tiffani's family plans to post bail and transfer her immediately to a secure drug treatment facility. The key word is *secure*. So, I think you can stop worrying."

This was welcome news, but didn't resolve the situation. Hopefully, the detective hadn't missed the key point. "That's fine," I said. "But what are you going to do with that one important piece of information?"

"Yes, That is important… if it's true. You know yourself that she could have, should have come forward with that information at the beginning of my investigation. If she had, I might have given it more weight, but she waited. Then pouf! Out of the blue, she fingers a respected officer—someone with an excellent reputation— for murder."

"She thought you wouldn't believe her," I said with disrespect, but I was too tired to care. "She said nobody takes her seriously unless it's about her artwork."

He let out a breath. "You know I wouldn't dismiss someone because she's just a wee bit of a thing and likes weird hairstyles. You know better."

I looked away, a little embarrassed. "She kept it a secret from everybody." My eyes returned to him filled with challenge now. "And she thought you'd ignore what she had to say because she uses drugs." *Okay, what are you going to say to that, Mr. Detective?*

He put his arms on the table. "Well, she might have been right about that. It's hard, often foolish, to take the word of an addict." I was disappointed that he wouldn't have given Tiffani the benefit of the doubt. Then again, he had more experience with users than I did. I stayed quiet and listened. "If the drugs were in the missing water bottle as we suspect, Tiffani was probably the last person who had it in her possession before Jack drank from it."

"She was afraid that you'd think she had murdered Jack, because she was the very last, but not the only one. If she filled the bottle and put it on ice, anybody could have tampered with it in the hour or so before she went back to get it." I spread my fingers apart as I pressed down on the table. "Don't you think it's suspicious that O.T. had the water bottle in his hands when she went to pick it up? She didn't look inside to see if anything had been done to the water. Why would she? She was handed the bottle by a member of a log canoe crew who was a cop."

"There you are. You've made my case. Thank you."

I wasn't done. "She trusted him. You trust him now so you're not even willing to consider that a good cop could commit murder."

Ingram shook his head. "Anything is possible, but he is actively assisting in this investigation. The lead he gave us—you heard it yourself—about the drug suppliers in Baltimore is legitimate. We're following up on it."

"I don't understand. How do Baltimore gangs or drug lords have any connection with someone down here on the Shore?"

"When State Police started moving in on their established pipeline of drugs to the small town north of the bay bridge, they needed to open a new channel. We're finding that Jack was part of it," he explained. "The people he'd chosen as business partners would not hesitate to hurt him and they certainly have access to heroin and fentanyl."

I felt like the walls of the small room were moving in. "It still doesn't make sense. I heard he was a sponsor of Project Purple, the county's drug awareness program."

"Why are you surprised? He was probably was trying to cover

his tracks or…" He pressed his lips together for a moment. "Or he was a man with a guilty conscience who was trying to justify the bad things he was doing for the money."

I felt like the air had gone out of my body. "Nothing is what it seems." I figured this was the time to put everything on the table. "Okay, we have a community leader who was contaminating his turf with drugs."

Ingram held up his index finger and added, "Maybe, it's still a maybe. We're still gathering evidence."

"Okay, maybe. And we have a cop who is respected for his work… doing what again?"

"He's an administrative property officer for the Maryland State Police."

"Does that mean he manages houses and apartments or—"

His chuckle helped relieve the tension in the room. "No, no, he's not a real estate agent. The short description is that he is responsible for evidence."

"So, his superiors put a lot of trust and faith in him."

He nodded. "Absolutely."

"You trust him."

Again, Ingram nodded. "I do."

"You even trusted him when *Flying Wing* was moved to the slip." I felt like I was on to something and continued the thought. "He was there, wasn't he?" Ingram frowned. "That would have given him the perfect opportunity to remove the water bottle."

"Somebody would have noticed," Ingram countered. He was still processing the possibilities.

I stood up. "I'm just saying, don't assume anything. You said it yourself. Nothing is as it should be, in this case." I went to the door and put my hand on the knob. "And please make sure that the 'wee bit of a thing' is safe." And I left, overwhelmed by the game of mirrors that was happening in front of own eyes.

CHAPTER 29

*S*cratches destroy the look of silver. They are caused by lack of attention to what you're doing.

"The Butler's Guide to Fine Silver"
Mr. Hollister, 1898

OUTSIDE THE JAIL, I sat in my car and closed my eyes. I needed to find the strength to drive home. I persuaded myself that Tiffani was safe. If O.T. was the killer, he'd have to be crazy to bust into jail and hurt her. Even though his laid-back attitude infuriated me sometimes, Ingram wasn't stupid. If anything happened to Tiffani, he'd be on O.T. in a minute.

My nerves were shot so I wanted to scream when my cell phone signaled there was an incoming text. I wondered if I could wait until morning to read it. No, not with everything going on. It might be important.

Please pick up my sunglasses from yacht club tonight. Please, please! Expensive! Don't want to lose. Thank you soooo much.

The wording was a little cutesy. Then again, maybe it wasn't considering it was from Tiffani. She'd been through a lot and since she was on her way to a secure rehab, it would be weeks or months before she could go to the club herself. It was the least I could do now that she was working hard to clean up her act. I texted back that I was on my way.

The main road through St. Michaels was quiet so I made it to the yacht club in almost no time. Thankfully almost all the parking spaces close to the main door were empty. I pulled into one and almost left the engine running. I would only be a minute. But a little voice said that it was an invitation for trouble and there had been enough of that to last me for a while. I went back, shut off the engine and took the key. I pulled on the front door. It was locked. Then I realized that the interior wasn't lit up as usual.

I heard the muffled ring of a cell phone. "The club is closed." A deep voice spoke behind me. I looked over my shoulder and saw a man standing in silhouette. The tall security lights threw his face in shadow. "Even servers and chefs deserve time off."

"Of course, they do." I tried to sound light and unconcerned. "Well, I'll have to come back tomorrow." I started to retrace my steps to my car, but the figure moved to block my way.

"They don't open until dinner tomorrow night, so we have lots of time to talk," he said casually.

Talk? With a stranger? In the dark? I tried to sound indignant. "I'm not talking with anyone now." I took a step forward, but the man didn't move. Fear started crawling up my back. "If you want, we can talk tomorrow, not here in the dark. Now, move out of my way, please."

He planted himself and drew his tall body, his feet apart to create a formidable presence. A tiny voice inside me said I knew this man and I should run.

He declared in a flat voice, "You know who I am."

He put his hands on his hips, now the Authority Figure, a role he filled every day. Because that's what Police Officer Oliver T. Smith did for a living.

He took a step toward me. "You're the woman Tiffani called tonight. I've seen you at the bar with her. You two were always so chummy. She told you things, didn't she?"

I dismissed his question. "I've no idea what you're talking about." I had to get away from this man. My car was so close, but he was blocking my path.

"She told you about the ice machine and how I handed her Jack's water bottle."

I tried to sound flippant to mask my concern. "What of it?" The words came out like a squeak. I took a breath and tried to settle down. "She told the police and they didn't think it's important, so what does it matter? Now, if you'll get out of my way." I took a step forward.

He didn't budge. "Of course, the police aren't going to take the word of a druggie."

I hated the way he dismissed her, because of her drug problem. His scorn triggered my anger. "She's getting clean." *Why, oh why did I blurt that out?*

"Still, the word of a drug user is like a scribble in the sand. It may be interesting one moment, but the next, it washes away as if it never existed, but you're different. You've got a relationship with Ingram. Sometimes I wonder why they keep him in homicide. He's slow, plodding. When I'm holding his evidence, he drives me nuts." I almost agreed with him, then

I pressed my lips together so no sound could slip out. I had to get away, but how?

He started to pace, one step that way, two steps the other, as he thought through the situation. "They'll believe you. You are what we call a credible witness."

If I kept him talking or persuaded him I wasn't a threat, maybe I could get away. That's what they do on TV. I could make a run for my car. Thank goodness, I left it unlocked. "You're wrong. Ingram doesn't take me seriously."

"He thought enough of your research that he came and talked to me." My stomach clenched. "I have to give you a lot of credit. Not only did you realize that I was the one who poisoned Jack—"

I covered my ears and shouted at him. "I don't want to hear any confession. Just shut up." I rocked back and forth like a crazy person then ran for my car.

He caught my arm. I struck out wildly with my fist and hit him on the ear. It was enough for him to let me go. He still blocked my way, so I took off like a shot in the other direction, down to the end of the building and around the corner to a tree. Dare I hope he'd lose me in the dark?

No. I could almost feel the impacts of his body on the ground. Then they stopped. I could hear him breathing on the other side of the tree that hid me.

"Come out, come out, wherever you are."

I put my hand on the rough bark and peeked around the side.

He lunged at me and I ran the other way only to see him jump in front of me and land on both feet. An unmovable object.

"Know what they teach us at the police academy?" His voice was relaxed. "It's called pursuit." He started bouncing on his feet. Leaning left, running a few steps right. Dancing around like Ali in the ring.

I wanted to sink to the ground and put my hands over my head. *Don't you dare!* I ordered myself. *You do NOT curl up and die.* The word *die* drove me action. My eyes followed him. *Wait. Wait. NOW!*

I sprang the opposite way and ran down the hill. I wanted to make a dash for the parking lot. He read my mind. I had no choice. I had to run to the docks. I moved faster. But where was I going? I skidded to a stop. The only thing at the end of this dock was water.

The sound of his shoes hitting the wood reverberated. O.T.

was walking toward me slowly. I turned and the broad smile on his face sickened me. He raced sailboats to win. He thought he'd won this race and my life was the prize.

I took a slow step backwards, then another. My head swiveled this way and that, searching for a way out. All I saw was the moon shining on the water around me. He'd boxed me in. A dead end.

He stopped and folded his arms. "Good, you realize you have nowhere to go. Shall we finish our conversation? I'd just come to the good part that you should appreciate. I was going to congratulate you."

"I don't want your congratulations." My only escape was to jump in the water and swim as if my life depended on it, because I was sure it did. In the water, he could hold my head under. He could use something to cave in my skull. He could slam me against a boat. He could...

My courage was seeping away by the minute. "I want to go home." My voice cracked.

He stood like a college professor, considering his failing student. "No, I'm afraid I can't let you do that. You'll just have to accept my admiration. You figured it out. You found the motive, means and opportunity. Your Mr. Ingram pointed the finger at Dominick right off. He was the logical choice, what with their very public rivalry. I enjoyed that. It almost worked. Too bad he had an ironclad alibi. Then Ingram looked at people on his boat. That Kevin guy got himself into a lot of trouble, doing business with a thief and committing fraud. He'll never work again as a programmer. Poor man, with a new baby and all." He shook his head slowly. "He made an excellent suspect, too."

I kept looking around for a way out, trying not to appear frantic, as we moved down the dock in a macabre slow-motion ballet.

"Then Ingram uncovered Jack's little foray into drug dealing. HAH!" O.T. bent over backwards, forcing a laugh at the top of his lungs. The sound bounced over the docks, against the club building and around the cove. Any other day, it would attract somebody's attention. Any other day. Tonight, members were at home or visiting another bar or restaurant.

"Your precious Detective Ingram. What a gullible fool he is. When I fed him that lead about the drug ring, he lapped it up like a dog. Everyone is comfortable blaming the obvious. Once they latched on to the Baltimore gangs, I was home free. Everyone was satisfied with the outcome…" He drew his eyebrows together and glared. "Except you."

Did this man have his police revolver? Would he use it?

"You had to keep digging. Even after you told Ingram about the family connection, he wouldn't go down the path. I am a fellow officer, a brother in blue. The only reason I'd kill someone would be in the line of duty to protect society. He's too thick to understand the bond of family. You do. I'm impressed."

"I wasn't the one—" *What was I saying? Would this cop-turned-killer go after Dr. Phillips?* "It was all about the log canoe. How long was *Flying Wing* in your family?"

"Captain Caulk had her built back in the late 1800's when he started tonging for oysters." He gazed into the darkness of the night, as if he saw his ancestor at work on the water.

"After he was murdered, what happened to *Flying Wing?*"

"She stayed in the family. His brothers and sisters didn't want to give up on of their last connections to the captain. But the ways of working on the water changed and she started rotting away in her slip." He threw his arms wide and shouted at the starry sky overhead. "Didn't they know the first rule of owning a wood boat? Use her, take care of her. Don't ignore her."

"She has to be loved," I said in a whisper.

He dropped his arms and looked at me as if seeing me for the first time. "That's right. Maybe you do understand."

Could I earn his trust? Could I still find a way out of this alive? "I've been reading a lot about log canoes. I've learned that boat owners, who really love their boats, feel a connection. I was there the morning Jack lost the race. It wasn't the canoe's fault." His hands twisted into fists. "It was Jack's fault." He drew his lips in so tight, they disappeared.

"I saw him kick *Flying Wing*."

Guttural sounds came from O.T.'s throat. Primeval. He stomped around, digging his heels into the wood planks.

I waited, then asked, "That's what pushed you over the edge, isn't it?"

"That's not how to treat a lady," he declared.

"Not a boat. Not a woman."

He stopped stomping around. "But Jack did both. He mistreated Nina and he mistreated my lady, *Flying Wing*. At least, Nina could fight back or move on. *Flying Wing* was his prisoner." His shoulders sagged. "He didn't deserve to live." His words pleaded for understanding. "It haunted me how that sweet log canoe fell into the hands of a bully."

"Tell me what happened."

He let out a long sigh. "The canoe left the family years before I was born. But she stayed on the Chesapeake Bay." He shrugged. "Where else in the world could a log canoe go? This is her home. I grew up with stories about Captain Caulk and his boats. He was murdered aboard the *Dream.* That schooner was destroyed by a fire set my his killer. And, of course, there was *Flying Wing*. When I heard the log canoe still existed, I tracked her down. And so did Jack. He thought log canoes were worthy of his attention." O.T. spat in the water. "I told the owner about my family's connection to the canoe. It seemed to make a difference, until Jack started throwing his money around." He dropped his eyes down to the dock. "The owner called us both to his dock and said we were going to hash out the sale right there. Jack made an offer that I couldn't beat. As I walked away, do you know what he said to me?"

"Tell me." Were we bonding? Could I persuade him to let me go?

"He said, You didn't think I was going to let you have the boat, did you? You're just a cop on a public servant's measly salary."

I gasped. "I'm surprised you didn't kill him right there."

"I didn't, even though he disrespected my family and my profession." His fingers flexed. "When he kicked her, I knew what I had to do. And I did it. You can understand that, can't you?"

"Yes, yes, I think so." I said in a soft voice and looked down, feeling defeated.

That's when I saw it. A boat hook, a long slim tube of aluminum used to fend a boat off a dock. I raised my eyes and met his. "Do you understand that I promise to say nothing and you can let me go?"

He tilted his head to one side and said in a gentle voice that matched mine, "And I should put my fate in your hands, because you're trustworthy and keep your promises?"

This cat-and-mouse game was terrifying. I took a deep breath to deliver the most persuasive part of my argument. I threw up my hands. "Why should you trust me when Ingram doesn't take me seriously? I'm no threat. I've already told him it was you. I gave him what I thought was evidence. And you know what he did? He brushed me off like some dirt on his shoe." I paused for effect then, as I brought my hands together as if in prayer, I said, "For the love of *Flying Wing*, I'm no threat. It's our secret."

He stood quietly and studied me. My heart leapt at the possibility that he would agree.

Then he bellowed, "You think I'm a fool." He laughed like a maniac again, walking around and away from me, throwing his head back.

NOW!

I grabbed the boat hook and, holding like a lance, ran at the killer with all the energy I had left. I aimed. The pointed end hit him right at the base of the skull. He staggered… right off the edge of the dock.

I ran, my feet pounding down the wood planks. Out to grass. Into the shadows.

Into arms that locked around me. Caught!

"NO! LET ME GO!"

"Abby, Abby."

"Help me! HELP ME!"

I was living the nightmare!

CHAPTER 30

*S*ilver is sensitive to light. Its shine and surface will disintegrate under intense prolonged exposure.

"The Butler's Guide to Fine Silver"
Mr. Hollister, 1898

"Abby, ABBY!" Arms closed around me like a vise.

"HELP ME!

"ABBY. You're safe." He squeezed. "SAFE!"

Safe.

"Abby, you're safe." Ingram's words were a cool breeze on my hot face.

Then I started to shiver.

What happened next was fuzzy. People yelling down at the dock. My body wrapped in a blanket. Hustled into a car. Delivered into Lorraine's soothing arms. Dawkins bringing a hot toddy, watching.

I awoke to sunlight glinting off the Miles River. A feather

comforter almost smothered me. The bed shook. A wet nose appeared, a wet tongue washing my face. I was safe. Simon was there.

Mumbling came from the other side. Lorraine was in a chair, untangling herself from an afghan. "The princess awakes." A smile touched her lips, but worry clouded her eyes. "I don't recommend that chair for sleeping." Slowly, she straightened her back.

"What are you—"

"Hush!" She looked at her watch. "No time for questions. Throw yourself in the shower. I'll get you something to wear from your cottage, if that's all right." She moved around the room, massaging the kinks from her body. "You have only a few minutes before he arrives."

"Who?" I managed to ask. My tongue felt wrapped in cotton.

"Detective Ingram. You were in no shape to talk to him last night. Dawkins and I threw him out after he brought you back to Fair Winds, but only after we promised he could return this morning." She looked at her watch again. "He'll be here in about twenty minutes. Simon, down. Abby, shower."

Serenely-calm Lorraine was a benevolent tyrant when she assumed control. I threw back the covers and followed her orders. So did Simon.

Bright rays of sunshine poured through the windows of the breakfast room. Detective Ingram didn't notice. The sleeves of his wrinkled shirt were rolled up to his elbows, the skin on his arms and hands marked with scratches and dried blood. His red-rimmed eyes concentrated on the steaming mug of coffee in front of him. Mrs. Clark stood next to him, her face strained with anxiety as she put a plate of fresh biscuits on the table. The man looked exhausted as he reached for the honey pot.

"They're better with butter," I said, slipping into a chair opposite the detective.

Mrs. Clark eyes searched my face, afraid of what she'd see

there. I touched her hand. "I'm fine. And will be even better now."
I reached for a biscuit and the butter.

Ingram studied me without a word. I looked down at my
biscuit, not ready to meet his eyes. It was an accomplishment for
me not to circle the drain in the shower, get dressed and walk
down the stairs. But I was here, surrounded by people who cared
about me. Lorraine sat down with us. Dawkins took up a position
by the door. Mrs. Clark fortified us with coffee, but didn't retreat
to her kitchen.

Ingram looked around at the people around me, alert, ready to
go on the attack if needed. He took a short breath, shifting into
his official mode. "Ma'am, I think—"

Lorraine's voice superseded his without yelling. "I think you
need to be gentle and let us support our girl as you do your job,
detective." It was clear she would not allow him to continue under
any other circumstances.

He inclined his head in surrender and took out his notebook.

I drew from her strength and asked for what I needed to know
first. "Before we begin..." My voice was raspy, my throat like
sandpaper. I took a sip of coffee and began again. "Why were you
there? What brought you to the club? "

He glanced at me, then at Lorraine and sighed. "You, it
was you."

I looked at Lorraine, confused. She closed her eyes and gave a
small nod to reassure me.

The man put his elbows on the table. "First, I owe you an apol-
ogy. It was your certainty that O.T. was the killer."

"You demanded evidence from me. Evidence. Evidence." I was
screaming at him. Lorraine put her hand over mine. I stopped and
settled back in my chair.

"You're right. Evidence is tangible, solid, something to grab. It
leads to answers about motive, means and opportunity." He ran
his hand over his thinning hair. "This case... I don't know. It's like
being in a fun house at a cheap carnival. What should be obvious

and straightforward is distorted. Your wild theories wouldn't go away, so I decided to go with my gut." He leaned back and folded his arms. "I stayed at the station last night to keep an eye on Tiffani. I spent the time trying to jam the pieces together to charge her with murder. They didn't fit."

"What happened to Tiffani?" I asked, afraid to hear the answer.

"She's a key witness now, just like you said. We transferred her to a secure rehab facility. She's safe plus she has the support she needs to stay clean and I know where to find her.

I sighed with relief. "Thank goodness." I looked out at the river and tried to let it carry away my fears about what could have happened to her. Feeling calmer, I turned back to the detective. "What's happening with the investigation? Are you still looking at a brick wall?"

"No, not anymore. I admit I was blinded by respect and loyalty to my fellow officers. Since nothing was making sense last night, I decided to follow my gut and I got lucky." He gave me a wry smile. "I now have the evidence to make the case."

The strain in his voice melted away now that he had confessed that he had discounted the information I'd brought him. "One of the officers at the barracks in Easton was asking around about an evidence transfer to Baltimore. He was worried. A call to property there couldn't confirm receipt. It's bad enough to misplace evidence, but when drugs are involved..." He shook his head slowly. "In this case, the drugs were heroin and fentanyl."

I perked up.

"Yes, the same drugs found in Jack's system. My internal alarm bell went off. I called Officer O.T.'s cell phone and didn't get an answer."

I remembered hearing a cell phone ring before O.T. said the yacht club was closed and I realized I was alone with a killer. I rubbed my arms, feeling the cold creep over my skin again. The call O.T. ignored was from Ingram.

The detective continued. "My call went to voicemail. I tried again, nothing. It's unusual for an officer not to answer a call from a superior during an active investigation. When the hairs rose on the back of my neck, I paid attention. I dialed your number and there was no answer." He pursed his lips. "Thankfully, I didn't wait. I had tech triangulate the location of your phone, hoping you had it with you. When they said your phone was at the yacht club, I knew something wasn't right."

"Am I the only person who didn't know they were closed yesterday?" Feeling as if I had walked into trouble with my eyes wide shut, I squeezed some honey on a biscuit.

Ingram glanced down at my biscuit and the corners of his mouth twitched. Then any sign of amusement fell away from his face. "I called St. Michaels police who sent some men and drove down the road like a bat out of hell. When I saw your Saab there and one of our official unmarked cars in the parking lot, I knew. I jumped out of my vehicle and started yelling your name. Your cries for help led me around to the back of the building. You were yelling, *Help me, help me!*"

"Aloud? I thought…"

"You were screaming! No wonder your voice sounds raspy now. You almost gave me a heart attack when you charged O.T. with that boat hook. What did you think you were doing, jousting?

With a quiver that betrayed her anxiety, Lorraine said, "It is the state sport, after all." It was enough to relieve the tension in the room.

"Well, you caught the brass ring, Abby. He went down and tipped over the edge of the dock. You took off like devils were chasing you and slammed right into me." He rubbed his chest. "I'm probably black and blue. And my arms…" He held them out for us to see.

"I did that?"

He nodded, but there was a playful gleam in his eye. "When I grabbed you, you must have thought I was somebody else."

"You scared me." My lower lip curled into a pout. "You wouldn't let me go."

"That's right. It was the only way I could keep you safe."

Lorraine took a breath. "And I'm forever grateful that you did and brought her home."

"What about…?" I didn't want to say his name.

"You don't have to worry about him. We took him into custody. The hospital says he needs surgery to repair some bone in his neck."

Lorraine whispered one word. "Good."

"I hurt him?"

He waved my question away. "Small price to pay, considering… He'll have plenty of time to recuperate. Between charges of premeditated murder, attempted murder, Tiffani's false arrest, possession and several other charges, I think he'll be in hell for a long, long time." He looked into his empty mug, seeing something we couldn't imagine. "A fine officer overwhelmed by circumstances and family loyalty."

Lorraine harrumphed while Dawkins picked up the coffee pot. "More coffee, detective?"

It was time to get on with things.

CHAPTER 31

*W*hen the table is ready to receive guests, take a moment
to appreciate the beauty of the silver pieces glinting in
the candlelight. It is the sign of a job well done.

"The Butler's Guide to Fine Silver"
Mr. Hollister, 1898

LATER THAT WEEK, I went to the club to see if I could locate
Tiffani's sunglasses. Still rattled by the events of Monday night, I
parked my car in the field on the other side of the swimming pool,
even though there were empty spaces close to the building. Yes,
the office had found her glasses. It was ironic that these dark
glasses with rhinestone frames led to the arrest of a killer. Instead
of thinking of what could have happened to me on the dock, I
thought what fun it would be to deliver the news the young,
quirky artist along with her glasses when she graduated
from rehab.

"Abby!" Nina called out from the lobby. It was unusual to see her here during the week. "I'm so glad to see you, Abby. I thought I'd have to sit on the patio all by myself." She put her arm through mine and started to walk us outside. I slowed my steps... and Nina read my mind. "Better yet, why don't we sit in the grill? It's cooler."

"You're not at the hospital today?" I asked, as we sat down at a table.

"I took a few days off. After what happened to Jack and all the emotion that swirled around it, I thought I'd stay and give Dom some support." She lowered her silky voice and leaned closer. "I learned how important that can be when my first husband hadn't the first clue."

We ordered tall glasses of iced coffee and sat back, content.

"I'm so impressed by what you did for little Tiffani." I felt my cheeks grow warm. "I never saw the telltale signs of opioid use. I don't think anyone took the time to notice much of anything about the girl. She was always the puppy running after Jack."

"Did you know she's an artist?"

Her eyes flew open. "I had no idea. Have you seen her work?"

"Yes, she's quite accomplished. She teaches a number of classes and has exhibited and sold her work at shows. She'd thinking about getting her Masters of Fine Arts, after she licks her problem."

"You were the one who helped her with that problem. Somebody else would have walked away. I don't think people don't know what to do when they suspect drug abuse."

"If it hadn't been for Charlie, I would have run away. I have zero experience with someone who uses. But Charlie told me about Project Purple and the pamphlet had the phone numbers I needed to get Tiffani some help. They even came out to talk with her when she told me she wanted to stop. It was amazing and I think it made all the difference. I didn't do anything you wouldn't have done. You're a doctor, after all."

Nina threw her hands up in the air. "I'm no saint. I've known the girl for more than a year and I didn't spot the problem. Believe me, I was taught how to give the antidote to an overdose victim in the ER. That's about all. I don't think I would have known what to do if she'd shown up on my doorstep. You're really something and I hope we can be friends."

"After all we've been through since the Governor's Cup, I think we are already."

Nina laughed. "You know, it's funny. When I first saw you, I watched you with green eyes."

"What do you mean?" I leaned closer. "Your eyes are dark brown."

"Not when they're filled with envy." I had trouble hiding my surprise. "You just fit in with everybody at the party here at the club. I didn't believe it when I heard that this was your first log canoe race weekend."

"It was my first time and I've got to say my stomach was doing backflips. I don't like crowds, especially when I don't know anyone."

"Oh, come on. Your good friend Charlie was by your side almost every minute."

I had to laugh. "My good friend? We'd met just a few hours earlier that day. A mutual friend arranged for him to show me the Governor's Cup trophy."

Nina shook her head. "Then my hat is off to you. You looked as comfortable as a swan swimming around in the cove."

"And you looked so casual and comfortable. You understood all the sailing jargon and how everything was supposed to happen."

She burst out laughing, almost spewing her coffee across the table. "How wrong you are. I can't keep port and starboard straight. You know what's happening here, don't you?" She smoothed her straight strands of raven black hair. "All little girls with straight hair want curls…"

"And those with curls want them to relax and go straight even just one time."

Then Nina raised her iced coffee. "Here's to new, unexpected friends." And we clinked glasses.

Later, at Fair Winds, Ryan and I walked along the shoreline together. I was pleased that he'd called first to ask if he could come. I didn't know why he wanted to come so I walked next to him in a comfortable silence.

As the minutes passed, thoughts about Jack's murder crept into my mind and chased away any feelings of contentment. Detective Ingram had said more than once that this was a case where almost nothing was what it seemed to be. The example of a majestic sailboat called a log canoe made his point and raised a question. "How do you really know someone?"

The muscles around his mouth tensed. "What do you mean?"

I licked my lips and started to think aloud. "Well, to have a relationship with someone, even a casual friendship, you have to trust that you know that person, the real person. Not some façade he wants you to see."

"I'm with you so far, I think." His words were hesitant.

"I mean, you want to know the real person instead of some illusion." I stopped and faced him. "Look at Jack, for example. We saw what he wanted us to see, a successful entrepreneur who had an original idea plus the nerve to run with it and made a lot of money. But he was a thief. He stole not only another man's idea, but also Kevin's feeling of accomplishment. When he was working for Jack's company, he thought he was doing work he point to with pride. Instead he violated his own values."

"To be fair, I understand that Kevin put the finishing touches on the code so it did more than expected. I wonder why he didn't suspect that Jack hadn't devised the original code." He moved his shoulder to dismiss the idea. "Sometimes people don't what to see what's right in front of them."

"That doesn't change the fact that Jack was a thief."

"And that he pretended to be this great businessman." Ryan was offended by Jack's poor business practices, as well. "He didn't share the credit or the money with the original developer. He didn't even have an agreement with the guy."

"Charlie told me the evening of the seafood feast that Jack wanted to be a pirate. That's why his crew wore black T-shirts. Little did we know, he was a pirate in the true sense of the word in today's tech world." I picked up the pace to relieve my disgust at being conned.

My eyes followed the shoreline of the Miles River. It would be so much easier if people were like a river, picturesque, with a surprise around each turn. A river could be moody at times with whitecaps whipped up by a nor'easter or frozen in place when the temperature fell. But, usually, a river was predictable with a defined path within its banks. If it deviated, the reason was obvious. A deluge of rain caused it to overflow or man had built something to divert it from its course. If only people were that predictable.

I wondered aloud, "How do you know if you're seeing the real person?"

Ryan walked beside me, silently mulling over his answer. "I'm not sure. I guess you look for the usual clues that someone lying to you. I like to think people are honest. I don't like to look for lies all the time. That would be a terrible way to live."

I nodded and out of the corner of eye, caught him looking at me, really looking at me. When he didn't stop, I stopped and turned to him. "What?"

"I wonder what draws me to someone. I guess it's a person's energy, aspirations, creativity… that's the kind of thing that really gets my attention."

"But is it the person or is it a lie?" I countered. "And if someone is using drugs, is the person's energy and enthusiasm real or chemically-induced?"

"Another good question. So, you're right. It's all about trust."

"And if you're brave enough to take the chance." When I realized what I'd just said, I clamped my mouth shut. I'd started this conversation to help me cope with the story of Jack, the made-up character, and his murder by a man who was tied to his family more than his profession. Somehow, our talk had veered to the sensitive subject of our relationship. We'd decided to let things develop naturally. It made me smile when our hands touched then slipped together as we continued our walk silently.

* * *

SEVERAL WEEKS LATER, I went to the post office to pick up a package and met a young woman who looked vaguely familiar.

"Abby! It's me, Tiffani."

It did a double-take and realized that this was the young woman, tear-streaked and desperate, who'd appeared at my cottage, asking for help. No wonder I didn't recognize her. Her face had a healthy glow and her chocolate brown eyes sparkled. Her hair was no longer pulled into some weird configuration. It had a professional cut that framed her face.

"Tiffani! You look great," I gushed. "How are you doing?"

She flashed a huge smile. "I'm good. I'm in IOP. Sorry, I'm spending a lot of time with people who know recovery-speak. IOP means Intensive Out Patient care. I go to the hospital three times a week for three-hour sessions. I spend time with people who have reclaimed their lives and are prime examples of what I can be. I'm managing my anxiety and building my self-esteem so I don't get sick again." A smile spread over her face. "I can do this, put my life back together and thrive without the drugs."

And I believed her.

CHAPTER 32

he tradition of fine silver carries a heavy responsibility. The Butler of the House must understand and preserve the history and traditions of the Family for coming generations.

"The Butler's Guide to Fine Silver"
Mr. Hollister, 1898

As THE SUN dipped toward the horizon, Lorraine and I sat on the patio sipping lemonade, a drink I would never give a child. Dawkins had played with Mrs. Clark's recipe to create an intoxicating version. I knew he added vodka, but there was a secret ingredient. "Just sit back, sip and enjoy." That was the only thing he'd say when we peppered him with questions and guesses. After such a hot day, it was the perfect libation to chill and celebrate the conclusion of Black Jack's murder case with Oliver T. Caulk Smith's guilty plea.

Lorraine took another sip and rested her head on the back of the wicker chair. "History follows you wherever you go. It's the winners who write it. The fact that our log canoe won the Governor's Cup has always been a proud part of my family's history. That's the way Daddy wrote that chapter. Now, I'm not so sure. Part of me wishes that I'd kept the canoe, taken more of an interest in *Flying Wing*."

"You weren't interested in sailing."

"I wasn't. But if I'd kept her, we would have avoided this horrid chapter about revenge in her history."

"Jack didn't buy *Flying Wing*, because he loved racing. He wanted to be Big Man on Campus, the envy of everyone around. He outfitted her with the best money could buy."

"Money that wasn't his," added Lorraine. "I'm still shocked that no one caught on that he stole somebody's computer code and made a fortune with it. Sometimes, we want to believe what we see and not question. It's easier that way."

"Sadly, things are not always as they seem."

* * *

I GAVE the engraved silver trophy a last rub to bring up the shine. This little silver bowl had brought me face to face with murder. The story had come full circle.

When I'd first found it, Lorraine wanted to display it with the print of the log canoe. Based on recent events, she put her plans on hold. For now, I was to return the piece to its dark corner in the silver closet. Not forgotten, just out of mind, for now. Maybe she was right, some things should be left to history.

Just as I was starting to think about dinner, Lorraine dashed by, her keys jangling in her hand. "Where are you going in such a rush?" I asked.

"I've decided to take up my mantle of civic duty again. I'm off to a meeting at about the proposed closing of Tilghman Elementary. They need everybody's support, not just the residents who live on the Island." She headed to the door. "Don't worry, I won't ask you to come…" After a dramatic pause, she added with a laugh, "This time." And the door closed behind her.

I had to laugh. Working at Fair Winds was not a nine-to-five job. It was a way of life, filled with people who gave me a feeling of safety and stability. I had room to explore who I was and who I wanted to be. At Fair Winds, it was more than friendship. It was family.

ACKNOWLEDGEMENTS

I had great fun researching this story and spent many hours talking to some wonderful people involved in log canoe history and racing, family genealogy, drug recovery and Project Purple: Talbot Goes Purple.

I really appreciate the time and attention given by Sheriff Joe Gamble of Talbot County, Maryland regarding questions of jurisdiction and homicide investigation procedure. He is the man leading the charge against opioid abuse in the county with a new program called Talbot Goes Purple. A visitor driving through the various towns and villages in the county will notice there is purple everywhere as the awareness of this terrible problem grows. He introduced me to Bruce Strazza who gave me crucial details to bring this story alive. Keep up the great work you're doing!

Many thanks to Chief Anthony Smith and his officers Lieutenant Jeff Oswald, Officers Jason Adams and Scott Kakabar of the St. Michaels Police Department, St. Michaels, Maryland for their insight into police procedure and the drug situation. And, course, Max the Wonder.

Special thanks to Robert "Bob" Murray, Captain of Rescue

Boat 40, Saint Michaels Fire Department, Talbot County Maryland. A former log canoe owner and racing captain, he gave me a truly realistic perspective on log canoe racing and rescue in case of a catastrophe. Best of luck with the new boat. She's a beauty moored in Saint Michaels.

Trauma nurse Kelly Runnels added the medical details of emergency response and opioid overdose, something she faces all too often.

LaSara Kinser, Librarian, Talbot County Free Library – Saint Michaels branch, provided quick answers about historical properties. Again, Shauna Beulah and Betty Dorbin fielded many research questions. As did Becky Riti, of the Maryland Room. A librarian's job is not to know all the answers, but know where to find them... and they do.

Lorri Wilson-Clarke, captain of the chase boat and Jon Clarke, captain of the *Magic* log canoe that has been in the same family and racing since the 1920's on the Chesapeake Bay. The story of the champagne bottle taken on board by the captain of a log canoe is based on one of the many antics of the much-beloved captain of *Magic*, Jimmy Wilson.

Thank you, Doug Abbott, Captain of *Flyer*, my expert on Dark 'n Stormy.

Betty Caulk Seymour, a direct descendant of Oliver T. Caulk, who kindly shared her in-depth research about the tragic incident that happened in 1899. Her family is blessed to have evidence of those who went before, thanks to Betty's tireless efforts.

Please note there a lot of people involved in log canoe racing and law enforcement. Any perceived similarity is pure coincidence. None of the characters in this story are based on real people, living or dead.

I took a little literary license with the small Revere Bowl engraved *Governor's Cup 1945* in this story. Log canoe racing on the Chesapeake Bay was suspended during World War II and didn't resume until 1946. I didn't want to step on the toes on an actual winner so I held a fictional race during that dark time.

Thank you to all who gave so freely of their time, stories and expertise. Any mistakes are the fault of the author alone.

AND TO MY DEAR FAMILY, as always your support makes all the difference!

*T*hank you for taking the time to read *Hammered Silver*. If you enjoyed it, please consider telling your friends or posting a short review on Amazon or the retailer of your choice. Word of mouth is an author's best friend and is much appreciated.

Thank you,
Susan Reiss

*S*usan Reiss trained as a concert pianist then worked as a television writer/producer for many years. Her work has received a Silver Medal, New York International Film Festival, the Cine Golden Eagle, three Tellys and numerous Emmy nominations. Named as a *Scribe of the Shore,* she participated in the Sheldon Goldgeier Lecture Series.

Her blog explores topics about writing, sterling silver, sailing and Eastern Shore life at www.SusanReiss.com from her home in St. Michaels, Maryland.

Facebook: Susan.Reiss.982
Twitter: @SusanReiss
www.SusanReiss.com

Silver Mystery Series
Set in Saint Michaels

FIRST BOOK

When software developer Abby Strickland receives an
unexpected inheritance sterling silver, her world turns
upside down. The police arrive when her
special cake server becomes a murder weapon.
With blood on the family silver, she sets out to find
the real killer. Lured to the crime scene in
Saint Michaels, a sailing destination
on the Chesapeake Bay,
Abby finds a different way of life filled with
quirky characters, boat races, a handsome guy
And a tangled web of wealth, greed and family secrets.

Silver Mystery Series
Set in Saint Michaels

SECOND BOOK

Sterling silver expert Abby Strickland wants to spend the holidays
curled up with her books and her puppy, Simon. When an antique
chalice disappears from a local church
with a puzzle of clues left in its place,
she is drawn into a dangerous treasure hunt.
Along the way, she learns about things that people do for love...
and some they shouldn't.
Can she navigate the maze of secret desires
in time to save the spirit of the season...
and a life?

Silver Mystery Series
Set in Saint Michaels

THIRD BOOK

Accidental sleuth Abby Strickland goes to
the Plein Air Art Festival
where gifted artists compete for big prizes and fame.
Elite art collectors eagerly search for their next acquisitions.
Tension between rivals runs high as all are drawn
into a net of creative envy, greed… and murder.

It's a charming summer event… until somebody screams!

BUTLER'S GUIDE

You've Read His Quotes
In Each Chapter

NOW...

See the Book

www.SusanReiss.com